CW00433447

First Training

FIRST TRAINING

WORDSWORTH CLASSICS

The paper in this book is produced from pure wood pulp, without the use of chlorine or any other substance harmful to the environment. The energy used in its production consists almost entirely of hydroelectricity and heat generated from waste material, thereby conserving fossil fuels and contributing little to the greenhouse effect.

This edition published 1995 by
Wordsworth Editions Limited
Cumberland House, Crib Street
Ware, Hertfordshire SG12 9ET

ISBN 1 85326 613 2

Printed and bound in Denmark by Nørhaven

First Training

CHAPTER ONE

I DO NOT recall the passing of my dear Mama, for I was then too young. I guard her likeness still, faded as it has become. That she was a gentle woman I have no doubts. I would have followed in her ways, perhaps, had not my father remarried when I was thirteen.

I remember well the coming of Stepmama, as I first called her. Father was then no more than thirty-five and she his junior by seven years. I remember her being all of a glitter, much taken with jewellery as she ever is, tight waisted, slender, and an allure to all male eyes. I remember that she awed me a little at first, for her voice, though well modulated, caused even Papa to take immediate notice of her at all times, it having a quality to it that is rare to encounter.

Strange were those first days, for sometimes there was merriment, social gatherings and parties, and at others a benign silence in the house which Papa seemed to accept as his due. My brother Robert was then fifteen and much taken with her. She would tease or even flatter him sometimes, but at others scold him and send him to his room. All things began to change. There was much alteration of furniture with carts drawn by great dray horses coming and going. This occasioned much excitement, but we were not allowed to express it unduly. There was too much clutter in the rooms, she declared, and so many small tables and whatnots among which the housemaids had to thread their way when cleaning were cleared away and more space made. In place of small settees, larger ones were brought in, their ornate coverings delighting me so that I loved to bounce up and down on them and feel their richly patterned surfaces.

I was not chided for this and felt myself perhaps my stepmother's favourite. Often she cast a most kindly eye on me and fed me tidbits so that my older sister, Sarah, and Robert became jealous, but she would have none of that. We could not but notice that Papa was quieter in her presence than he had been before, and had it not been for the social proprieties I am sure she would have taken her place at the head of the table.

"I wonder she does not wear the trousers," Sarah once remarked crossly, though the words were said without malice for it was difficult to withhold admiration from her.

My stepmama's name was Julia. The name suited her for its richness. She was above middling height and indeed when she wore boots or shoes of a certain type was to be seen as tall as Papa. Her hair was sometimes taken up in a bun which revealed a lovely swanlike neck, though I preferred it when down and would beg her to let me brush it which she did, to the annoyance of Smith, her personal maid, who could often be seen glancing at her with awed eyes.

Picnics she was much fond of and would take us on them when father was about his business. From such as I learned, he had been more lax in the past with his affairs but was spurred on by her and indeed she would sometimes tell him when to go and when to return. He abided meekly by her decisions as we all did, and so as may well be imagined we looked up to her and perhaps I believe were all a little in love with her.

My special pleasure as I grew older and attained my fifteenth year or thereabouts was to occasionally assist her in dressing. Poor Smith would be sent out and I set first to help undo the hooks and eyes in her gown. This being removed revealed a delicious frothing of lacy petticoats and underskirts. As I helped remove these in turn I would sometimes find myself touching her thighs and feeling the perfumed warmth of her body, which made me quite enamoured of her. Occasionally when divested to her corset, stockings and bootees, she would even utter a little cooing sound as she held my hands to her plump silky thighs and moved them up and down while smiling at me.

"Do you like the bodily pleasures?" she asked me once quaintly, seating herself before her dressing table mirror. As she spoke she slowly unlaced the front of her corset and therewith unveiled two large firm breasts of such marbled whiteness that I could not help but gaze upon them in awe and envy. The brown nipples upon them, set in large aureoles of sweetly crinkled flesh, stuck out boldly, being conical and finely-pointed. With a little sigh as if taken herself by her beauty, she then cupped them and gazed at me smiling. "One day yours will be as large," she said, whereat I blushed and knew not what to say. "I believe they must be very pretty already. Show me, Clara," she went on and turned about on her stool.

I turned my head towards the door and felt flustered, thinking that Smith might return.

"No one will come in. Take off your dress," I was told.

The sunlight came softly into her room and made a haze of all, casting its milky shine through the dusty curtains. One is not of course ever flustered at undressing in front of another of one's own sex, but perhaps some flickering of intuition told me of something that I could not have expressed.

"Let me help you, dear," she murmured and with that her fingers were busy all about me so that in no time at all I stood in my chemise. "Take this off, too," came her words. When I did so, my bubbies—already proud and firm—were revealed. Her eyes opened slightly in admiration, which of course pleased me. My titties had already grown well and would not have scorned the title of pumpkins, the skin velvet smooth and rich, and proud to display my strawberry nipples. That at least is what my stepmother called them while gently tweaking the tips until my face grew flushed and I felt them stiffen. "How well they come up," she whispered, "shall I show you something nice?"

I nodded, my cheeks suffused. There was a hot feeling in my eyes as she drew me towards the bed, lay down suddenly upon her back with her legs dangling over the edge and pulled me upon her so that I stumbled and fell between her stockinged legs. Holding me so, she gazed up at me quite dreamily and cupped my face in her hands.

"What a beauty you are becoming," she murmured and then so adjusted herself with a supple movement of her body that my nipples came upon her own. "There—is that not nice?" she whispered. Her lips were immediately under mine and I could scarce speak for excitement. Slipping one hand beneath my chin and so keeping my mouth directed to hers, she stroked with the other down my back. I wore by then only my drawers, white stockings and strap-over shoes such as had just come into fashion. Our nipples tingled together and brushed like rubbery thorns, for I can think of no other description for the feeling. Without speaking further then, she pouted her lips prettily and brushed them lightly all about my own, making me feel quite swoony. Our breaths intermingled. My breasts seemed to swell. "I have been longing to kiss you," she whispered against my mouth, this being said in such a soft, seductive tone that I moved my arms around her neck and felt distinctly the burr of thick curls around her pussy pressing into mine through our drawers.

Did I like it, I was asked, and I nodded as best I could in my posture, felt my face suffused still, though with excitement rather than embarrassment, and a nice tingling in my belly. Never having done such a thing before, the richness and warmth of her body felt superb under mine.

"I want to teach you. Will you let me?" she husked.

I knew not the real meaning of her words, but the helpless wonder in my eyes spoke for me. Tremulously I felt her fingers pulling on the ties of my drawers which she then began to wrinkle down. I started a little at that, but she purred something incomprehensible into my ear and then worked them so quickly down that in a trice my nudity was pressed into the cotton of her drawers where I could more distinctly feel the hump of her cunny. Then she pressed me up a little so that I had to use my hands to support myself and gaze down upon her.

"Can you feel mine better?" she asked.

"Yes," I said, quite in a daze, but much excited. I could not resist wriggling a little which pleased her for she laughed softly.

"I like doing it through my drawers and so will you, for that is how I mean you to be fondled first, Clara. Keep your belly pressed in tightly to me while I keep my legs open. Now I shall teach you to kiss. Part your lips a little and protrude your tongue into my mouth, then you will feel my own. Move it all around so that I can feel it."

I gurgled, I panted. What I was experiencing was so beautiful and unbelievable that all the world's other pleasures seemed as naught to this. Her tongue, wet and long, coiled about my own, causing me the most exquisite sensations as our cunnies ground together. Hers, being veiled, exuded a slight moisture which seeped through her drawers, creating an oiliness between us. Her own hips began to work more yet her movements were gentle and undulating so that it was as if I were upon a fleshly sea of wondrous curves and bumps. Her breath hissed through her nostrils in a fine spray of heat.

"More," she choked.

I had intruded my tongue further. All time ceased and I could feel only the luring moisture and the slow circling of our mouths. Gliding down slowly, her hands began caressing my smooth bottom cheeks. I quivered as she felt delicately down and into the tight groove between the chubby halfmoons, which caused her to clamp my mouth the more on to hers.

"What lovely bottoms you and Sarah have. I am going to make them do such nice things," she whispered, though only afterwards was I able to gather myself sufficiently to recall her words, which appeared to infuse her with even greater excitement for of a sudden she rolled me on to my back and, cupping her hand under my moist quim, rubbed the ball of her thumb around my spot, making me writhe. "Keep your legs open," she admonished me, her globes rubbing suavely over my own.

So determined was her tone that I obeyed. My eyes and mouth were open. The ceiling swirled above me, the plaster cupids on it appearing to move of their own accord. Finding me quiescent and with my thighs held apart, she stroked my brow.

"What cocks are going to throb and spout in this warm little nest! Have you seen one yet?" she asked while rubbing me gently all the time.

I shook my head. Speech would not come. My belly was melting. I began to jolt my bottom, poised as it was on the rolled edge of the bed.

"I wonder who I shall put you to first?" she then mused. My fingers clasped and unclasped, my head rolled from side to side. Completely prey to the exciting movements of her thumb and fingers, I could but utter little gasps. The room grew ever hazier about me. I sought nothing but fulfilment, as she well knew. The firm fleshy bumping of her titties upon mine was delicious and added to my delirious sensations. I gritted my teeth. "Come on, come on, Clara," I heard her utter. A thin whine escaped me, or a sound more akin to mewing. I raised my bottom, arched my back, and then her tongue plunged into my mouth, swirling all around my own, while I, panting madly, loosed a fine salty rain upon her fingers and—uttering a croaking gasp—all but swooned. I was dissolving as if in a pale white luminescence, my body limp and seemingly boneless. "Good girl," she murmured. I made to clutch at her tightly, but she rose suddenly and sauntered back to her dressing table where she sat heavily, bowed her head for a moment and then turned towards me.

"Dress yourself, darling. It was but your first lesson," she said, which made me feel so exposed and guilty that I sat up and quickly snatched at my chemise which lay crumpled near the foot of the bed. My drawers being by then dangling around one ankle caused her to laugh fondly. "Slowly—always slowly, Clara. Ladies do not rush," she admonished me, then with a laugh rose, bent over me and kissed my moist brow. "I will teach you everything. Will you obey me?" she asked.

I wanted then to run and hide, was in two minds about everything, yet so pleasurably pulsing between my legs that I fain would have had her do it to me all again.

"Yes," I heard myself reply.

While she straightened, turned back to her mirror and began humming to herself, I made myself decent, as the curious phrase has it. Lest the reader think me a natural wanton, I must take care not to write too much from hindsight. I was between my fifteenth and sixteenth years and innocent of all save what had just happened. I was not, though, a goody-goody and had begun of late to toy with myself when abed, though never with such delirious results as my stepmother had afforded me.

"You are my favourite—d'you know that?" she ventured while brushing her hair.

"I love you," I said impulsively, never having used those words before.

"Of course," she said simply, "but we must remember

that love and obedience go ever hand in hand. Will you remember that ever? I wish you to. I am obedient to my principles and to those that my dear Mama instilled in me. I may even be obedient to your desires when they are more aroused in you."

The import of such words meant little enough to me then. I was all of a-tremble with pleasure at what she had done and though standing docilely enough, her womanly intuitions told her so. Standing beside her once again as I was, she tenderly felt all round my bottom and thighs through my dress and was pleased, I believe, that I stood submissively to this.

"Do you love me because it was nice? Answer quickly and truthfully, Clara."

"I love you and it was nice," I answered impulsively and again I glimpsed a look of admiration in her eyes such as flattered me greatly. While I had admired and gone in awe of her, even of course felt affection for all her kindnesses and even her occasional sternness, I had never felt towards her as I did now.

"You do not stutter and stammer your replies. I like that," she said. "Sarah is different from you, more fey and more awkward, but she will train well—in due course."

Indeed yes, I remember well the first emergence of that word from her lips. At that moment I had no cause to dwell on it, yet it embedded itself in my memory so that when I later lay in bed that night it recurred to me constantly. I knew now that something had happened between my sister and stepmother, but could not of course bring myself to ask. Then, as girls will, I persuaded myself that it was but a careless remark. I was as one who longs to say many things but does not know what they are. Sensing this, she was most patient with me.

"There is naught that anyone else need know of such things, Clara—not at least until I wish it," said she.

The image of Papa immediately sprang to mind, most

naturally, for I had no doubt that she intended him as well. I was aware, as were Sarah and Robert, that he had become quieter than I somehow remembered him before his remarriage and that he deferred to her. It is said nowadays that women of our time were ever meek and dutiful, but that is not so. I have known perfect harridans who made their spouse's life a misery so that—as I also now know—they turned to gay girls for comfort. A woman then, of the time of which I speak, could not so easily be thrown out of her own house as hitherto had been the case, and if she could not vent her marital wrath upon her husband then she would do so upon the servants.

As time passed my stepmother explained all such things to me, not by lecturing but by quiet remarks that she knew would make an impression on me, as they did, for females absorb more in such matters than do males. Girls are closest to their mothers and I became now so to my immediate female guardian.

While I now helped her to dress for the afternoon, she gave me a little tickle between my thighs—though through my dress—and laughing asked me whether I thought what we had done was naughty.

"I don't know," I replied, very confused and more shy when not within the heat of it.

"Well, it is not," she told me bluntly, "all pleasures are to be looked upon as pleasures provided they do no eventual harm to anyone. Did you know that I had caned your sister?"

I was startled and showed it. I did not even know that we had a cane about the house.

"She was wilful. A girl must not be wilful. She must learn all for her own benefits. That is the purpose of being taught. The road may seem hard at first but soon it leads to pleasant meadows and there one may disport oneself as one wishes."

Perhaps the most astonishing aspect of this was that

Sarah had said nothing to me, though we always normally confided in each other, as sisters do. Curiously enough—and such was the strength of our stepmother's personality—I believed it all the more for Sarah's strange omission. Besides, and though this was only what might be called a side thought, the remark about my sister's bottom had intrigued me and now was cleared up.

"Oh, did it hurt her?" I asked out of curiousity but also out of protectiveness.

"No more than it will you, my pet, when I have to do it."

"She did not tell Papa though?" I asked, though my tone of voice was rather in the form of a statement than a question.

"Certainly not. She knows better than to do that," came the reply. With that she took a Turkish cigarette from a box beside her table and lit it. With a quite merry smile she offered one to me but I shook my head. "You will come to like them I believe; what a pleasant perfume they give off," I was told.

I wanted then to take a puff; but it was too late to ask and I dared not. Then with quite a flourish she swept past me, opened a wardrobe and from a shelf took down a whippy cane, the sight of which truly made me quiver. Told to feel it I extended my hand timidly and touched its polished surface.

"I tingled her up with it well, Clara. Do you know what being naughty is?"

"Why, yes, it is doing things that one shouldn't," I replied naively.

"Oh? Do you think? It is also not doing things you should do—but that is a mystery saying, as my Mama used to call it, and you will learn the meaning of it soon enough. Suppose after dinner tonight when we are all in the drawing room, I told you to raise your dress and push your knickers down. Would it be naughty to refuse?"

"In front of all? Oh no, I couldn't!"

"Be not disturbed, I shall not ask you to. There may be occasions—other occasions—where I shall, however, and if you do not then I shall cane you."

"Oh!" I stepped back. I truly believed her. "You would not," I gasped.

Instead of replying, she ran the cane lovingly across her palm. "It stings beautifully. You should have seen Sarah's hips waggle!"

"But what did she do?"

"Does it matter? Perhaps it was something she would not do. Will you not trust me to behave in your best interests always?"

"Yes."

I could reply in no other way. Most curiously or not, after what had occurred I trusted her completely. I knew no strain of cruelty in her and so was more intrigued than fearful at her words.

"Let me lay it a little across your own adorable bottom. Shall I?"

Was it in truth a request or a command? I stood rigid and in that moment squeezed my nether cheeks together.

"Please don't," I stammered.

"You are refusing? What a naughty girl you are!" But her tone was only that of a tease, then she beckoned me and I softened and moved back to her. "I would adore to cane you, Clara—to make your bottom hot and ready," she murmured. Quite as one mesmerized, I stood still though my legs trembled as with slow but certain hand she raised my dress inch by inch until first the back of my thighs and then my knickered bottom were revealed.

"Stand still," she said severely. I blinked and did so. Then, holding up my dress higher, she laid the cane at a right angle across my chubby cheeks and there held it as if to give me the feel of it. I did not move nor could have done without her command and knew it. "The cane may be cruel or it may not. It may act as a punishment or a spur. I use it only as a spur, Clara, and never cruelly. You trust me in that, do you not?"

I nodded. Though wary at that moment, I did trust her. She tapped the cane lightly across my pert moon, causing me to utter a sharp "OOOOH!" though I felt little from it.

"Now again," she murmured, "bend forward, keep your dress up and your bottom well stuck out."

"B . . . b . . . but . . . ," I stammered. This briefest of rebellions was however quelled by a single look from her. As she stepped to one side of me, I obeyed a little miserably, feeling that I had somehow been trapped. Withal, however, I also entertained a certain sense of daring and excitement that I could not explain. Keeping my legs straight, I reared my bottom and waited.

"I adore your obedience, Clara. Remain obedient still."

I knew then that she meant to cane me. My dress slipped but was soon drawn up again. In a businesslike manner she then turned me about so that I found my hands placed on the side of the bed. I wanted desperately to speak, to plead with her, but could find no manner of words to utter.

"Now your drawers down again," I heard, and as recently as they had been donned so now as easily did they cascade, gliding down to my ankles and there subsiding in a forlorn pool. Her hands touched my bare bottom and I wilted. This gesture of defensiveness was ignored.

"You will learn the correct posture, my pet. Make a hollow of your back so that the moon of your bottom is made the more prominent thereby. Do not arch your back in the reverse direction for it looks absurd and is indeed naive."

Her words were smooth enough but firm. Obeying hesitantly, I presented myself in the best fashion.

"Have no fear. I do not mean to scorch you," came her

voice. I heard then a hiss as of the cane slicing through the air.

"THOOO!" I squealed, for light as the stroke was, and full across my young orb, it stung me and I reared.

"Still now, Clara!" she barked.

I gave a little wailing sob and waited. Then my next and longer wailing cry was uttered as this time I received another scorcher, though in truth I know it to have been but a skimming motion of the cane at which she was so adept.

"NA-NAH-NAH!" I heard myself sob and worked my hips madly, endeavouring as one does to shake off the tongues of fire that were leaping through me. Even in the midst of my cry, however, a third bit into me, and this time truly did for I leapt and clutched at my bottom, not caring about my posture nor indeed about obedience. I was not however admonished for this nor did she attempt to still me but instead cast down the cane and drew me about so that I sagged against her and sobbed my protests to the world.

"Dear little one, it is but your first taster. Did I deal with you so harshly, my sweet little dear?"

I blubbered only because the thought of it had proven perhaps worse than the deed. Her hand stroked my hair, my face was pressed into her perfumed bosom. Her words ran over me like softly drifting leaves as, instead of chiding me, she praised me for my fortitude. This causing me to sob louder, I was kissed on my moist and wobbling mouth and once more found myself clinging to her.

"Are you not grateful that I did not really sting you? It does not hurt? Does it really hurt—really, really?"

I cried on for effect a little and she knew it, stroked my hair continually and kissed my nose and brow.

"You come up well, darling—you lift it well. We call it presenting, you know, and I shall teach you a little more about that later. There now, let me soothe your nice hot bottom. A little hot, is it not, but you cannot say that I truly hurt you, can you?"

I shook my head, face hidden. It had stung me awfully, yet I could not describe it as a pain.

"Now, darling, the final salute. Your tongue, quickly," she breathed. My face was lifted. I surrendered anew, but therewith her forefinger found the tight, warm cleft of my bottom and rotated its tip around my puckered hole. Feeling the strange sensation of that touch I pressed myself into her involuntarily, which was what she desired for her finger followed and gently rubbed me there again all around the rubbery rim of my secrecy. Thus our bellies and legs were tight together and I could not escape, intoxicated anew by the sweet lashing of her tongue. Curiously enough I felt then with her progressive caressing a slight moisture in my bottomhole and my knees sagged. Then, withdrawing her mouth from mine but keeping the tip of her finger ever pressed demandingly there, she smiled down at me.

"Oh yes, truly you are my favourite," she whispered, "and you have now had your first trials."

CHAPTER TWO

I WAS LEARNING a new vocabulary: first "training," then "presenting," and now "trials," but at the time could scarcely have given much thought to them. My entire concern in this moment was that my bottom still stung and tingled and that I had actually been caned, as I thought, for nothing. Indeed, after a few more moments I ventured to say so. My stepmother regarded me gravely.

"Yes, it must seem so to you, Clara, but all has its purpose. You did far better than Sarah, I am pleased to say."

"Perhaps you caned her harder," I murmured. I still felt resentful, yet an intense excitement burned in me at what had gone before and the instinctive knowledge that I had not been dealt with vindictively. To the contrary, I felt that her true love for me was now emerging.

"No, I did not," she laughed, "though in fact I did give her six to your three, but it was not in any event as with you and I."

I had no need to ask what she meant. Sitting gingerly on the bed, I wriggled my bottom, constantly tightening and relaxing my burning cheeks. Those who read this may wonder at my sudden advancement at my age. Girls of tender years can indeed be led, but they also have a greater instinct than males of similar age. I was being led, but not misled and little by little my confidence in asking questions increased.

"Why did you cane Sarah?" I asked. Without replying immediately she drew upon the bellpull which summoned Smith, who glanced at me somewhat curiously, I thought, which caused me to have a little anger at her, though I did not show it. She was about twenty-three and reasonably comely, having a fresh country complexion, a narrow waist and good hips.

"Her bottom is fair to be caned or at least leathered," my stepmother remarked after she had instructed the maid to bring up wine. I was flattered to be handed such remarks and even more so that I was to be allowed to tipple. Smith returned as quickly as she could, perhaps wishing to overhear something she should not, but in that was not successful and, departing, banged the door a little which caused my stepmother to say that she would pay for that.

I hugged myself at that remark. Perhaps it was that Papa had been too weak with us that I turned the more eagerly to Julia, whose strength and strength of purpose was apparent. She, knowing this, took less advantage of it initially than she might have done, for in such scenes as followed, I—being seemingly impressionable and indeed even submissive—might have appeared as a more central character if such had been her wish. I wanted to ask desperately whether she had been lovey-dovey with Sarah as with me, but as moments went by there was no need. The very inflexions of her tone told me that I was her chosen one and of course I gained great pride from this.

"Why did I cane Sarah? I would not reveal such a confidence to anyone but you, my pet, nor must you think that anything we say or do together will ever be revealed to a living soul without your knowledge. I required to know of Sarah two things: whether she has been handled yet and whether she has seen a cock. I know you have not and believe you. Sarah very foolishly took umbrage and was impertinent. She is overproud, Clara, but thus also easier to handle than she thinks. I had some trouble in putting her over and removing her drawers."

I tried to imagine such a thing. Sarah was slender but taller than I. Unconscionably I giggled and asked if she struggled much.

"The discipline I brought to her was not as I might have wished it for it was needful to grasp the nape of her neck and hold her down. The cane did not have its proper reach. Even so, she knew its sting all right. As to Robert, it may be another matter."

"R . . . R . . . Robert!" I exclaimed involuntarily. He was approaching nineteen and a fair, muscular boy.

"I have not dealt with him yet, darling," I was told and was softly kissed. "I shall do so in quite another manner. Do you wish to share a secret?"

I nodded eagerly. There were too few secrets in my life, except those I pretended that I had, and the question met my youthful yearning neatly. My hand was taken and warmly clasped. To my pleased astonishment it was even raised to her lips.

"I am taking such a chance with you," she sighed, to which I responded vehemently that she was not. She laughed and asked slyly, "Does your bottom feel nice now?" I nodded, for it was true—there being a most pleasant and electric tingling now—and by gently squeezing my cheeks together I gained a most delightful sensation. Side by side we sat on the bed with her arm around me. "When I fingered you, you did not jerk away as Sarah would have done. I was so pleased, Clara."

I blushed and bent my head, but did not answer. Had it been anyone other than she it might have seemed horrid, but I had to confess to myself that the subtle titillation had really given me pleasure.

"I did not mind," I said shyly.

"You know that your Papa does not actually share this room now, for I found it not always convenient. Of course it does not mean that I do not love him still. I can be quite ardent when the mood takes me, I promise you," she said frankly, "but having separate bedrooms does provide certain conveniences of privacy. I do realise that you have not thought of such things, but it is best to make you aware of them and besides, we are going to do a lot of things together now, are we not?"

"Oh yes," I replied eagerly, for I was utterly flattered at such confidences and being treated as an equal. Again my instinct told me that I was alone in this, though having greater innocence than might be suspected from my narrative, I did not suspect what was to come.

"Listen carefully then, for all hangs initially upon your confidence and your co-operation. This evening I am going to handle Robert as I believe he needs, for I will not have your sister, nor he, nor your sweet self go into the world untutored. Immediately after dinner your Papa will be playing cards with some friends of his. I have given him permission so to do. You will excuse yourself and come up here. The dressing room adjoins and I will leave the door ajar. You will place yourself within and observe all that passes through the crack in the doorjamb. You will make no sound nor betray your presence until after I have dismissed him. Should you do so all will fail. Do you understand?"

"Yes," I breathed. All doubts as to our complicity in such matters had vanished.

"Very well then, I believe you. I shall be an anchor and refuge to you, Clara, in the months ahead," my stepmother averred solemnly, "but you had best go down now or Sarah will become inquisitive. Say that we have been discussing needlework."

I giggled and put my hand to my mouth. The wine had gone down very pleasantly within. "I promise," said I and moved to the door, whereat she rose and stayed with me.

"You will see Robert's prick tonight," she said gently. I gaped. My hand slid from the doorhandle.

"Wh . . . aaat?" I gasped, but received only a laugh in response. Her hand smacked my bottom lightly.

"Go on with you," she smiled and pushed me out. There upon the broad landing I stood in a daze. All seemed as but an hour before—the cypress trees framed through the window where the stairs turned, the polished bannister, the almost cathedral like quiet of the house, its many rooms mainly empty and with closed doors. A scent of lavender came to me from a china bowl on the windowsill. Sarah, who was reading in the garden, would ask me pettishly what I had been at. For a moment I turned my head back but my stepmother's door was shut and looked forbiddingly so.

In what a mood I waited for the evening! Having no trepidation for my brother in our stepmother's hands, I felt safely detached from what was going to pass and very excited. Indeed I found myself looking very naughtily at that part of his person where his trousers hid his cock, which was certainly something I had never done before. There is a special thrill in being made an accomplice in such matters, but withal I was calmer than I thought I might be.

At the appointed hour then, I slipped upstairs and hid myself as I had been told. There was no fear that Robert would at any time touch or open the door to the dressing room which gave immediately on to the bedroom. I had not been in there before and was fascinated by the several chests it contained together with two wardrobes, a couple of armchairs and various items of my stepmother's clothing laid casually about. There were patterned stockings of black and grey, several corsets with lace frills, long boots, garters, and much else to tempt my fingers. While waiting in the silence that surrounded me I lifted a chemise and a corset that were crumpled up together and saw beneath to my profound curiosity a small black whip that had not one thong but many—like snakes, I thought. The thongs were thin and plaited, being no more than some twenty inches long and attached to a handle of ebony which was serrated for grip. It looked strange and alien and yet I could not help but touch the handle and wonder a little that it should lay so openly there.

Then footsteps sounded and my stepmother entered alone. I wondered if the venture were not to proceed for she moved about the bedroom for a moment and then opened the door where I stood.

"Be quiet, be still and do not move no matter what is said or done," she said and with that all but closed the door again in such a manner as left a gap for me to peer through. The bed ran parallel to the wall where the door was and she seated herself upon the side of it in such a position that I could not fail to see her. Then almost immediately came a knock to which she responded in a clear voice.

Robert entered then and closed the door which added to the fraughtness of the moment for myself at least. Then, as she patted the bed beside her, he came fully into view, looking I thought a little pale and his face full of wonder.

"Sit!" my stepmother said sharply and, as he did so, adjusted her posture so that her curving hip touched his. His complexion flushed then and his hands clasped themselves together nervously. He knew not where to look and seemed to wish to avoid her eyes. Smiling, with no little condescension in her face, she laid one hand upon his upper thigh, making him start. "Are you nervous?" she asked. A perfect thrill shot through me then for I divined instinctively that something had been said and done between them before and that I was about to share in a secret that would otherwise have been hidden from me.

As she spoke she used her other hand to raise two fingers beneath his chin and draw his face around to hers, at which he most distinctly blushed.

"No," he quavered, but I knew him to be lying.

"You have no need to be. Remember what I have told you, Robert. You have but to obey me and all will be well. Do you not wish to obey me now?"

He bit his lip. I could have sworn that tears sparkled in his eyes. Bereft of speech, he nodded, though the movement of his head was constrained by her touch.

"Robert—answer me!" Her voice was level but sharp, her bosom rising and falling visibly beneath her grey and white gown that gave full prominence to her breasts and allowed their upper, milky surfaces to be seen in all their swelling glory.

"Yes," he replied, his voice thick.

"I beg your pardon, Robert?" Again her steely tone.

"Y . . . y . . . yes, Mama," he croaked and again a thrilling sensation ran through my veins.

"That is better," she purred. "You must give constant thought to everything I tell you, for you will be guided and instructed now by none but me. Do you wish to pay penance now?"

Robert's face suffused, his hands trembled, for in that moment I distinctly saw our stepmother's forefinger extend itself where her hand lay on his thigh so that it passed just once over his genitals. A sound that could only imply assent came from his throat. At that she stood up in such a position that she was facing me and no more than eight feet from the small opening through which I peered. It seemed then that all heaven waited for what was to occur next.

Robert rose in turn, his shoulders bowed. First he removed his jacket and, while she stood supremely silent and upright with her feet placed apart, he folded it and placed it on the bed. He was shaking, as I could see. I thought perhaps that she was to cane him, and yet her posture did not indicate it, for the back of her legs were close to the edge of the bed and she gave no hint of moving.

"Down, Robert," she then intoned and he moved as might a puppet, with a shaky stiffness in his limbs.

There, before my astonished eyes, he stood before her, head bowed, and then sank slowly to his knees so that his forehead all but touched her skirt. Gazing directly at me then, she smiled a little and—raising her skirts to just above her knees where her black stockings glistened—threw them right over Robert's head so that he was enveloped as within a tent.

"Now," she commanded.

Eyes glazed, I saw a movement of his knees and back that betokened that he had moved further into her. Indeed, her eyes half closed and her lovely mouth for a moment assumed a petulant look. I knew then that Robert's face was pressed against the most intimate part of her person, only a small part of his calves, his ankles and feet showing where the broad skirt had cascaded down over him. Her legs being well apart, she held them thus for a moment and then to a muffled groan from my brother she clipped them quickly together so that his head was tightly gripped between her thighs. Her hand then moved down to where the bulge of the back of his head just showed and she pressed upon it, not gently but demandingly, bringing a snort from him.

Dumbstruck, I could not really conceive what was happening save that our stepmother looked glorious and victorious in her stance, her hand held firm to him and her shoulders back, her face slightly flushed and lifted. Her hips moved a little and then stayed themselves. Once more came a groan from Robert, for evidently her thighs had tightened against his ears and I could well imagine the ruffled rims of her garters there.

Suddenly she jerked. "Ah! not your tongue, you little

beast! I shall whip you, Robert, for that. Keep your mouth open, and your tongue well hid."

Then did both her hands clamp themselves against the back of his head, her legs parted anew and she threw her head back, a look of perfect pleasure on her face. I could hear faintly the gasping of my brother's breath. A full minute passed and then another. Stepmama's beauteous expression looked soft and fulfilled, I of course being quite dazed but not a little stirred and excited by this strange, strange event. Then with sudden decision she flipped up her skirt from over him, stepped back and immediately let it cascade down to her ankles while the red face of my brother—or rather in the first instance his flushed neck—came into view.

"Up!" she commanded him and, trembling more than ever, he staggered to his feet, whereat she took his shoulders and spun him around so that he stood in profile to me.

I could not help but let my eyes seek where I knew they were to do so and saw immediately the considerable hump in his trousers. Thereupon, our stepmother passed her hand lightly over it, standing as she was face on to his left shoulder. He gurgled, started and stared straight at her door.

"Show me, Robert. Show Mama," she said quietly.

Robert's hands moved. With shaking fingers he prised open his buttons one by one, I holding my breath as each was loosed. Finding him too slow, she gave an impatient tug at his shirt just above the waistband of his trousers which seemed to act like some sort of trigger or release, for then out sprang his cock in full erection, the crest positively glowing with pride and I drinking in every inch of the fleshy stem.

"Good," my stepmother said quietly. Poor sweet Robert, I could see his legs shaking still and his face high flushed. A gasp escaped him and his head quivered as in ague, for her fingers then ringed it lightly, ran up and down the throbbing stem and released it so that it quivered its pleading to the empty air. His face was sheened with perspiration still and his brow positively glistening.

"You like the scent of me, do you not, Robert?" she asked, and he nodded.

"And the taste of me?" This time she laughed, but not cruelly. So saying, she grasped his stiff weapon tightly and then again let it go.

"Y . . . y . . . yes, Mama."

"One day, Robert, if you are very good and obedient, I may remove my drawers for your exercises. Would you like that? No, do not answer, for I know your rising lust. How wicked you are and how you must be punished for it!"

A rippling laugh escaped her and however bizarre the situation was I could not help but feel a thrill of deep affection at the sound. Her eyes met mine again deliberately through the crack between the door and the frame and a little smile as of pride and pleasure wisped over her ruby lips.

"Now show me your balls, Robert."

At that he pushed a little frantically at his trousers, let them slide down and was so uncovered to just above his knees where they crumpled and hung. His shirt being tucked up, I could now see all. His testicles hung like two rich plums close beneath the root of his erection which seemed to me not lewd but beautiful to see with its mingled white and pinky colour and the rubicond head from which his foreskin was drawn tightly back.

"Has Sarah seen it?" she asked and made him quiver terribly as she passed alluring fingers underneath his balls.

"N . . . n . . . no," he stuttered.

"You are well hung, Robert, for your age. Be mindful that your prick rises well when you think of me, but do not play with yourself nor make yourself come for your shirts and sheets and kerchiefs are ever being examined and my wrath will truly fall upon you should you disobey. Guard your liquid treasures, Robert, for such moments as I ordain and I will judge you a good boy. Have you a question to ask? You are permitted one, as I told you in the summerhouse of late."

The summerhouse! Had she meant to say it or was it a slip of the tongue? I recalled now her strolling there once or twice with him but had thought nothing of it, thinking her presence with him but a maternal one. Now perhaps I knew that its walls held secrets that I longed to know.

"M . . . m . . . may I k . . . k . . . kiss you, Mama?" stammered he, though not daring to turn his head but facing ever forward.

"What a request! With your naughty prick up and your balls out? What would the world think of me? Would you have me raise my skirts while you do it and press my thighs to yours? Well?"

"N . . . n . . . no."

I felt truly sorry for him. His expression was utterly forlorn, yet at the same time I was seized by a feeling that his behaviour was at least unmanly. There was no tie of blood between them and despite the disparity in their ages he might well in the circumstances have risked a kiss, even though it meant a caning. So my befuddled thoughts ran. I both loved him and yet felt a distant contempt for him which, had I but known it, was exactly the concoction of emotions that she wished to engender in me.

"You bad boy," our stepmother said softly and then, placing one hand beneath his bare buttocks so that her forefinger distinctly moved between them, took light hold on his straining penis and frotted it gently, causing his mouth to gape and a low moaning sound to issue from him.

"In a little while, when you are gone, Robert, I shall remove my drawers, which you will find well warm and musky with my scent, and will toss them quickly on to the landing. You will wait there and catch them and may take them to bed with you if you wish. Would you like that?"

Her voice, so tender again, stirred my heart anew. Her hand continued to rub, lightly and maddeningly, I have no doubt.

"Yes. Yes, Mama," he croaked.

"Very well—cover yourself and go. Be quick on it. I may exercise you again tomorrow if you are good. Beware that you do not spill your lust into my drawers, for I shall know of it. You may suck upon them, but that is all."

I heard all in a daze, conscious of a melting moisture in my own most intimate garment and unable to tear my eyes from my brother's rampant pego until it was fully covered and his jacket on. Turning away from him, our stepmother waved her hand airily in dismissal, at which he literally slunk out and closed the door. I then burst out, unable to contain myself and fell into her embrace.

"Oh, how naughty!" I exclaimed involuntarily.

"Wait," she laughed, "let me give him his little treat."

Most boldly then she doffed her drawers, easing them off over her bootees. The crotch was damp as I well expected to see it. With almost a giggle she waved the cotton before my face, bringing a deeply feminine effluvia to my nostrils, opened the door a little, tossed them out, and closed it. A scurrying sound came to our ears and she laughed and said, "You see!" Then her expression changed and became one of seriousness.

"All men and boys are so if properly taken in hand," she said, and asked—as though I were much older than my years—"did you not know?"

I bit my lip, feeling embarrassed at her question yet wanted withal to appear bold.

"It is too soon for you to understand," she said gently, "but I mean to progress you quickly. The choice is simple, Clara. You may live what Society is pleased to call the normal life. You will marry, suffer the boorishness of your husband, become infinitely bored and wonder what to do with all your days. As you grow older he may desert you for other women. Do you wish that?"

"Oh, no!" I must have looked more deeply concerned than I felt for she kissed me all about my mouth.

"Robert has a good cock, has he not?" she asked. Before I could think of how to frame a reply she went on, "I cannot let it remain unmannered, you see, and by that I mean that he requires training, as all males do. Some females, too." Her eyes twinkled. "It is a precious thing to be able to guide the destinies of those who would otherwise live haphazard lives and become so dull that they bore all about them. Robert is really happier than he has ever been for he waits upon my ministrations and knows that I will finally comfort him. I have given him a direction and a purpose, you see, and have concentrated his mind wonderfully, if I may use dear Dr. Johnson's phrase. Stern and remote—though also sometimes teasing—I may seem to him, but were I to leave him to his own devices he would soon begin to poke every girl in sight. He would come too quickly and afford the girls no pleasure. In a word, he would be uselessly ruttish. That would not be good, would it?"

I shook my head, so persuasive were her words and so urging her tone. Most of all I wished to know Papa's place in all this and how we might keep our secret from him, for all three of us had now been in her hands.

She saw the wonderment in my eyes and said carefully, "There are mysteries, are there not? Does it not make life more exciting? Think on it."

"I don't need to," I said impulsively, whereat her eyes glowed.

"I truly believe you do not, Clara. I judged you well from the start. You display neither bewilderment nor incomprehension. Truly were you born to the part I mean to have for you—that of a Mistress of many households and of many eager souls. Go to bed now. Judge levelly the events of the day. Tomorrow I must begin to bring Sarah to fruition."

"Oh!" I exclaimed, but there were to be no more confidences that night and I was firmly ushered out. Going to my room I thought again and again of Robert's waggling cock and blushed—yet it was so nice to see. Perhaps in my imagination I even put my fingers around it as she had done.

CHAPTER THREE

BREAKFAST was ever a quiet affair, broken only by the movements of the servants about us, the tinkling of cups and spoons and the careful sounds of knives and forks such as are made by gentlefolk in eating.

Papa looked as dapper as ever, his goatee beard being well trimmed, though his face a trifle pale. My stepmother appeared to defer to him, being gentle in her talk, though now and again it seemed but a cloak for the proddings she gave him such as to his business and the estate. Occasionally he would appear to begin to offer a light opposition to her views, then her magnetic eyes would meet his and he would wipe his mouth hastily with a napkin, take a further sip of coffee and say for all the world as if he had made the suggestions himself, "Of course, my pet—this is how things should be."

Indeed when he made that remark I saw Sarah's lip curl a little and positively hated her for it. Our stepmother, I believe, did not miss the facial gesture for she gazed at her sharply, went on eating for a moment, and then said, "We shall go to the summerhouse immediately after breakfast, Sarah."

"Oh, I do not wish to," replied my sister pertly.

"I said we shall go," came the quiet and cutting reply. Papa gazed from one to the other.

"Sarah might prefer to go riding," he murmured.

"She will have plenty of riding to do, William—I shall see to that as I shall to all else," came the reply whereat a silence fell. Sarah flushed and pushed a piece of bacon away with her fork. Robert appeared to be in tremulous excitement. As for myself, I seemed to draw strength from merely gazing at my stepmother who radiated as ever a positive aura and glow of confidence such as I believe is given to few women. I thought of strange things—the roundness of her bottom on the seat, Robert's prick upstanding the night before and how he might have disposed of her drawers without the maid finding them when she did his room. I glanced at Sarah's breasts and saw how beautifully rounded they were. Such thoughts had never entered my head before and yet I felt no strangeness at them nor even immodesty. All was surely as it was and must be. So perhaps was the basis of my own philosophy then formed. Above all I bathed in the glow of our stepmother who I knew would be victorious, though if asked in what I would have been unable to answer.

"Robert, you have my instructions," she next said and, though there was otherwise silence, it seemed to deepen as her voice ceased.

He nodded and appeared too awed to speak. No sooner were we done and Papa risen—for in such small matters all etiquette was observed—than my brother went out, passing through the conservatory into the garden where I wondered much what he was to do. Our stepmother rose next.

"Come upstairs, Sarah. I wish to speak to you," she uttered in a tone that brooked no refusal.

My sister stirred pettishly in her seat, avoiding my glance, then got up and followed. As my stepmother reached the door with Sarah in train, she turned and said gently to me, "You will be in attendance, Clara. Wait in the conservatory."

"Yes," I replied simply. The door closed and I wished to move but could not. Some urgent wish impelled me to know what my sister's fate might be and so after a moment I daringly followed, creeping up the wide staircase until I was within sight and sound of our stepmother's room.

"Take them off this moment, Sarah!" I heard her say and then a smacking sound and a small cry from my sister.

"Oh, why must I?" she wailed, then another smack.

"Because I tell you. Leave them on the bed now. Are you not cooler thus without your drawers? You have no need to wear them in the house, nor in summer out of doors. I am mindful as to all your ways, Sarah, though you believe it not. Tidy your hair again—you may use my brush—I wish you to be looking your best. A little rouge upon your cheeks now."

"I don't like it, though."

"It is not a question of what you think you like, Sarah. Rub it well in and smooth it out towards the edges—so. Let me look at you. Your eyes do not glisten as they should. I shall have to smarten you up. Come!"

Oh good heavens, with what fearful trepidation I scurried down lest I be caught! All too breathlessly I reached the conservatory and stood demurely, giving Sarah a sweet smile that she appeared to resent for her mouth was set and quite a scowl upon her face. As she went out upon the lawn my stepmother paused and murmured to me quickly, "In three or four minutes, Clara, come—come to the summerhouse." A swish of her skirts and she was gone, following Sarah at a pace and indeed I saw my sister glance half anxiously once over her shoulder and then quicken her steps.

There was to be discipline of sorts, I knew that—and no doubt for the way she had curled her lip at table. I did not wish her hurt, though, and so waited with one finger in my mouth as I was still then wont to. I was far from calm and felt my pulses ticking. A small seizure of panic came over me and I wanted to run after them but stayed myself. I trusted my stepmother devoutly and knew it. I believed all she had said and was in her hands.

The summerhouse was placed too far from the house for sounds to be heard therefrom, which in the circumstances was as well. As I finally approached and found myself trembling a little, Sarah's cries came distinctly to me. I began to run, but remembered my stepmother's instruction that a lady never hurries. So I paced myself anew.

"How dare YOU!" reached my ears from Sarah as I reached the door. Her voice sounded really wild and plaintive. My palm was moist as it touched the doorhandle, but it would not budge. "NO-WOH! Oh, the shame of this!" I heard and then at my somewhat feeble though excited rattling the door was opened and there blocking my view within was, of all people, Bertha, the wife of our coachman, who was some forty years of age and buxom of form.

"HA-AAAAR!" screeched Sarah then and all was revealed to my startled gaze while Bertha moved and thrust the door to, putting a bar across it.

There across a small deal table, so narrow that it supported but her shoulders and her tummy, hung Sarah, bereft of all save her stockings, shoes and her chemise which, being well and tightly tucked up about her hips, gave full display to the naked orb of her bottom. To her rear stood our stepmother, flourishing the selfsame black whip of many thongs which I had seen the night before. Yet this seemed itself as nothing to what else astounded my gaze. Bound to the wall immediately in front of Sarah and but two feet from her was Robert, his trousers down and his shirt wreathed fast about his waist so that his risen penis and balls were wantonly in full view. His hands being tied behind his back and fastened, as I soon saw, to a ring set into the wall, he could move not, no more than could Sarah whose legs had been stretched out in a wide vee so that her ankles might be secured to each of the legs of the table.

"Let me go-woh-oh!" Sarah screeched, having our brother's cock in full view.

For her cry she received a hissing stroke of the whip and I saw then how the thongs splayed out, their little knotted tips biting into her bottom as might have done two score of bees. This causing her to writhe as best she could and squeal loudly, my stepmother turned to Bertha—who had approached closer to the table—and asked, "Is this not the best way?"

"It is that an' all, m'am. I have my own daughter seen to likewise and the better she is for it. She don't spurn a hand at her bottom now nor a little feel which gives her a nice tickle. They has to be brought to it, though, and the proud ones the more. Miss Sarah now, she'll come up well, though she don't know it."

"YAAAAAH! I shall tell Papa! Oh you wicked things," cried my sister, whose cheeks were tinged a most pretty pink where the whip had caught her, as again it did now.

"Be quiet, girl, or I shall have Bertha do it and she will do it harder."

SWEEEE-ISSSSH! sounded the thongs and then again, coursing first from the left and then the right while I, utterly bemused and frozen in my attitude, stood ignored behind them. Sarah did not know I was there, I could swear. I did not wish her to, though could not help a stirring in me at the luscious vision she presented. Her long legs, being wide apart, gave full view to the sweet lips of her quim, surrounded as they were by a bouquet of curls. Her bottom, round as an apple and indeed more sensuously appealing than I ever thought it to be, positively glowed as SWEEE-ISSSSH! SWEEE-ISSSH! the small whip sang again.

She had ceased to try to speak now. Sobs, moans and all sorts of little cries were rent from her. Head bent over the edge of the table, she avoided looking at the cock of Robert which prodded manfully up to her view. His eyes were blank yet had a staring of wildness as well they might have done. It occurred to me that he must have been already bound—by Bertha obviously—while Sarah was being stripped and so all her charms had been presented to his gaze. He has seen her snatch, I thought, and he has his prick up. It was a wicked thought, but I could not avoid it.

"NO-NO-NO—-PLEASE!" Sarah howled, finding voice again while the crest of our brother's penis seemed to quiver ever more eagerly.

"Cup his balls, Bertha, and hold them tight. I wish him not to come. He has had a fine sight of her and will be rampant for hours," my stepmother said, thus echoing my thoughts.

"A nice pair he has and full of cream, I'd lay a wager, m'am," Bertha chuckled, doing as she was told while Robert's eyes bulged. His testicles looked like two large eggs on her palm which she kept tightly pressed up.

SWEEE-ISSSH! The whip sounded for the last time, on this occasion coming well up beneath poor Sarah's burning bottom so that her hips jerked violently and a shrill series of wild sobs were rent from her.

My stepmother turned to me then, a finger at her lips and pointed to a side table on which stood a small pot. I gazed bemused for a moment but then she clicked her fingers impatiently and so I hurried to it and handed to her the little glazed receptacle that I saw was filled with cream. Having done so, I stepped back, fearful that Sarah might somehow see me. Letting the whip slide to the floor, my stepmother dipped her little finger within and then deftly applied the cream to the little wrinkled orifice that peeped between my sister's nether cheeks.

Sarah's head shot up immediately and she screeched

and tried in vain to wriggle madly. At that she received such a slap on her bottom as made her howl, whereat the cream was applied more generously and then to my awed gaze a forefinger was eased up within her bottomhole, half inch by half inch. At that Sarah's mouth opened wide as did her eyes. A gritting screech escaped her. Her bottom waggled, but being invaded as it was could do no other than accept the salute.

"Very well, Bertha, " said my stepmother amid Sarah's gargling sounds.

At that, Bertha loosed the bonds behind Robert's back and prodded him firmly forward. Seeing his stiff cock then so close, Sarah waggled her face madly from side to side the while that her legs strained as the forefinger eased now more powerfully back and forth in her tight fundament.

"Hold her nose, Bertha, and put it in," snapped my stepmother.

I could not believe what I heard, but with that Bertha took hold of our brother's pulsing tool with one hand and with the other pinched Sarah's nostrils so that her mouth was forced to open. As deftly as a plum might be inserted in the mouth, so then was Robert's prick between her lips. His eyes appeared to come out on stalks and his head hung back with a look of perfect ecstasy on his face.

"GAAAAR!" Sarah choked, but so swiftly was the introduction made that a full four inches of Robert's thrumming stem were now buried between her lips. To add to her sensations then, our stepmother removed her finger with a faint PLOP! and gave my sister's bottom a hearty smack.

"NOW, my dear, you will remain so. Bertha will release your nose and I shall stand steady with the whip. Should you attempt to eject Robert's prick from your mouth, I shall whip you hard for a full ten minutes and without a pause. Be certain, Sarah, of my determination in this matter. Very well, Bertha. I shall give her but one more taste of the thongs to remind her of her fate should she choose to disobey. So!"

The cry that came from Sarah as the many thongs hissed across her now fully pink and quite adorable bottom was of course utterly choked back and suppressed by the throbbing rod within her mouth. True to her word, however, our stepmother let the whip hang loose to her thigh whereat Bertha released her hold on Sarah's nose.

"Keep your prick in her mouth now, Robert, but do not come. You hear me!"

Robert could not reply, of course. His mouth hung open like a yokel's. Moving slightly sideways I saw that Sarah's lips were compressed tightly and no doubt desperately about the fleshy stalk. Her eyelashes fluttered and her eyes were closed. She moaned interminably in her throat. I loved her then—so strange a thing to say but so defenseless and so beautiful she looked.

"Suck a little on it, Sarah. Come, dear, do it. I shall know by the movements of your cheeks if you are obeying," came softly from our stepmother who quite tenderly then stroked my sister's hair with one hand and her quivering bottom with the other. I could but guess however dimly at what then was passing in Sarah's mind and how scorched her poor bottom must feel. I felt compassion for her, and no less tenderly than the urging stroking of the hands about her. Hot flushed as she was her cheeks sucked in once and then with a gargling cry puffed out again.

"Very well, that will do. Out with it, Robert, and turn your face to the wall. You have seen today more than you have merited."

Turned about he then was by Bertha and quite roughly. Poor thing. I did feel for him. Our stepmother bent then to untie Sarah's ankles, but then suddenly appeared to recall my presence. Motioning Bertha not to let my sister turn her head—though such would have been exceedingly difficult for her to do—she ushered me out through a quietly opened door.

"Return to the house. Sarah will soon be out. You must comfort her, you know," she said almost quaintly.

I wanted to. It was my task to do so, as I saw it. I would kiss her poor bottom and comfort her indeed.

"We shall have time to talk later," my stepmother added, which saying gave me a feeling of ever greater importance so I took myself quickly back into the house and there awaited Sarah's return. Indeed so impatient was I that I peeped from my bedroom window which gave out on to the garden and in but a few moments saw her stumbling back, her hair awry and bodice open. She was not crying but had a hollow look on her face.

I left my door open, pretending to be busy and of great innocence. Upon mounting the stairs I heard her give a little wail which I knew was intended to draw my attention and so hurried out on to the landing and gazed down in seeming wonder upon her.

"Oh, Clara!"

It was then that she gave way fully to emotion and so stumbled against the wall that I ran down a few steps to her side and supported her.

"Sarah, what ails you? How dusty your dress is!"

"You d . . . d . . . do not know what has h . . . h . . . happened to me!"

"Come to your room, dearest, and lie down. Tell me all."

Led sobbing into her room, she fell upon her bed in a posture of abandonment, lying on her tummy. I sat beside her and stroked her hair, much indeed as our stepmother had done but long moments before.

"Tell me all. What is so terrible? Where are the others? Have you been attacked?"

So well did I act my part that I chided myself inwardly for my duplicity. As I sat back, Sarah's head moved and slumped into my lap. At any other time the gesture would have been one of great innocence, but I was no longer in that state. The side of her mouth was upon my thigh, above my stocking top. I felt its softness and its moisture through my dress and could not but help think that these were the same lips that had enfolded themselves around Robert's cock.

"Oh, Clara, I was wh . . . wh . . . whipped!" she burst out.

"What? Oh, you could not have been! Who would dare do such a thing?"

"Why, Stepmama, of course. Oh, and Bertha was there and she held me over! My poor bottom, and I had done nothing, Clara, nothing, I swear!"

The strain of hysteria in her voice aroused me and I moved her so that she lay full upon her back, a perfect cascade of shining tears rolling down upon her cheeks. Her bottom moved fretfully. Her whole posture demanded comfort and attention. I cast myself upon her as though to restrain her in her movements, making to affect great agitation at her news. She had not mentioned Robert, though. I thought that strange and yet could understand her motive.

"Of course you have done nothing," I soothed. "Come, let us have off with your dusty dress and make you pretty again."

"I hate her, I hate her!"

"Yes, darling, yes."

"Don't undress me."

Her plea was all too late. She was willing, it seemed to me, to be bundled about a little. Females in a certain state of excited distress are often so, as I was since to learn. I had to rumple her much in removing her dress and then her chemise, my exclamation of apparent surprise bursting out when I pretended to discover that she wore no drawers.

"Oh, you poor thing, she took them off!" I burst.

"St . . . st . . . stop it!" Sarah jerked. Her garters were white and pink, most pretty in appearance and matching well with the creamy shade of her stockings. Her legs, being long, were finely tapered, though swelling voluptuously at their junction where a proud and well-furred bush flourished its dark brown curls.

"Show me," I urged and rolled her over on to her tummy. The sparkling pink of her bottom was still evident. It bumped a little as I touched it with my fingers and a mewing sound came from her while her fingers clawed into the quilt. Since she was clearly in no great physical discomfort, I divined instinctively a sense of excitement in her that she would have preferred to hide yet could not help but let seep forth. Murmuring my condolences, as it were, I bent over beside her on the bed and applied my lips to her quivering halfmoons which had all the appearance of strawberries and cream.

"Don't, Clara," she whispered, but I knew her frailty now for she did not kick nor endeavour to roll over.

"Shush—let me comfort my poor baby," I murmured and in so doing put on a greater maturity than my years indicated. Soothing my lips all about, I slyly observed the relaxing of her shoulders and a shy hiding of her face which she effected by crooking up one arm and burying her head in the fold of her elbow. "Now it feels better, now it feels better," I intoned. The warm silky surface of her well-cleft moon enchanted me. The taut smooth skin seemed to stir willingly under the moist blessing of my mouth. "Is it nice?" I asked a little daringly. Her cheeks contracted and then relaxed.

"No," she answered pettishly, but I knew it not to be true.

"I will make it nice, truly I will," I whispered and began to stroke her naked back which rippled agreeably to my touch. My other hand I cupped gently beneath the lower bulge of her firm bottom so that she might not move and then with a rising thrill of sensuousness dipped my tongue into her cleft and wisped it up and down.

"C . . . C . . . Clara!" she uttered in pretended shock, "wh . . . wh . . . what are you doing?"

There was no strength nor rising reprimand in her voice and then came to me such words as our stepmother might have uttered.

"Be quiet—it is for your good," I said. The die was cast. I was tasting her and finding the sensation wickedly exciting. Without further ado I parted the springy cheeks of her bottom with both hands and twirled the tip of my tongue all around her puckered rosette.

"N . . . n . . . no!" she blathered, yet her bottom gave such a little jerk as betrayed and denied the refusal of her cry.

Such being my arising nature, I suppose, I pressed my fingertips tighter into her and thereby exposed her nether aperture more fully. Indeed, it opened a little, which permitted me to flick the tip of my tongue within. A frantic moan came from Sarah and she kicked, though not viciously. It was rather as though she were endeavouring to avoid something that she found pleasurable. So very much indeed can be read by such febrile movements of the body. I was determined as it seemed to me then to conquer her now and held her bottom cheeks ever further apart. As I did so she made to rise by pressing up with her hands, but in that moment the bedroom door opened and a voice sounded above us.

"It is called *feuille de rose*," I heard my stepmother declare. So quick was she in response to the revealed situation that her words were immediately followed by the snapped command, "Hold her!"

I shrieked in apparent alarm as did Sarah, but prevented her from rising and indeed pressed her tightly down once more by appearing to collapse upon her. With great presence of mind, however, our stepmother made it seem that I would escape for she then spat, "Hold her, I say, Clara, or I shall whip you in turn!"

"Oh!" I quavered for good effect while Sarah drummed with her hands upon the quilt in dismay.

Then with the swiftest of steps we were joined at the bedside. Bending and taking hold of Sarah's knees while I slyly relaxed my weight upon her for a moment, our stepmother deftly swung her over on to her back wherewith I fell across Sarah with a well-considered shriek. Thus having my face hid and my back turned upon our intruder, I felt only a flurry of limbs and then a soulful cry from Sarah.

"AH-OOOH! Don't let her!" she cried, but already our stepmother had knelt and—thrusting back Sarah's legs until her knees all but touched her tummy—applied her lips and tongue to her moist honeypot. "NOO-NOOO-NOOOO!" hummed Sarah. Her wild face was jerked from side to side, the tendons on her neck straining.

A soft lapping sound came to my ears. I held my arms around my sister's neck as though in bewilderment, my grasp restraining her head from twisting so much and my cheek finally coming against her own velvety one. She snuffled and gasped. I felt the jerking of her hips and heard the steady, succulent sound of our stepmother's tongue all about her cunny.

"DA-DA-DAH!" Sarah moaned. I appeared as one dazed and yet at the same time a little excited at what was happening.

"Oh, darling," I whispered. Her eyes glazed, her movements becoming less frenetic. I felt a quivering throughout her entire body. Her back arched and strained. Had I but known it, her bottom was now firmly cupped and her cunny already spurting its juices.

"OH-WOH-WOH!" she whimpered and then as if by some divine chance our mouths came together. I sought her tongue. Shy as it was at first it came at last to meet mine. Violent tremors shot through her. I stroked her breasts and found her nipples hard, passing my thumb sensuously back and forth across the quivering tips. She was utterly lost. Her moans wafted into my mouth. A gurgling cry and she came again, quite flooding the lips and tongue that were assuaging her. Then as if in a swoon she loosed her mouth from mine, sank down and lay still whereupon our stepmother rose, delicately wiping her mouth.

"Draw her full on to the bed," she murmured.

"Oh, what is to do?" I asked, playing my role well.

"Be quiet, child, for you too will learn soon enough," she replied in skilful complicity and in a trice Sarah lay naked to her stockings between us while our stepmother dealt with her most lovingly, stroking her hot face, kissing away her little sparkling tears and passing her lips over her own.

"You know how I have longed to kiss you, Sarah," she whispered, bringing my sister's eyes beneath her own. Truly Sarah looked most beautiful in that moment, her inner thighs glistening with her spendings, her breasts swollen and her nipples erect. Laughing softly, our stepmother traced the curves of my sister's lips with her fingertip and caused them to part in peachlike sweetness. "You will keep your mouth open when I tell you and you will keep your legs open, Sarah, when I tell you. Do you understand now?"

"You wh . . . wh . . . whipped me," Sarah moaned as though in blank astonishment still that such a thing could happen.

"And shall again if you are wilful. You see now how I have spurred you to fulfilment? You are in course of training, as soon Clara shall be. You will play filly to the stallions, my love, receive the libations from their throbbing cocks and learn to handle them at will."

So saying, our stepmother smothered Sarah's mouth with her own and, gliding one slim hand down her belly, commenced to play her fingers amid her curls. Sarah spluttered, choked and gasped—might even have wrenched her lips away had the hand not been insistent.

In a moment she quivered, straightened down her legs, and spilled her juices out anew.

CHAPTER FOUR

"I HAVE BEGUN drawing Sarah over the hills and plains of understanding," said my stepmother a little later, having left Sarah quiet and huddled up upon her bed. "Do you understand?" she asked.

"She will be whipped again, you mean, if she does not let someone do it with her?" I countered naively.

"It is not so simple as that—not so simple by far, my pet. You were willing to attend to her. I am doubly pleased with you at that. *Feuille de rose* . . . did you hear me say that when I entered? It means the pointing and luring of the tongue around the nether orifice that Nature intended for our pleasures as much as our cunnies. However, that is a diversion. Such subtleties will come to you better later. As to your 'someone,' that is precisely how it must not be. You have seen now Robert twice in rampant state. How easy it would be for me to satisfy him, to draw forth the spurting juice from his cock. Ah, you blush—but that as you well know by now is the major purpose of his tool. Men stride about the world like conquerors. Women are docile to them when they should not be."

"Oh, but you whipped poor Sarah in front of him and now he will lose all respect for her," I objected.

"Why you sillikins, could I not have let him have her if I wished? It is far from my intention to degrade my own fair sex. My purpose is to uplift and make them strong. Scarce a man lives who is not a schoolboy at heart and who does not wish the forbidden sight of skirt uplifted, drawers at droop. Some are fondlers and others sniffers. They behave indeed like dogs on heat. As for girls, they know not how to comport themselves and believe that in order to please the males they must surrender to them, bear their children and become haggard and unlovely in the process. You mark what I am saying, Clara?"

I nodded and again felt awed. She knew well enough that I was imbibing her every word.

"The mastery of males begins—mostly oddly perhaps to your mind, my sweet—with the mastery of females. Only another female may set herself to this task, for otherwise a male would merely wreak his will upon her and then pass on to others. A girl thus must be taught to receive the cock while the male himself is seen, observed, controlled. At first she may be in a perfect frenzy at it and buck truly like a young filly when his prick is to her. This inspires her in turn with a certain disdain of the male, though his weapon itself may have given her final pleasure. In arranging matters thus I bring the male to certain subjugation—performing as it were the role of his Mama whom he reveres and scolding him for his sins while yet occasionally ensuring that he commits them. For such commissions of sin he is punished and knows he will be. He is like a little boy for whom the pantry door is ever held ajar, so all is tempting to his view."

I found myself wriggling. "Have I . . . have I got to do this?" I asked nervously.

"Of course," she replied crisply, "what else? I shall bring you through fire yet, and you will thank me for it. Should you of course prefer to live a dull life such as Society has in store for you . . . "

"Oh no!" I interjected.

"Well then," she smiled, "matters are settled. Once you have a long, thick stiff prick nestling in your pussy or buried 'twixt your cheeks, you will know well enough the pleasure of it. Moreover you yourself will learn to control the male—that is to say, the number of thrusts he affords you and how steady or fast they may be, for all is designed to afford the maximum of pleasure to the female. He, poor worm, slumps limp afterwards and can do nothing more whereas the female, glowing with health and voluptuous desires, may take another and another at her will. That is the secret of our supremacy, Clara."

All was new to me and yet I understood, or if my understanding was not comprehensive then at the least I believed her every word.

"A demonstration will suffice better, dear. Wait here upon my bed."

With that she bustled out and long minutes passed. Some inkling of what she might be about stirred in me and I fain would have run. Indeed I started up but then sank back upon the bed whereupon a curious lassitude seized me and I felt as I did when lying in a meadow in the sun, toying with buttercups and having not a care in the world. Even when my stepmother entered again—alone—I did not stir but ruffled my head into the pillow and smiled at her with a sweet pussycat look as she afterwards said.

"Draw your skirt up beneath your bottom and take your drawers off," she told me.

Such was my mood that I obeyed without question and even mischievously spread my legs the better to show off my slit at which she laughed, asked me to sit up with my back against the headboard and to draw my knees up a little.

"Stay now," said she gently whereat I was all of a bubble at what was going to happen and braced my feet into the coverlet. Then she turned about again and was gone, but this time more briefly for when the door reopened it was to admit herself followed by Robert and Bertha.

Oh my heavens, what a sight! The upper hallway must well have been cleared of servants and he prepared in secret quiet. For my brother wore only his shirt which at the front was tucked back so that his erection was in full view. Seeing me in an apparent state of readiness he blushed deeply and might have retreated had not Bertha given him a push and closed the door. The greatest of my amazements however derived from the fact that around his neck was a thick and studded dog collar to which was attached a leash that Bertha held. Some sound escaped my throat but it was scarcely coherent.

"Be still and be quiet, Clara," my stepmother said briskly as though to infer to my brother that I had no option other than to obey. For all he knew perhaps I had been whipped as Sarah had been. I was thus in a sense excused in his eyes, though he had seen me well enough as a watcher in the summerhouse.

Stepping in front of and to one side of him, Bertha gave a tug on the leash and drew him forward so that his bare knees bumped the side of the bed and his balls swung. My stepmother stood with arms folded near the head of the bed and close to me.

"Up with you, Master Robert," Bertha said.

I felt he must have been coached in this, for somewhat awkwardly—and not apparently being allowed to use his hands whereby to lever himself up—he got upon the bed on his knees so that one of his legs nudged mine, making me start.

"Open your legs more, Clara," came from my stepmother.

I gulped and obeyed. Clearly I was making room for my brother who by various murmurings from Bertha and tugs on the chain was brought in closer to me, but not so much that our bodies touched. I in a half-reclining position found my eyes level with the bulbous crest of his cock and saw more clearly than ever how the faint blue veins stood out upon the noble column of flesh. Bertha then moved behind me and at such a distance that the leash was taut, so preventing him, as I divined, from jerking forward.

"Now, my love, you are about to see in a matter of minutes how the male is pleasured, how brief that pleasure appears to the females—though I may say that I believe it to be intense—and how he is enfeebled afterwards. Robert—you will not move now, sir, or I shall have your buttocks made redhot."

My lips were parted, my own face suffused. I knew not where to look yet ever felt my gaze drawn to the wondrous weapon he displayed. It was then already some good eight inches long and of fair girth. His balls were heavy and reminded me of ducks' eggs, though hairy. As our stepmother's hand approached his tool, his teeth gritted and he stared straight out above my head. A snorting sound came from his nostrils in the moment that her beringed fingers enfolded it, the tips running gently up and down the swollen shaft before she took hold of it more purposefully.

"This, Clara, is called 'milking,' " she said to me quietly and then began to frot him, luring her ringed fingers up and down his prick so that his breath panted and flowed out in longing moans. "One may take one's time about it, Clara. You will learn in due course how to modulate the movements of your hand, whether to bring the male on quickly and to make him gush or to quell his sense of urgency, for if the cock is held tightly—so!—then he cannot come in any event."

"GAAAR-AH!" my brother choked and his head hung back.

"Be QUIET!" she scolded him and now, cupping his balls with her free hand, tickled them beneath with her little finger, causing his hips to rock.

I swallowed and my eyes grew bleared. The most itching and tingling of sensations made itself felt in my cunny so that I longed to toy with myself but had not the daring to do so in front of him. I confess that I let my thighs sag even wider so that my cuntlips veritably pouted at him and so no doubt increased his mad desires. Certainly he panted more and his mouth gaped the while that her luring hand worked steadily.

"There will come a time, Clara," said she—while all the while Bertha stood silent in the background—"when I shall modulate his explosions of sperm the more. He will learn to come only on a certain count—which is to say perhaps fifty strokes of my hand, or the same number when embedded in a quim or bottom. Should he, or of course any other male in training, give way to his lewd excitement and eject his sperm prematurely, then punishment will follow and he will receive no pleasuring during a disciplinary period. For the moment, however, since Robert has not been milked before, I propose to give him a certain leeway."

"NEEE-YNNNNG!" Robert gritted. He was plainly near his tether for our stepmother's hand was warm and comforting and, being soft as velvet, must have teased him beyond endurance. The poor soul, he did not try to disgrace himself, but having for the first time his younger sister so lewdly displaying herself to him the while and the lips of her pretty cunny to his view, he could not help himself. The breath literally whistled through his nostrils and her finger, I swear, tickled his balls the more.

"Oh, you bad boy—you naughty boy," she breathed, which words as I learned are manna to the yearning male, whether he be fifteen or fifty, for they deem them both encouraging and exciting while yet obtaining overtones of admonishment. Our stepmother now was watching his face. She knew the signs.

"I c . . . c . . . can't help! Oh, Mama!" he whined.

"Come then—come—spill your juice. Let us see how

fiercely it spurts," she commanded and to his profound dismay, no doubt, loosed her hold on him around his prick while still couching his balls on her palm.

I had of course never seen the male sperm erupt before. Perhaps by instinct I slumped down a little, thus inadvertently showing as much of my bottom to him as my slit. Desire must have raged in him for then with a croaking cry a veritable jet of white creamy liquid shot out and up in an arc that seemed to poise like a seagull in mid-air before it splashed down on my belly and my bush. So warm and lovely did it feel that I was entranced and, being just as quickly followed by another and another, so that the stream seemed endless, I felt myself inundated and all of a sticky swimming while Robert juddered, his hips jerking violently.

"More, you young brute, more," our stepmother intoned.

"HAAAR!" shuddered he. The jets were weaker now in their erupting. I could see them clearly bubbling out of the tiny hole in the knob of his cock. His thighs quivered violently and his jaw sagged the more. The bulb glistened deliciously with his spendings, and all the while our stepmother firmly cupping his balls while Bertha continued holding the leash taut to keep his head up. Then at last he was done and the last dribblings fell and spattered on to the bed. A long shuddering sigh came from him and his expression softened, his body slumping as much as the leash would allow.

All was then still and quiet.

"Very well, take him out, Bertha," our stepmother ordered. Limp as a reed he was drawn off the bed by a tugging of the leather strap. He looked cowed and yet his face appeared angelic, perfectly unlined and smooth.

"They are best when young," my stepmother observed, "yet the older men are equally amusing in their ways and can be known to ream a girl more vigourously. I prefer my beginners to be put to older men. Ah, what a froth you have from him upon your bush! It will be a full half hour at least before his young cock can be urged up stiff again. A man twenty years his senior may take even longer, yet no woman is exhausted in any wise by having a single fuck and, as I told you, can have several in a row, enjoying the last as much as the first and mayhaps more so. You had best bathe now, dear."

"Yes, Mama," I assented, though I so rarely called her that.

As ever, she turned away as if the entire matter had passed already from her mind and I knew that I was simply to imbibe what I had seen. Casting off my dress in my room and feeling a pleasant stickiness all between my legs, I put on a robe and went along to the bathroom—which is to say the one that I and Sarah used, for Stepmama now had her own, and a third and smaller one was for Papa's use. Finding the door locked, I shook the handle impatiently.

"Who? Who is it?" came Sarah's call. Her voice sounded nervous. When I answered, there was a splashing sound, a noise of grumbling, and then the door was partly opened and she stood holding a towel about her.

"Oh, is the water warm still? Have you finished?" I asked.

"Yes, but only just," she replied crossly and blushed. Not speaking, I cast off my robe and then my chemise and stood naked. The water was perfumed and inviting. Only recently then had we had water to come through taps in the bathrooms and it was a perfect joy, though made much heat and work for the servants in keeping the stove going to heat the water. Being cautious of her mood I got in and laved myself, sinking back with quite a smile upon my lips, for I knew more than she and indeed had learned more.

"Clara, what is to do?" she asked nervously.

"Why, you were very naughty and so was I. Mama was not displeased with us really," I replied simply.

"She is not our Mama—not our true Mama," Sarah said crossly and let the towel fall and began to brush her hair. Standing upright as she was her bottom protruded delightfully and I thought of how I had had my tongue there and teased her up while she wriggled. I did not doubt that she had enjoyed it and chided her inwardly for being a hypocrite. Besides, she had been tongued as well and could not now pretend that she had struggled overmuch against the insistent protrusion of our stepmother's tongue.

"Did you not like it?" I asked and soaped myself all over.

"No, of course I didn't, it was horrid. I did not know before that people did such things. If she whips me again I shall tell Papa."

"Will you not blush to tell him all?" I asked slyly whereat she spun around and scowled at me, though looking lovely still in doing that.

"What do you mean, Clara?" she spat but all was then bravado. I shrugged.

"Mama will say, I am sure, that she kissed you afterwards and all was well."

"Oh!" exploded Sarah and stamped her foot. Facing me then as she was and naked, her tits bouncing a little in her anger and her bush well fluffed out from the drying towel, a sudden wicked fantasy came to me that I would like to have Stepmama or Bertha hold her arms the while I knelt between her thighs and tongued her cunt. Perhaps this very thought drove me a full measure beyond what I had already learned, been taught, and had instilled into me. I wanted her cunny to sparkle on my tongue, to bring myself pleasure in doing it and hear her wild cries as she was forced to surrender.

"Let us not fret too much for I did not mind it really. I, too, have been caned, you know," I said proudly.

"You? Oh, you have not! What a story you are!"

"Oh, Miss Clevercuts, so you believe you know everything, do you? She took my drawers down and caned me stingingly upon my bottom—so there—and then she kissed me all about as she did you and it was nice," I said rather breathlessly.

That she believed me I did not doubt.

"I don't want to hear about it," she said crossly. "I think she is so awful for she will not allow me to wear drawers now."

I laughed. "Well, you can scarce tell Papa that, or shall you run to him and say, 'Look, Papa, I have no drawers on.' "

"Bah! you are as horrid as she sometimes, Clara," was her response, and gathering up her clothes got into them as quickly as she could, for my last words had clearly flustered her and she must have felt trapped. Well—she was trapped for a purpose and that to bring her pleasure, I told myself and found myself surprised by my own thought. Yet even then a sense of resolution was invading me and taking hold of me. I was conscious of our stepmother's aura and personality as though from a distance. It is said that now, in my twenty-fifth year, I also possess such. "I could feel you coming even though you had not then entered the house," a girl has said to me in midway or advanced passage of her training, and I have sensed it to be true, for I know the spell that my stepmama can still at times cast over me.

So perhaps one counts the steps of one's progress. Had I not had that conversation with Sarah in the bathroom I might have been left in limbo with her, wondering how to converse with her and what to do. As I dried myself, however, I was no longer in doubt. Robert's prick was quite adorable and I dreamed of the heavenly sensation of having it spout within me. Therefore, I decided, Sarah must also. It would be for her good. Her bottom and her cunt would be nourished by his libations, as would my own.

I, of course, was powerless to hasten matters. All lay

in our stepmother's hands. For three days nothing further happened that was untoward. Sarah appeared wary; Robert was quiet, though his eyes frequently fell adoringly on her. Upon the third day after she had tongued Sarah and milked Robert, she took us upon a picnic. Knowing how to beguile, she even drew Sarah out of herself and once or twice made her laugh.

I alone perhaps sensed or knew that the female spider was still weaving her intricate web.

CHAPTER FIVE

UPON OUR RETURN that afternoon we learned that Papa was to absent himself for a week. He was to Paris, it seemed, upon business, and privately I had no doubt he was being dispatched there. So perhaps did Sarah for she looked querulous. Little as we saw of him, yet she looked upon him in some way as her protector and thus asked him what he was to do there.

Being all seated in the drawing room and drinking tea, we were at ease. Papa looked very smart, I thought, in a white ruffled shirt and cravat and black trousers that had a broad silk seam down each side in the military fashion.

"Why, Paris is a city of wicked ladies," our stepmother laughed and looking at him asked, "Is it not true?"

He blushed faintly and looked, I thought, disturbed. Sarah bit her lip and clearly considered that such a remark should not have been made, but nothing missed our stepmother's ever watchful eye. Having finished her tea she plucked a peach from a cutglass bowl that stood upon a table at the side of her chair and rolled it in her hand, so drawing our attention to it in the silence that followed. As many peaches do it had a cleft in it which her thumb gently rubbed.

"How smooth it is and how round," she murmured. I held my breath. Sarah shifted in her chair. Women have a fine intuition of things not said or perhaps about to be said. Robert appeared uneasy, got up and with a mumbled excuse went out, more I believe to the relief of Sarah than myself. "Do you know what it reminds me of?" was asked and our stepmother extended her palm so that the peach stood as if in waiting upon it with the cleft—which I must say looked wickedly naughty and symbolic—pointing towards us.

No one answered. It was as though we were on a pinpoint of Time and the room very hushed. Papa opened a silver casket, rustled within and drew out a cigarette, though he smoked rarely. As if by deliberation she waited until he had struck a lucifer and lit it. The blue smoke coiled up silently.

"Do you not know?" she teased, and Sarah clenched her hands. "Why, it is like your bottom, Sarah, so perfectly rounded, so smooth, so prettily the cheeks parted and yet not."

"AH-OH!" exclaimed Sarah almost as if she had been bitten and jumped up and ran out as fast as a cat might when disturbed by a sudden loud noise.

"My dear!" Papa quavered.

"Why? What have I said?" Stepmama taunted. "William, you have not seen. . . . " And then she paused. I knew the meaning of her pause.

"I must see to my crochet work," I blurted and followed Sarah out, but she having gone upstairs all in a flash I loitered by the door.

"The poor girl, you have dismayed her terribly," I heard Papa say, though weakly I thought.

"Oh tush, as I was about to say, my pet, you have not seen her bottom. Perhaps a peach is not a good comparison—a polished apple might be better, the skin polished and smooth."

"I say, really!"

"The boldness of its protruberance! What a pert thrust it has, though perhaps no less than Clara's. Why, that dear child's *embonpoint* is perfectly exquisite—a mere tickle of it and she jerks and laughs, so merry is her pleasure to be fondled there. As to Sarah, her silly pride disdains an affectionate fingering round her nether globe and yet she trembles not a little when. . . . "

"P . . . p . . . perfectly improper," I heard Papa declare and then he uttered a little gasp.

"Like silk, my pet, or velvet. Her thighs are warm and fulsome, and such a bush between as springs against the hand and tickles up the palm as does a tuft of grass."

"J . . . J . . . Julia, I beg you. . . . "

"Is it not nice when I tease it so, William? How stiff you have become and that is very naughty of you. I trust you will not disport yourself so in Paris, for you know my wrath in such matters. I can be very cold to you, my love, if I choose. You are keeping these dear receptacles full for me, are you not, when next I choose to empty them."

"Ah dear God, how you taunt me so!"

"She wears garters of pink today, William. Very tight about her thighs they are. The frill of her chemise barely covers her tuft. Ah, do I make it quiver thus or is it the thought of it?"

"We sh . . . should not t . . . t . . . talk thus, my dear."

"Your foreskin is so taut by now I can barely move it! Hand me your kerchief. Shall I make it bubble? Restless she lies in bed at nights, her nightdress full drawn up about her hips, her legs atwist and bottom bumping. By morn her sheet is creased and moist. Do you not think that the effluvia which emanates from a proud young girl on heat is quite delicious? Stop it, you bad thing, you must not come. You know I forbid it."

"J . . . J . . . J . . . Julia!"

"Why, my pet, you are stuttering! What agitations!"

"L . . . l . . . let me! Oh, I beg you!"

"Most certainly not, William. Your mind is clearly overheated with wicked visions. Sit still, I tell you, for I am removing my hand. We shall discourse upon your return. I shall expect to find you in as fine fettle then as I do now. Fasten your trousers lest you disgrace yourself. Would you present yourself to Clara so, should she return?"

"Wh . . . what imp . . . impossible thoughts you have, Julia!"

"And what nonsense you talk, dear William. How can they be impossible if I have uttered them? Logic should be arranged as neatly as cups and saucers on a dresser, should it not?"

"You b . . . b . . . bewitch me and dismay me and . . . "

"Excite you? Did you not believe me when I said that Sarah has a delicious bottom, and Clara as well?"

I crept away. My ears burned, my face was full flushed. Running up to my room I doused my face in clear cool water from the bowl upon my marble washstand. The laving of the water settled me a little. Not only had I heard but I had envisaged her stroking of him as she had stroked dear Robert. Her power it seemed was infinite, her sway upon Papa complete. Yet he had not admonished her for it as strongly as he might. Thus I realised and thus did I contemplate. He was but putty in her hands. There was but one ruler of the household now, and she the one whose lips I longed to taste. Would she know that I had listened? It seemed to me that she knew all. Upon coming to me later and seeing to my appearance, she gave no hint of it.

"Your Papa will depart in the morning. There will be visitors," she said mysteriously.

"Are they nice?" I wished to ask, but the question would have sounded foolish.

"They are not known to you but soon will be, Clara, as also to your sister and brother. I have decided on a course other than I first set myself. I shall inculcate both you and Sarah by example."

At that I pouted, for it seemed to me that she was treating me once more as a mere beginner. I told her then of my conversation with my sister in the bathroom, whereat her eyes shone.

"Do you think I take you for a sillikins, a muff? I know you not to be. You set the finest of examples. Better however for the moment that Sarah and Robert do not think us both in league. Though we are, are we not?"

"Oh yes! What will happen? Who are the visitors?"

"A young lady and her guardian, my dear. They come by close and secret invitation. She is not unlike Sarah in appearance, nor as I understand in her ways. Bertha will assist in all. I have but a week to prepare the maiden who is called Clarissa. Her guardian will say little to you. I wish you not to speak to him."

"To keep him in his place?"

"How quick you are! You will not be dismayed by what you see, I know. Sarah may be difficult, but I will deal with her accordingly. If I have to deal with them together. . . . " She paused, then added quietly, "It may be necessary, of course."

"All right," I said quickly and felt with an upsurge of excitement that she was in part seeking my permission.

"Very well, then. You know I will bring Sarah to no harm. It is for her good—and yours."

"Yes," I replied dutifully.

Sarah, of course, being all put out, would not speak to her and avoided dear Papa until the moment of his leaving which seemed to worry our stepmother not a whit. She had made herself look lovelier than ever in a cream gown of some daring deshabille with such a plunging neckline as almost made her nipples peek above the lace and caused a dull flush to appear on Robert's cheeks at every wobbling of her tits. Of the visitors, she said nothing to my brother and sister and so their surprise was the greater when at precisely three that afternoon a carriage rolled up on the drive and there deposited them both.

All introductions being effected, I observed both closely. Clarissa had indeed the same figure as Sarah, though being even more patrician in features. Calm as she held herself I sensed her inner tensions as I did those of her guardian, a large quiet man of middling years whose voice ran deep upon the few occasions that he spoke. Clarissa looked slightly bewildered and sought to sit near Sarah, but my stepmother placed herself deftly between them and spoke of everything other than that which I guessed was on her mind.

Wine having been dispersed and drunk by all, my stepmother after half an hour rose, smoothed down her gown in such a manner that all eyes fastened on her and said to the guardian, whose name perhaps was Harold (for I have since learned that identities are oft disguised), "Shall we then go up?"

At that, Clarissa appeared to grip the arms of her chair but was gently prised into a standing position.

"My husband's study will be best," opined my stepmother who then led the way while Robert and Sarah sat in wonderment. I hesitated, but then in the doorway she turned to me. "You may come—as chaperone," she laughed. Two pairs of eyes followed me as I went out. Clarissa cleared her throat. A faint flush appeared on her smooth cheeks and she gathered up her skirts delicately as we ascended. The door to the study being open, my stepmother led the way in and closed the door, giving me a nod as an indication that I should take my seat on a couch, which I did. The desk was of mahogany and a wide one. It was a room I entered rarely, for its bookshelves then interested me not, imposing as they looked.

"Clarissa, you look very sweet. Come and stand by me," my stepmother said, seating herself in Papa's chair which had a round back and swivelled all about.

Hesitantly the young woman did so and thus faced her

guardian over the barrier of the desk. My stepmother then most unexpectedly looked across at me and asked, "When did I last cane you, Clara?"

"Oh, I—er—three days ago, or four perhaps," I stumbled, having been caught quite unawares.

"Are you the better for it now?" I was asked. "Yes," came out like a little bolting rabbit so that she laughed, half turned and looked up at Clarissa, asking, "And when were you?"

Clarissa blushed to her eyebrows. "Oh, I have not been!" she answered, shocked. My stepmother dotted, making a tut-tutting sound, and turning to Harold asked, "Have you not been lax with her?" As she spoke so she raised the arm that was just behind Clarissa, swept her hand up the backs of her thighs and gently tested the firm globe of her bottom so that the young woman jerked.

"I have—er—tried," stammered her guardian.

"You have removed her drawers?"

The question came so smoothly that it seemed a long interval passed before Clarissa uttered a shocked "Oh!" and went more pink than ever.

"Do be quiet, please," my stepmother urged her gently and then quite deliberately circled her hand about the girl's bottom, feeling no doubt its warmth and silkiness.

"There . . . there were objections," he stammered.

"From you? From you, Clarissa?" was uttered by my stepmother in astonishment. "Have you not let him put you over? Do you fear the cane? Would you prefer the birch or strap? Have you been mishandled? Is that the truth of it?"

"Madam I never. . . . " began Harold but was quieted by a steely glance and the words, "She will answer for herself." All the while her palm circled as if reverently and appeared to calm Clarissa a little though I would have sworn she wished to move.

"It is r . . . r . . . rude," she stuttered and tried to gaze everywhere but at her guardian.

"Rude?" my stepmother echoed in amazement. "All young ladies—or at least those of comely forms and merit—must be put up to it and before your age. Come, dear, let me see your drawers."

"Oh, I beg you no! Not in front of him!"

A perfect flurry ensued. I sat as still as a stick insect which pretends to be a twig. Clarissa made a wild dash around the desk, my aunt crying "Hold her!" which her guardian did. Head down and back bent, she struggled fiercely, but his strength being much the greater and with a fierce flush of his excitement in his face he had her bent full over on the desk the while that my stepmother, getting up, gripped the nape on Clarissa's neck in steely grasp.

"Leave her. I have her," she snapped at him, whereupon he took several paces back, his complexion unpleasantly florid and a certain bulge making itself to be seen already in his trousers. Then, clicking her thumb and finger at me as though I were but a servant (such was her manner to be at times), she commanded me crisply, "Uncover her."

Have I need to detail Clarissa's plaintive cries? She sobbed, expostulated, all but swore indeed as, crouching down, I took her gown and underskirt and raised them with a flourish to her hips. At that she screamed wildly, but by clamping her free hand over her mouth and keeping her head pressed down, my stepmother suppressed her cries and, bending slightly back, observed the beauty I already saw. Or I should use perhaps the plural. Clarissa's white drawers were quite thin and so moulded themselves to the outswelling of her halfmoons, delineating each and crumpling tightly into her groove. The pink ribbons of her drawers hung loose and prettily as oftimes is the case. Withal her ruffled garters, too, were pink—a colour much affected by young ladies, for it shows off well the white silk of their stockings. Her thighs swelled up, all richly creamed. Not a mole or other flaw showed upon her milksmooth skin, the whole bulge of her derriere being most enchanting.

"Oh my God, I shall die from this!" moaned she.

"Stuff and nonsense! Why should he not see your bottom and put it to a tingling of occasion? Have you not been tupped by some young gallant, eh?"

"I know not what you mean, I know not!"

"Nary a hand, Madam, so far as I know."

Unwisely the guardian had interjected. He had not been invited to speak. My stepmother's eyes flashed.

"Can you be sure? Very well, you shall have a glimpse of it and then you will retire, sir, if you please, and join my son and daughter in the drawing room again."

"NO!" came a muffled shriek from Clarissa. Her hips waggled madly, which could have done nothing but urge on the gentleman's fairly stiff condition. My stepmother held her tight, however, and my fingers were already busy. Perhaps my eagerness to see her well-cleft orb was little less than his.

"AH-HAH-HAAAR! NO!" sobbed Clarissa in despair but it was already far too late. Deftly I peeled them down and smoothed them to her knees. The fig of her quim peeped out, much nursed by curls. Her bum—for it is just occasionally a sweet word to be used—was pure perfection, larger by an inch or two than one expected and the gleaming pallor of its cheeks giving way to a faint gingerly hue where the hemispheres inrolled. I longed to palpitate them with my fingertips which I felt tingling for the task.

"I shall die!" came from Clarissa again, though the words were only just to be distinguished.

She was, of course, ignored. "You may go," my stepmother observed coldly to her guardian whose eyes were hot with wonder and with lust. He turned stiffly away, as well he might in his condition. At the door his gaze faltered and returned to the ardent moon of his desiring and which I do not doubt he had waited long years to have revealed to him. His fingers groped for the handle, for he seemed blind to all but the sight of his ward's naked bottom. My stepmother shook her head impatiently at him and a dull cast came upon his features as he exited.

"Beneath the cushion on the armchair seat you will find a paddle, Clara. Take it out," I was told.

Until then I had thought of paddles as merely instruments for propelling a boat along. What I soon found myself clasping was something not unlike a tennis bat and with the round part made of heavy leather.

"Now, my pet, attend to her bottom well with it," my stepmother said and I stepped back half a pace behind Clarissa, my palms not a little moist with excitement, to better judge my distance. A certain awkwardness obtained in my first using of the implement but upon meeting the girl's refulgent, bulging cheeks it made a most resounding SPLATT!

CHAPTER SIX

THERE IS an element of glee, I do confess, in warming up a young lady's bottom, particularly when she is fey or shy. Men are so rarely dab hands in this sort of exercise, for their enthusiasm for a different kind of sport soon overtakes them. The exercise brings up the cock and swells the balls and ere she knows it and before her bottom is brought to proper condition, the female is plugged or corked or reamed.

I am using here of course terms that I learned later. My stepmother told me that there was a wondrous gleam in my eyes as I stung dear Clarissa's bottom, perhaps enjoying doing so the more for knowing that her ardent cheeks had not been so treated before. Upon receiving the first, her head shot up but quickly was pushed down again. Firmness in such initiations is all.

SPER-LATT! I smacked a second time, the roundness of the paddle covering almost two-thirds of her bottom and bringing a rare shade of pink to the cheeks.

"The left cheek, then the right, then full across her orb, and then beneath," I was instructed.

How privileged I was to be so taught and with such an elegantly-formed pupil as Clarissa! Her face turned violently from side to side, my stepmother permitting the movement but ever keeping her palm clamped over the girl's mouth. My strokes beneath, coming up under her bulge, were not so effectual for I had not yet learned the particular and subtle wrist movements that since are second nature to me. A certain cushioning of air prevents the paddle by its very nature from belabouring too hard and yet it has a perfect sting and at the same time affords a deep sensation of heat.

Tears rolled from Clarissa's eyes over my stepmother's fingers as she strove by wild undulations of her hips and bottom to evade the strokes. As so often in such moments, a chance swinging of her hips would often bring her nearest bumcheek in perfect contact with the leather and so she was stung the more.

"Now, darling, three beneath. Bring them up well," I was told.

Clarissa's rounded derriere was by then a bright pink and merging into red. This time I measured the angle of the paddle and brought it up well, causing her to reach right up on to her toes under the impelling sweep of the paddle. "GAR-HAAAAR!" I heard her choke at each one and saw her burning cheeks contract and then relax. A nod from my mentor and I dropped the paddle. I wanted dearly to kiss those heated hemispheres and my stepmother could not miss the fact, so gave yet another nod and a little smile. Her lips distinctly formed the words, "Feuille de rose!"

Enchanted and quite unable to resist, I fell silently to my knees behind the sobbing girl so that her luscious bottom loomed before my face. How violently she bucked when first she felt my lips! My stepmother, anticipating the movement, pressed her free hand firmly down into the small of sweet Clarissa's back and so restrained her movement, though her hot bum still bumped agreeably to my nose.

Thereupon I grasped her cheeks and, thumbing within

her groove on both sides, drew the plump elastic half-moons just so far apart that her crinkled orifice came into my view. I heard the snorting of her breath though her nostrils, delved my tongue and found her coy, tight hole, Twirling my tongue, I felt a sense of ecstasy as the rimmed ridge came to my touch. What a mélange of scents I experienced—that heady *odor di feminina* of which only the most knowing and subtle think to write! Then perhaps in that moment the true meaning of *feuille*, or leaf, came to me and I curled my tongue upwards on both sides like a leaf that has drawn up its edges, and worked it tight within.

"THOOOOOO!" I heard Clarissa whine.

"Very delicately, dear, just back and forth. Reach in as far as you can," I then was told.

Again and again Clarissa's bottom bumped my face, but I held her. Then, reaching up one hand, though not instructed to, I felt her quim, its softness, its rolled lips, its moistness. Running my forefinger between the oily cleft I sought her spot and there rubbed gently as my stepmother had done to Sarah.

"NEEE-UUUMPH!" Clarissa exploded, yet her most intimate parts were divulging secrets that her mind would not. Her legs began to tremble as I circled my fingertip and felt her bud erect itself the more. My tongue squirmed in her bottomhole, drew out and then invaded once again. At that her bottom began to rotate a little rather than to rebel, and of course my stepmother was watching like a hawk her every move. The urgings of Clarissa's hips were a little more womanly now rather than merely childish. The bulging flesh of her bottom glowed to my face and her exudations were becoming excitingly sticky. The breath rattled in her throat.

"All right," my stepmother snapped. She sensed exactly, it seemed, when Clarissa might come on and spill her dew. I had been about, in fact, to delve my face up right between her thighs and bring her fur upon my mouth.

A little disappointed that this final pleasure had not been afforded me, I rose, quivering with excitement, while with a sudden movement my stepmother swung Clarissa up into a standing position and whirled her around so that their bodies bumped together, face to face.

"Now, my dear, you will be quiet," came in a steely tone.

"You . . . you . . . you . . . " moaned Clarissa wildly, her skirts still wreathed up and her bottom a perfect glory of pink and white.

"Yes, I—I, Julia," came my stepmother's response and with that she dragged the young woman's head back and forced her to stare full into her eyes. Even as I had been, Clarissa appeared mesmerised, her chin gripped commandingly and one hand cupped beneath her naked bottom.

"Go, Clara—I will bring her down in a moment," I was told. Disappointment showed clear in my expression yet I did unquestioningly as I was told. There are moments, as I learned, when there should be no witnesses to what is said or done. Descending to the drawing room, I felt an air of awkwardness obtaining.

"What is to do?" Sarah asked me rather pertly, though I could have sworn that she knew very well what was to do, for some scuffling at least must have made itself heard.

"Clarissa is being tutored," I said casually and gave her a slightly cold look for asking so open a question. A silence then obtained as if no one knew what to say, all minds being busy above stairs, so to speak. "Will the gentleman not have more wine?" I asked and then in a sharper tone than I intended, said to Robert, "See, please, to his glass."

Clarissa's guardian cleared his throat, his eyes not being above perusing both Sarah's breasts and thighs as well as my own. It was the first command, if it could be called such, that I had ever given to my brother, he being more used to ordering me about, and I was no doubt as much surprised as he when without question he rose to oblige, not so much out of courtesy I felt as at receiving an order from a female. Going to the sideboard, he obtained the bottle and was in mid-stride with it when our stepmother appeared leading Clarissa, who looked unconscionably pale.

"That will not be needed, Robert," we were told. My brother then stared from her to me and then back to my stepmother, which I was vaguely pleased at, as though he were caught between two fires. Being urged forward gently, Clarissa sat in a chair neighbouring that of her guardian. We were then as an audience might be that waits the rising of the curtain. The bottle was replaced upon the sideboard.

"An air of expectancy reigns," my stepmother smiled. Totally in command of us as she was, she took the centre of the floor so that we gazed on her as pupils do a Mistress. Her words were cleverly put, for no one could comment upon them. She waited a moment as if daring one or another to do so and then clapped her hands, making us jump, or making at least myself jump. At that Bertha appeared, dangling the little whip in her hand, and with her a tall, slim youth close to Robert's age whom I had seen about their cottage on the estate. I knew him as a labourer but upon this occasion he wore what might have been styled his Sunday best—narrow black trousers and a white shirt.

"Excellent," my stepmother said and, while all looked a trifle apprehensive as Bertha turned the key in the lock, went on blandly, "We now have three males to three females here. Of them all perhaps Charlie is the better trained, for you have seen to him well, have you not, Bertha?"

"That I have, m'am. He's allowed a sniff or two around me but no more than that if you don't count his queenings."

The meaning of that last word being unknown to me, I sat fair still. Sarah and Clarissa had turned into statues. Robert was transfixed. As for Clarissa's guardian, he made play at first to be intrinsically interested in a tidying of his cravat.

"Yes," my stepmother said. She crooked her finger and the young man approached, looking neither wary nor nervous but as one in a dream who is hailed to step towards a goddess. "Do you like it, Charlie? Do you like what is done to you?" was asked him softly.

He shuffled thereat, seeming not to be able to meet her eyes—or wishing so much to do so that he did not dare. "I have my obediences, m'am," he murmured, the statement producing a broad smile from my stepmother who, turning, asked of us, "You see? One here at least knows his obediences, as you all shall. Robert—you will lie down in the centre of the floor as will Charlie. Head to feet I will have you, and about a foot apart."

I heard Sarah swallow. Clarissa shifted in her chair. No sooner were the words spoken, however, than Charlie slid down on to his back and I saw now the reason why my stepmother had disposed of so many oddments of furniture. There was room for all to move. Robert was hesitating, but a further snapped command brought him up. He moved stiffly, shaking not a little and then laid himself down in the manner ordained so that his head came level with Charlie's feet. At that, Bertha moved into the room and came closer to my stepmother, so that I knew a further drama was to ensue. All eyes were on her whip.

Clarissa's guardian made as though to rise and then sank down again. "I think. . . . " he began.

"You may indeed do that but be quiet about it," came the cold reply. "I will have no arrogance of male wishes here. Think you that you have come to a playground for your lusts, or a brothel? Has he learned to dip?" my stepmother asked of Bertha, inclining her eyes towards

Charlie who lay quiet and supine, his fingers clenched, as did Robert.

"Full well he has, m'am, and keeps it there long minutes when he is called to."

"Good. The art is one that Robert has to learn, but soon now shall. Sarah, Clarissa—get up!"

"Oh! can I not go upstairs?" Sarah wailed.

"Later, my dear, when you are fit and ready for it. Stand forward both of you and side by side. Bertha—tie their hands. I will have no nonsenses."

"Mama! I beg you!" cried my sister, but Bertha was already bustling past her to the sideboard where—all having evidently been prepared in advance—several lengths of cord were to be found. A quavering"No!" came from Sarah who stared over her shoulder at what was revealed, whereat my stepmother, advancing on the pair, seized both their chins and all but barked, "Heads up! Look straight ahead! Hands behind your backs!"

Sarah began to cry. I expected her to. Clarissa paled but did not struggle, In a trice they were bound with arms behind them. The young lady's guardian appeared as one spellbound.

"P . . . p . . . please do not whip us," Sarah burst, and was ignored.

"Draw their dresses up and wreath them to their hips, Clara."

"NO!" came a screaming cry from both, yet all was done in a flash and Sarah—having no drawers on and Clarissa's evidently being left upstairs—both stood with bellies, pussies, bare, and thighs unveiled. Their heads hung. How sweetly desolate they stood!

"Sir—you will sit upright and upon this chair," Bertha then said, bringing forward a plain wooden one with straight arms. Her words were of course directed to Clarissa's guardian who looked as dumbstruck as a man might be.

"Look here, I say!" he expostulated, but at that my

stepmother moved quickly to him and so grasped his hair at the back of his head that he cried out and flailed his arms, though not daring to strike her.

"UP! UP!" she spat, whereat like a craven schoolboy he allowed himself to be raised (I swear with tears starting in his eyes at the way she tugged) and was rapidly flopped down into the plain deal chair to which Bertha then swiftly tied his wrists and then his ankles which were secured to the legs of the chair. His knees thus being drawn apart, he looked a total prisoner.

"M . . . M . . . Madam, if I had known!" he spluttered, whereat my stepmother wheeled on him, her face a perfect fury and her half-veiled breasts rising and falling.

"Had known what? That you might take Clarissa's drawers down and pummel her at pleasure with your prick? Does your wife know of such tricks? Be silent, sir, and observe."

My surprise was no less great than that of Sarah and Clarissa who both peeped up from their shameful stance and then dropped their heads again.

"Very well, to their queenings," my stepmother said. Very gravely then she removed her gown as did Bertha who—plumper than she—was still well modelled in her fulsome curves. My heavens, what a sight! Both were corseted and tightly so, their breasts full bulging naked over rims of lace, nipples erect upon the ripe and creamy mounds. Arrogantly their bottoms moulded full into their directoire drawers whose crinkled legs were tightly spanned about their thighs.

"Make them look up, Clara. Hold their heads back!" my stepmother ordained so that I—a minor Mistress in my realm—stepped behind my sister and Clarissa, drawing on their hair and doing so, whereat both cried out and Sarah would have spat at me if she could.

"I h . . . h . . . hate you, Clara!" she hissed but was heard and received a sharp smack on her bottom from my stepmother who stepped forward and intruded her hand between us. "Oh-woh-woh!" Sarah sobbed and writhed her hips.

This done and all settled, as it were, there began what seemed to me on this first occasion to be a most bizarre ceremony. Moving to the two prone males and standing imperiously astride their forms, Bertha lowered her knickered bottom full over Charlie's face while Robert received the same salute from our stepmother. I held my breath, wondering what they were at, and had no doubt that both Sarah and Clarissa were staring equally with wide-open eyes. Within seconds those two closely-sheathed moons had settled firmly upon the mouths and noses of the young males, Robert giving a great start but his companion remaining docile.

Down they thrust and there settled, knees fully bent and hands on hips while all sorts of splutterings and gaspings came from beneath. My stepmother wriggled a little and then settled herself even more firmly, as did Bertha, a look of utter triumph and pleasure on their faces.

This then was "queening," when the female so subjugates the male in shameless fashion and asserts her full authority over him by thrusting the most "shameful" part of her anatomy over his face, keeping it there the while that he gasps for breath and with his nose thrust up between the plump, splayed cheeks. Each facing the feet of her "victim," the two women stayed so for a full minute while great puffing sounds were heard from Robert and Charlie. Then, leaning forward, fingers found the young men's trouser buttons, flicked them open one by one and displayed to our eyes the already stiff bananas of their pricks.

"OH-WOH-WOH," Sarah sobbed again at that and would have swayed had I not held her hair. Truly, I was most impatient with her, for the cocks—being of almost the same size and with foreskins drawn back and knobs displayed—looked most beautiful. Were they to be milked now? No. Having so revealed the shameless excitation they had caused, both the illustrious females then sat up again—for so I thought of them even though Bertha was of lowly social rank. The suspenders of both strained twixt stocking tops and corsets, thus somehow giving to the view an even lewder appearance of voluptuousness.

"GAAAAAR!" choked Robert in most muffled fashion. He was clearly at the end of his tether and even his neck becoming purple. Aware of this, my stepmother lifted her bottom an inch or two clear of his face and instructed him quietly to lick at her crotch and all else he could find with his tongue.

Sucking in his breath and flooding it out again, how eagerly he did it! Despite the ardent titillation, however, she remained perfectly still as did Bertha who had the same performed on her. Their eyelashes fluttered a little as though in token of the pleasure they were receiving from their "slaves"—for such I later knew males often to be called. Their crotches grew distinctly moist so that by peering closely between the shoulders of Sarah and Clarissa I was able to see how the rolled lips of their cunnies then impressed themselves through the fine material of their drawers, no doubt maddening their "slaves" the more.

My stepmother breathed deeply then as though controlling her excitement. I had seen my brother put under her, as had Sarah. It was such a demonstration as we never could have dreamed of. I sensed the power of Woman then in all its majesty and my heart beat the faster. I was translated into a new world where Woman was the Queen and her "King" but subject to her bottom's weight.

Bertha rose first. There was a certain look in her eye that betokened something else.

I was soon to learn—as were Sarah and Clarissa—what it was to be.

CHAPTER SEVEN

As SHE MOVED towards them, my sister and Clarissa twittered and swayed nervously on their feet, though they could not have helped but feel some little excitement.

"Put them over!" she commanded, walking around to the back of Clarissa so that I was then immediately behind my sister.

"Don't you dare!" cried Sarah, but all in vain. Struggling to no purpose at all they were moved but a few steps to an accommodating, broad settee and pushed into a kneeling position upon it, their bottoms jutting over the edge and each with her shoulders held by Bertha and I.

"Up, you young curs!" then came from my stepmother to the boys. At that Sarah screeched and tried in vain to wriggle free, but no time was wasted in the due performance of "dipping." Led stumbling to the girls, Robert was placed behind Sarah, and Charlie put to Clarissa, which is to say that their cocks were taken—my stepmother standing between them and using both hands—and nudged against the maidens' bottomholes.

"HAH! HOOOO! NO!" cried Sarah, but by placing one knee in the small of her back (whereby I imitated

Bertha) she was held almost motionless and her lovely bottom rearing up.

"Your knobs within and then an inch beyond—no more!"

So ordained my stepmother and purplish indeed was my brother's face as he found his swollen plum invading his sister's nether aperture. Charlie, being quieter and more set in the face, had clearly done it before.

How dearly I wished I could better see! In my position, facing the two young men, I had only the vision of their cocks bent down a little into a straight position and disappearing up between the fulsome cheeks. Their penetration was, though, but a symbol. Gritting his teeth, Robert urged his inch within—so Sarah then held more than two in all and yelped and squealed galore.

"Hold!" my stepmother commanded the young stallions. That they were being put to exquisite torture I had no doubt. As to the feelings of Sarah I could not then imagine them for she was receiving at last her brother's tool in her bottom.

"Ho, ho, ho —MAMA!" sobbed she.

"Darling," I breathed to her, though whether she heard or cared about my tender word I did not know. I wanted her truly to enjoy and knew perhaps some day she would. Her frettings and her pullings seemed to me unnecessary, for I wanted it myself. His cock was in—just in—his balls were cupped. So patiently did my stepmother hold them both, and neither dared to move.

"When the girls are quiet," she breathed, "you will take them out."

In truth Clarissa had uttered scarce a sound, was mute. She was to become a darling of my heart for that, proving herself eventually to be ever so and maintaining ever her pride thereby even when her Papa—for so I discovered her "guardian" really to be—was put to her, his cock full up her orb.

"Be quiet, Sarah, now—did you not hear?" I asked.

"Silence, Clara!" I was admonished, and properly so.

Such events are ceremonies proper and should not be interrupted. Despite our stepmother's stare, I stroked Sarah's hair. Her sobs were low and pitiful, yet came not from the heart, but broken pride. Robert gave a little jerk and a twitch and was scolded, though gently. I sensed that Sarah was gripping him tightly. It was an excellent preparation for what she was to receive when her pleasure finally mounted—not then but later on when she would allow herself to be mounted. The present, febrile jerkings of her bottom were insufficient to dislodge her brother's cock and this she finally learned and buried her face with a great sobbing sigh till all was still.

"Yes, my beauty," our stepmother breathed at her then, and as if in approbation.

Not fully understanding the purpose of what she had called "dipping," I waited then for what seemed to me the utterly desirable moment when both pricks would be fully sheathed in the girls' bottoms—but it was not to be. They were but being given a "taster," while as for the males this was a discipline. A hint of promise lay therein, yes, but in all it was to keep them thoroughly obedient to the Mistress of their fate.

Even so, my stepmother allowed them to remain so embedded for another long minute, their thighs quivering much and their eyes quite agonised.

"Out now, slowly, and down with you again!" she then commanded, and with the most haggard of expressions and thickly-waggling weapons they obeyed, the process of uncorking bringing a soft "OOOH!" from both Sarah and Clarissa. "Up now, girls!" my stepmother said then almost merrily and much as their legs, too, quavered, they were doubtless glad to, though would not have turned about to display anew their furred nests to the males had they not been swiftly smacked and brought around.

The face of Clarissa's supposed guardian was of course a picture to see in all this, but no one really paid him heed, and as Robert and Charlie sank upon their backs upon the floor again, so Bertha magically produced two pairs of drawers which, being thrust into the hands of my sister and her companion, they all too gladly put on.

"You have seen the males queened and perhaps by now know the purpose of it, or if you do not your minds will come to it soon enough," they were told. "You may now take greater pride in your femininity than you have done in these past minutes. You, Clarissa, go down on Charlie even as Bertha did. Sarah—you will teach your brother a similar lesson!"

Both girls stood frozen for a moment, though left free to move. Perhaps some semblance of understanding came to them then, for it was my sister who moved first. The psychology of it then made itself better understood to me. The male had taken advantage of the female, and though he had been bidden to mattered not. Now the female could reassert herself. So my thoughts spun as I hoped Sarah's would, too. Reaching within a foot of our brother who lay biting his lip and trying to outstare the ceiling, she appeared to hesitate but was spurred on by the quite gentle voice of our stepmother saying, "Yes, Sarah, NOW, Sarah."

Her shapely form wobbled a little as with a constrained look on her lovely face, she placed one foot over Robert's body and then, as if casting a beseeching look all around, sank slowly down. Urging herself awkwardly upon her knees, she gritted her teeth slightly and threw her head back as one might in appealing to unseen angels of deliverance. She could not help but be thinking still of his prick in her bottom. The sensation would still be there, both shaming and exciting her. Would she now take the revenge that was offered her?

At that moment Clarissa, being firmly taken in hand by Bertha, was being carefully positioned. Her knickered bottom hung like a full moon over Charlie's face, but neither yet had touched.

My stepmother and Bertha saw to it that they did.

"When a girl learns to queen the male and does it thoroughly and well and with a sense of satisfaction, she is more than halfway there," my stepmother told me afterwards, saying that it was a moment of crowning glory to be achieved, whether with a stranger or one's kin. Indeed, she demonstrated it upon me so that I knew for myself the sense of utter submission in being so imperiously smothered by that fleshy globe.

"Sometimes," she told me, "they first take the scent of you that way and will follow ever after at your skirts with their tongues lolling like eager hounds."

"Are they allowed to put their tongues up?" I asked.

"Only when commanded to, Clara. To do so otherwise is to call down punishment upon themselves. The wearing of drawers is a sign of contempt and of protection. The thicker that garment is, the greater the punishment, particularly if the female keeps her bottom as cool as possible before going down on the male. Should she wish to excite him and frustrate him the more, she will wear the thinnest possible drawers and make sure that she has been well seated on a chair beforehand and warmed her orb so that the effluvia of her cunny and bottomhole comes the more pungently to his nostrils. There are variations, of course, but you will learn these in due course and may even invent a few yourself."

I became eager to, yet at this moment now I was watching my sister's bottom as, by sudden pressure of our stepmother's hands on her shoulders, it was plumped down firmly on Robert's face—she enjoining him fiercely to keep his mouth closed and his tongue in.

"PMFFFFF!" I heard from him the while that the deep colour spread up into Sarah's face and she wriggled inanely as though to get up, until my stepmother stilled her and bent and whispered something in her ear at which Sarah bit one corner of her lip and obeyed. Clarissa, being by then well down on Charlie, sat inert, her expression proud as ever or perhaps now even a mite more so than heretofore. Then did my stepmother place one leg astride Robert and sit down firmly on his stomach so that she faced Sarah whose lips quivered.

"There, my darling, is that not better?" she was asked quietly. Tears brimmed in Sarah's eyes, her mouth opened as though she might cry. Our stepmother's arms enfolded her shoulders tenderly and Sarah's head sank upon her offered shoulder. "Is it not better?" was whispered to her then, "to have the male under you and not rampant at you, Sarah? Yes, my dearest, urge your bottom down upon him well. Has he not been wicked?"

"Ho, yes!" sobbed Sarah and clung to her, her fingers hooked as though frantically into her stepmother's arms.

Poor Robert—he was puffing madly, but I could not doubt that even Sarah felt a certain victory in it. Her nostrils flared as his own breathed fire into her bottom, and yet she had him as certainly as a cat has a bird and must have sensed it, while her erstwhile enemy had now become her friend who stroked her hair and murmured sweet endearments to her.

Of course the act of queening produces a complementary warmth between the parties and so cannot fail to stir the female somewhat, though, as I have since learned, she does well to hide her emotions and to concentrate upon the proper disciplining of the male. Thus it was that my stepmother appeared to give not a jot for Robert's role in this and did not even glance down at him when finally raising Sarah to her feet.

"Come, dear," she murmured, "we will bathe you now. Clarissa, too. Bertha will see to the males."

My sister was indeed subdued as was Clarissa who bore a look of concealed wonderment on her face. Upstairs then and to the bathroom we adjourned where both were refreshened. Then did we repair to my stepmother's bedroom where wine was dispensed and at first drunk in an almost cathedral-like silence. Sarah knew not what to say any longer nor how to protest—if indeed she still wished to—while Clarissa, being a guest, was bound to remain quiet.

"You did well, Clara, to obey me," was said and thus I was made to appear, if not guiltless, then at least in part innocent, for the subtle menace in my stepmother's voice was patent for all to hear. "Do you then enjoy obeying me?" she asked craftily.

I played my part well, at first hesitating, then darting a glance at Sarah which seemed to beg her forgiveness. I sought for reply that would give credence to my appearance not as an accomplice but as a submissive.

"I don't mind if Sarah doesn't," I replied, thus endeavouring to convey that my sister had not struggled, screamed nor protested as much as she might have done.

"Oh, I do," Sarah blurted, but realising that she was all but one against three immediately took on an awkward expression, compressed her lips and toyed with the bedcover as though her thoughts were really elsewhere.

"You are bound to. All of you are bound to," my stepmother replied, "yet every step I take and every form of guidance I give you is for your own good. You have seen the lusting of the male and how he never frets to put his cock to a bottom or a cunny. Think you that we are to encourage such behaviour? Well, Sarah?" she asked sharply.

My sister showed retreat. "I don't know what you might make us do now," she mumbled.

"I shall MAKE you pleasure yourselves and in so doing will guide you along such paths as will teach you how to discipline pleasure itself, how indeed to weave a net into which you will not yourselves fall victims, but will learn how to use it as a snare and a weapon. Let us take a practical case. You, Clarissa, would have fallen victim to your guardian in due course. I doubt it not and believe you do not also. You would have tired of struggling to keep his hands from your skirts and the warm bulge of your bottom. In due course apathy would have overcome you. A fumbling descent of your drawers would have occurred. Some errant fingering of his might have aroused you against your will. Torn between excitement and the fear of intrusion by another, you might have yielded haphazardly and taken the steaming cock in your quim silently and quickly until his lust was expelled and you were creamed."

"Oh!" exclaimed Clarissa and cupped her face in her hands.

My stepmother took her wrists and drew them away slowly. "Swear to me that it could not possibly have happened and I will absolve you, Clarissa. Look into my eyes as you speak!" she declared solemnly.

Clarissa's lips twisted. "I don't . . . I don't know," she uttered lamely, whereat a victorious look came over her questioner's face.

"Once he has rodded you, my sweet—as he surely will—you will become prey to his lusts, will lie in waiting for his coming, too timourous to object and having no one to run to. In part you will desire what you will receive and so will be the fluttering butterfly in his net. Your cunny, oiled by his sperm, will throb so appealingly as to make you forget your scruples."

"Oh, scruples, indeed! How can you speak of them after what you have subjected us to," burst forth my sister whom I expected to be immediately smacked at the least for that, but our stepmother spoke to her most softly.

"A stave of good wood hardens in flame, my love, and so shall you. Remember this as a precept all your life. Do not give way to emotion for it is the worst of teachers, producing only abject pupils whose minds run hither and thither and have no resting place. Clarissa knows the truth of what I speak—do you not, Clarissa? Say quickly, girl, what lies immediately in your mind."

"Yes," Clarissa said simply and would again have covered her face but was prevented.

"Your truthfulness, my dear, is like a shining light amid

so much duplicity in the world," she was told, no doubt to her great surprise. "I propose then," my stepmother went on, "to hasten events, though entirely to your advantage. You have freely confessed that the lips of your cunny, and—I have no doubt—your succulent bottom-hole as well—will open in time to your guardian's cock. So be it, but it shall not be in circumstances of shame and wonder, but of womanly pride and, yea, victory!"

"You . . . you do not mean NOW?" gasped Clarissa.

"What better time, my dear, now that I have made him subject to my whims? Let him be subject to yours also. He will be duly punished afterwards, while you yourself will be feted."

"Madam, I cannot!" expostulated Clarissa, this interruption being however ignored.

"Have Bertha bring him up," my stepmother said to me, accentuating sharply the command *bring*.

"Oh! I cannot watch THIS!" jerked Sarah, who sprang up.

"You cannot? Really?" came the cold reply. "Very well, Sarah. It cannot be said that I have not done my very best to bring you to the true way of womanhood. You have, then, a week to mend your ways or I shall have no recourse but to put you under to as good and stiff a penis as I know. Go to your room!"

Hot-cheeked, my sister fled—I tactfully allowing her to before descending the stairs and entering the drawing room. Robert and Charlie were not to be seen. Clarissa's guardian had been loosed from the chair but not from his bonds. His wrists now were secured behind his back and the movements of his legs were impeded by a hobble, which is to say a short length of rope tied to both ankles that permitted him to take only a short step at a time. He was also now gagged.

"He is to go up?" asked Bertha who appeared to know everything and who must have been in league with my stepmother for quite a while. I nodded and stood to one side as she snapped around his neck the selfsame hound-collar that Robert had worn and led him stumbling forward. His eyes appeared glazed, as well they might, though his erection threatened to burst his trousers. All a-gog, I followed them up discreetly, his passage being necessarily slow.

The bedroom door to my stepmother's private abode was closed. Bertha knocked in true servant style and waited. An interval obtained before the command "Enter!" was called. "Close the door!" she commanded me as we went in, and there upon the bed I saw Clarissa kneeling, naked to her stockings and shoes and with her bottom jutting moonlike over the side of the bed.

Her guardian's eyes bulged and his complexion took on a crimson hue. It was as well perhaps that the gag impeded his speech, though hollow sounds were to be heard coming from beneath it. Receiving a sharp smack on his brawny buttocks, he was pushed forward by Bertha until he stood in waiting immediately behind his pretended ward's luscious derriere which gleamed its pallor most invitingly, the sprouts of cunt-curls showing dark beneath.

Holding her head up and with breasts proudly heaving, my stepmother addressed him.

"A new word is about to enter your vocabulary, sir, for I doubt that you already know it. Clarissa is to be serviced, or—as a farmhand might put it—she is to be covered. Your bonds are intended to assure that you do not otherwise defile her sweet form with your mauling hands. Spread your knees wider, Clarissa, for a lady need have no hesitation in doing so before a serf. Have his trousers down, Bertha, and let us see his equipment and whether I deem him sufficiently well hung for the task. Ah yes . . . a reasonable exhibit. His balls weigh well, do they not?"

"Fair as big as my husband's, m'am," said Bertha, who for a moment brought them from under his upstanding tool on her palm and then let them dangle again. The man's head shook wildly, but no mute gestures could avail him now. The prize he had so desired was well displayed before him, but in circumstances that I doubt he could have dreamed of. He snorted as my stepmother took hold of his big leathery prick and rubbed it suavely with her fingers. The knob glistened in its huge swelling and the veins upon the stem stood out fit to burst.

"The principal pleasure is to be Clarissa's," my stepmother informed him briskly. "You will not therefore come before you have afforded her at least fifty full strokes of your cock. I shall guard your motions well. Fail to pleasure her and you will receive this a dozenfold!"

Thus saying she produced a cane which looked most fearsome in its aspect, causing his head to waggle as though it might fall off. I gathered that he was denying any intended weakness on his part.

"Clarissa henceforth will be your true Mistress, which is to say that she will ordain your movements, your monetary disbursements, and such pleasurings—or not—that she feels in a mood to dispose. Should you at any time choose to disobey her, you will know my wrath, sir!"

With that, my stepmother placed her hand upon Clarissa's head and gently urged it down, the better to see her bottom mounding up. "This is agreed between us, is it not, my darling?" she breathed, whereat Clarissa nodded as blindly as might be. Her hair having been loosed of all its pins, virtually naught of her profile was in view on either side. In the superb thrusting out of her bottom and the displaying of her figlike quim, which both combined with her sleekly stockinged legs and smooth, dipped back, she appeared as a totally anonymous symbol of supreme femininity. How dearly would I liked to have licked up between those ivory-smooth cheeks and then sought the moist bouquet beneath!

"Put him to her then, Bertha, and may he have marked well what I have said," came my stepmother's words while the cane moved menacingly in her hand.

Bertha cackled and, even from beneath the gag he wore I could hear a coarse croaking sound as the plumblike knob of his penis was brought close to the pouting lips of Clarissa's quim. For an eternity it seemed to hover there, my stepmother placing the palm of her hand gently between the young woman's shoulder blades, then—to an upward jerking of her guardian's chin—the swollen crest was nosed between the rolled lovelips, causing Clarissa to jerk a little and utter a moan. Mouth open—as if I wished to absorb the succulent male fruit myself—I watched it urge within, the pulsing stem being severly controlled in its forward motion by Bertha's ringing fingers.

"ZOOO-OOOH!" came from Clarissa, but the sound was quickly bitten back, for which I much admired her.

In such circumstances of control, there are few more enervating sights than to see a long, thick, erect penis entering a female's honeypot. The lips of Clarissa's cunny urged apart, like two small waves that encounter the prow of a boat. Her fingers clenched and her nose buried itself in the counterpane.

"Half in and hold!" my stepmother said and with that Bertha with her free hand pinched his big buttocks and so made him give such a start that Clarissa received a full four inches of his cock, her cunny becoming even more distended while her hips waggled rebelliously, but at a soothing of my stepmother's hand were bravely still again. Her guardian's legs trembled mightily, his thighs resembling small treetrunks and his calves quivering.

"She's going to be lovely at it, m'am. I knowed it the first time I saw her. See how still she is, how nicely she comports herself."

This from Bertha, of course. From my stepmother a mere nod, as though it was what she had expected of her pupil all the time.

"Let him proceed," she murmured. "Take the cane,

Bertha, and station yourself behind him. I shall begin the count . . . ONE!"

"FEEE-OOOH!" came Clarissa's muffled hiss as now the big banana of flesh sheathed itself slowly in her quim until his balls hung down beneath her curls.

"TWO, sir!"

Out it withdrew, and with full majesty until the knob hovered almost beyond the figlike entrance and then drove up again.

The knuckles on Clarissa's hands distinctly whitened, but my stepmother was scarcely watching her as such. Having full faith in her, as it seemed, she monitored such tiny signs of Clarissa's hip movements which might seem to have indicated that she wished to expel the invader. My cunny itself moistened all the more and surreptitiously I stood with my legs parted.

"The male is but a penis-bearer and a provider of our means of livelihood and our luxuries, Clara," my stepmother told me later. "True, he may be taken up in conversation sometime and, if proving witty or in any way informative, may be listened to though not with respect. For a woman listens to a man's mind as much as his words and, given that she is ripe of figure, will divine the speech that goes on silently in his head, that being concerned solely with means of taking down our drawers."

That which was happening before me now I wished never to end. As he came upon his twentieth stroke, his movements seemed bolder—so much so that Bertha seized the short hairs at the back of his head and hissed a warning in his ear. As for Clarissa, her cunny had distinctly moistened, for I saw her exudations glistening on his shaft as it emerged and the distended lips seemed positively to cling around its girth.

"Twenty-one—twenty-two—a little faster now for a moment—let her feel the slapping of your balls, sir. That she will empty them for you I have no doubt," my stepmother said. Her lovely face showed no emotion whatever save that there was a glistening in her eyes that came, as I surmised, from pride in her accomplishment.

He was breathing more heavily now, as the snorts from his nostrils betokened. I had little doubt that he wished to spill already and so did my stepmother for she halted him with his bulbous knob just inside Clarissa's nest and thrust his chin up.

"You will receive now, sir, one cut of the cane as a warning of your fate should you sperm her prematurely."

Oh my goodness, what a yell he would have uttered if he could as then Bertha whipped the cane in full across his buttocks! His head jerked further up so that his chin pointed to the ceiling, and his eyes came out on stalks while in trying to evade the whippy cane his prick thrust full up Clarissa's quim and held there tight.

"Thirty-one," my stepmother intoned mercilessly even while his eyes creased up in a grimace and a red streak showed across his bottom.

True, she was putting him to his task severely, for the male serf's cock is usually nursed over a period of time until he learns to have it rubbed more and more beguilingly, but without coming save on command. In the first weeks of disciplining, the male is not permitted to come at all and so learns that the hand that soothes him is also the one that masters him and which he must obey, whether it is nursed in the palm, urged up the female bottom or sheathed in a clinging cunny.

I will not, though, detail the sweet agonies of Clarissa's guardian—if such he was—at any greater length. No man could have wished to reach the post more urgently than he.

"Fifty—and NOW!" came from my stepmother whereat, the tendons on his neck straining violently, he brought Clarissa's bottom to smack against his belly and injected his tribute in long throbbing spouts of such abundance that both of them quivered and rubbed together for ages before his dripping spout was finally withdrawn, whereupon Bertha gave him no time for settlement but simply led him out.

His task was done. I saw the meaning of it then better than any words that might then have been uttered to me. The whole role of the male had changed before my eyes. Such food for thought is rarely given to a girl of my then young age.

Immediately his steaming weapon was withdrawn, Clarissa sank down and wriggled on her belly where she lay supine. At that, my stepmother raised her fingers to her lips and motioned me to withdraw. I did so, but lingered at the door, hearing murmurings and kisses.

"Yes, if you want," I heard Clarissa say and then came a rustling of clothes and I guessed that my stepmother was undressing. It was a full threequarters of an hour before they reappeared, both looking cool and faultless in appearance as my stepmother ever intends after such an event. As to my brother and Charlie, Bertha had tied them up back to back in the potting shed, nursed their cocks, and then left them so. They were more severely in training now.

Clarissa's guardian sat transfixed and knowing not where to look, being completely attired and unbound, so free to move.

"You may escort Clarissa back now, but you will return within two days so that I hear what she has to say. Kneel, cur, and kiss the toes of her shoes as a token of your obedience!"

There was a moment's silence, as may well be imagined, and then he stepped forward to his "ward" who looked now utterly demure.

"My dear . . . " he began.

"You were not summoned to speak, but to obey, sir!" snapped my stepmother who made such a small, menacing movement in his direction that he fell to his knees upon the instant and, raising the wide hem of Clarissa's dress, laved his mouth greedily over the polished toes of her shoes. Feet slightly apart, she did not stir.

"You may have him kiss your thighs before you retire tonight, Clarissa. He will kneel to do so, but his lips will attempt nothing else."

"Yes," was Clarissa's quiet response. She stepped back smoothly but quickly then, causing his mouth to fall upon the carpet so that with the most foolish of expressions on his face he rose awkwardly and stared as though lost from one to the other.

"You may go," my stepmother told him distantly. "Follow three paces behind her at all times."

"Of course." He stumbled and sought rather humbly to meet Clarissa's eyes but she had turned away and swept in ladylike fashion into the hall.

"Another convert!" my stepmother laughed as their carriage departed. My mind, however, was on other matters.

"What did you mean about Sarah?" I asked, whereat her eyes took on a different look.

"She is to be put up to the cock in a manner that will teach her the best of lessons," I was told, but could gain no more from her.

CHAPTER EIGHT

FOR THE NEXT few days Sarah avoided me as much as possible and spoke coolly to me only when necessary. When I mentioned this to my stepmother—who was equally distant with her—she waved her hand airily and said, "She will learn."

"When shall I?" I asked pertly, making her laugh.

"Do you want to?" was her response, and we both knew what was meant. I was torn for a reply and she, seeing this, asked, "Who with?" Again I could not bring myself to answer.

Finally I blurted out, "I want to. Like Clarissa."

"How grown up you are in all reality, Clara! I mean to take you by the hardest route now, for nothing else will suffice. So far you have obeyed me. Do you promise to continue to do so?"

I nodded, being eager to please, though little knew my fate.

"What a pity," she went on, "that Sarah has proved recalcitrant and quite unexciting, though I mean to get her over the hump. It brings me to a solution I did not yet intend, but sooner or later the full circle must be drawn. So long as it remains incomplete then we cannot draw other females and male serfs into the arena. You understand what I am saying, Clara?

For a full minute my mind remained blank, then as some intimation came to me of what she meant by completing the circle, I swallowed and stared at her and my lips quavered.

"It will be all right, you know," she said gently.

"B . . . b . . . but . . . Sarah," I blurted.

"She *has* been difficult, hasn't she, but she will soon get over it. There is nothing nicer in all the world than bringing all together and having things nice and trim. One day you will wish to make your own way in such matters and I shall not impede you. You will see then even better how necessary it is to have free rein and not to have forever to arrange the training of young ladies and, of course, of males behind closed doors. The sense of freedom you will obtain will be infinite. You will, as a sage said, wear life like an old cloak."

Until then perhaps it had all seemed to me like a bizarre game, but now it was clear that her intent was wholly serious.

It was at this time mid-morning and I had seen nothing of Robert whose manner remained pleasingly dutiful and quiet to us both. Upon asking where he was—which I did partly to distract my thoughts—my stepmother gave a mischievous grin and replied,

"I believe Bertha has made him ready. Come upstairs with me."

On the stairs we passed Bertha who gave my stepmother a nod as if to say that all was well and then passed down. "You are going to milk him," then was said to me and with trembling excitement I followed along the upper hallway and together we entered his room.

There to my profound astonishment he sat upon his bed attired in a chemise that I recognised as one of Sarah's—a rather pretty blue one with white lace at the hem and neckline—stockings and shoes. His hair had been well brushed and there was rouge both upon his cheeks and on his lips which doubtless Bertha had applied. At our entrance he sprang up, the flurrying movement of his feminine garment betraying the gathered legs of a pair of white batiste drawers around his thighs.

"Robert! How sweet you look!" our stepmother cooed while he stood awkwardly with hands to his sides and blushed to see me regarding him. "Does he not?" came then and the door was firmly closed. While I scarcely knew whether or not to nod, she snapped to my brother to hold his head up well and stand in the centre of the floor the better that "she" could be inspected, as she said. So shuffling forward—and being then reprimanded for not stepping more daintily—Robert presented himself the better and gazed past me at the door. "The sweet thing is not yet fully accustomed to her new attire, but soon will be. Do you not like the feel of stockings up your legs, Roberta?"

"I d . . . d . . . do not m . . . m . . . mind," stammered he.

"Do not mind indeed! Why they are lovely and of the finest silk. Feel up under her chemise to feel her garters, Clara!"

I would have blushed myself had I not now known better, but knew I must put a boldness on in front of him. Besides, being slim of figure and having a remarkably smooth skin, my brother indeed did look sweet, though his toes moved uneasily in the tight feminine shoes. Steeling myself and not without an intense fluttering of excitement, I approached close to him and ran my hand up beneath the lacy hem of the chemise, causing him of course to tremble. I felt the ridge of his stocking tops, the ruffling of the garters and then the warm skin rising up above.

"Go on, Clara. See if he is hard. I know you want to."

My fingers crept like spiders to their prey. Robert jerked his hips but otherwise kept still and I knew that I was tickling him a little but could not help myself, so tentative at first my explorations were. The drawers being thin, I could feel first the heavy hang of his balls with my fingertips which felt all around and beneath them. My breathing sounded softly and I could feel my pulses racing as he stood passive under our stepmother's eyes while I sought the stem of his prick.

"Yes," I husked.

"Yes, what, Clara?"

"His prick is hard," I managed to convey.

"The naughty thing, and one pair of drawers already wet in his excitement. Should she not be spanked?"

I giggled. Robert's prick was thrusting out mightily through the soft cloth of his drawers and felt like a tent-pole.

"As you said downstairs, Clara, a naughty girl does need to be. Turn her around and pull her drawers down. Make her bend over the bed!"

I thought Robert would resist, but he did not, though his eyes pleaded, but not entirely for salvation, I thought. Beneath the urging of my hands he turned full about and placed his palms upon the bed while I, flipping up his chemise with rising pleasure, untied his drawers and let them flutter down. In profile his penis was now to be seen at full stand.

"Now, Clara, stand to one side of him—that side, yes—and cup his balls firmly while I smack him."

Robert's gender seemed to change from moment to moment, but it did not matter. His plums nestled warmly on my palm, and heavily. I did not squeeze them, for some instinct told me not to, then heard his wincing cry as our stepmother's hand landed SMACK! upon his bared bottom. Then came SMACK! again and I saw a glinting of tears come into his eyes which I divined were not entirely of pain. A pink hue showed on his white skin where her palm had blasted in.

"Now, Clara, hold his cock loosely. Ring it in your

fingers and let it move back and forth while I spank him. He will come soon enough, for it stimulates as much as it stings, does it not, Roberta?"

"I d . . . d . . . don't want to be a g . . . g . . . girl!"

It was his one protest, being followed by a howl and then a gasp as simultaneously our stepmother's hand smacked in again on his out-rearing bottom and his stiff pego nestled in my warm hand. Ah, the ineffable thrill of holding it! I had little time for my thoughts, however, for I was constantly being instructed, and indeed taught.

"Your other hand under his chin. Hold it up, Clara. As for you, Roberta, it is not what you want, my girl, but what you are going to get. Some things will be quite nice for you provided you obey me." SMACK! SMACK! SMACK! "Is he throbbing well, Clara?"

"Oh, yes!" I gasped, for indeed he was, all the veins pulsing warmly to my skin and the knob shiny and emergent. My other palm formed a rest for his chin and held his gaze straight forward. With each SMACK! his hips of course jerked forward and thus the full length of his pego made a thrilling journey in between my ringing fingers.

I expected him to be smacked harder—perhaps naughtily I wished it so—but then of a sudden our stepmother ceased, opened a drawer while I held him still, and laid a large white kerchief on the bed beneath his prick.

"Milk him, Clara. He will not move. Work your fingers back and forth until he comes and Bertha will then take charge of him again."

"GOOOOO!" choked he, for no sooner had she spoken than I was eager to obey. That he was naughty—though I knew not in what way, and it did not matter—I convinced myself. It is easy so to do when one has experienced the overlording of the male. Many times in the past Robert had teased me and played awful jokes on me and now I was getting my own back. Stepmama moved away and watched, no doubt approvingly, for I had wilted not.

My teeth set a little as I spurred him on and even, to her delight, murmured the words, "Come on, come on," as though impatiently.

Naturally I felt his weapon throbbing all the more and tightened my grasp beneath his chin. How glorious it is to so subdue the male! How weak he looks when in a woman's hands! His jaw sagged, impressing its weight upon my hand, and a mad, breathless sound came from his throat while his hips jerked the faster to my titillations. Then, taking two steps forward, our stepmother gave him two hard smacks indeed and with that he let out a cry and a helpless gasp, the engine of his tool seeming to expand in girth in my grasp as a long cannonade of sperm leapt from his knob, arced in the air and spattered down upon the waiting handkerchief, there to be joined by another and another while I—hotly observing his virility—madly wished it up within my quim. Again and again he spouted, his buttocks tightening visibly, my fingers being frothed with his spendings and his cock like a greasy pole.

"FEEE-OOOH!" he moaned and then the last spurt came and after it a dribbling as the thick drops fell.

"Leave him!" my stepmother commanded, and I learned again that after emission the male is not to be coddled except in special circumstances but is to understand that his duty is performed and that the attendant female or females have more important matters to attend to than his momentary satisfactions. Handing me then another kerchief, my stepmother saw to the wiping of my hands, which were pleasantly warm and sticky from his effusion. Robert remained bent over, not having been told to do other, though his legs trembled a little in the aftermath.

"Come, darling, shall we take some wine?" I was asked and thus we departed as smoothly as we had come. The door closing, my stepmother seized me and hugged me on the landing. "You liked it, Clara? You did?"

"Oh yes," I responded hotly, and quite truthfully.

"You see, then, you have nothing to fear. They are all alike. In their hearts they adore to be subdued by us and some would give all the world to be, for it releases responsibility for their actions on to *our* shoulders and permits them often to do what is otherwise forbidden. Should they be punished then it is their joy to be so. Do you remember what I said to you about the little boy and the larder door?"

"Yes!" I responded gleefully and could scarce contain my excitement for I was now more fully converted than ever to her cause.

Putting her arm around me as we then went along to her room, my stepmother explained: "The naughty boy reaches for a cake or biscuit, although he has not asked if he might have it. Being apprehended by his Mama or perhaps his elder sister, he receives a smack on his bottom. Although it stings, he feels certain secret pleasure in the fleeting pain which serves to stir his cock a little. So he resolves to be naughty again, although he may not fully recognise the reasons for his actions. He wants to be smacked, you see, and his cocky to get hard, for he wishes it to be seen and taken hold of. Then he will be even naughtier and so progresses until his Mama or sister takes him more in hand, just as you have done with Robert."

"I could not have done it on my own, though," I confessed.

"What is to that? It will come in time and sooner than you think, Clara. Each step you take imbues more confidence in you. In time there will be no male whom you will be afraid to take in hand."

"But as to girls . . . ," I began, for after her treatment of Sarah I was a little lost and had not got the jigsaw all together, as it were.

From her cabinet my stepmother took a flask of wine and poured two glasses. "As to girls, Clara, there are generally three sorts. Those like Clarissa who know their destiny and put themselves in due course to the cock while having the male believe that affairs are quite the other way around. Of course, it may take a while for they do not all have mentors such as myself. As matters progress, however, and as they come to a clearer understanding of their role, so they take the male or males in hand and reverse the quite unnatural order of things. Hence they are able to take charge of their domains. One must divine by instinct—such as you will slowly gather—whether a girl is such or whether she needs some sterner treatment. In Sarah's case the latter obtains. She little knows that pride is one of her best possessions. It must be broken in order to make it whole again and stronger."

I brooded on this a while as we drank and then she continued: "So you see, Clara, there are those who will themselves to destiny and others who are wilful and must be guided to it, however hard the path may seem. As to the third category, I must confess to you that some females are born to be submissives. So be it, for they make excellent slaves and willing bedmates. The shy ones are quite delicious and ever wish themselves to be seduced. Now that you have had Robert's prick in your hand and felt him come, which do you prefer—the male organ or the female tongue?"

"I like both," I responded unthinkingly, and this pleased her.

"So it should be, my love. Such inclinations become a woman, for she then may take her pleasures as she will with either sex. What a delight it will be for me to tongue your cunny while you have a cock up your bottom."

I rolled my eyes and could not imagine such a pleasure, though it was soon to be. Already I could feel the piston urging in me and longed for it as I did the agile lapping of her tongue.

"Shall I have to tie you?" she asked teasingly. Love showed as strongly in her eyes as ever I knew.

I laughed and felt quite choked up with excitement.

"No, but you may smack me first for I shall feel very naughty," said I.

"Once his cock is up you, you will feel more than that," she replied solemnly and bore me back upon the bed. Our lips met in the hottest of kisses. Our tongues swam together. I parted my legs as her hand crept up beneath my skirt.

I knew well enough whose prick she meant.

CHAPTER NINE

SARAH was immured in her room when Papa returned. Robert was put to work in the scullery in cleaning all our shoes—a chore to which he gave himself devotedly. I had looked in on him once or twice and watched him in his kneeling and polishing. Raising his eyes to mine, he pleaded dumbly with me but I shook my head, though not unkindly. I believe he saw a promise in my gaze for a certain fleeting hope came over his features which he dutifully did his best to disguise. In turning away from him, I drew up my skirts a little, for I sensed that he liked my legs and the thought even then struck me that there might one day be a certain jealousy of possessiveness between Sarah and I. I took it then as a strong presentiment, though it was not in fact to be. As the choices became wider, so we ceased to differentiate, though would have protected our own from all.

Upon Papa asking after my sister and brother, my stepmama merely replied that Bertha wished to see him.

"Bertha?" he exclaimed in some astonishment, for he had naught to do with the comings and goings of servants. My stepmother had long seen to that.

"She is waiting in your room, William. Will you not

go up? You may tell me of your affairs in Paris later. Sarah has been wilful, if you would know. I have smacked her bottom several times. What a pink glow it has offered up to my hand!"

"Really, Julia!"

"Go upstairs, William."

I being present all the while made it plain—even though by my silence—that affairs were now shifted a little more into the open. The gauntlet was cast down. I felt uneasy, tremulous and yet expectant.

"If it is to see Bertha, of course," he responded weakly, to which she gave a short, "Yes," and moved away. I pretended to be much wrapped up in a novel by Mr. Thackeray.

More hesitations and clearings of throat and then Papa made his way upstairs. Why Bertha, though? I was puzzled. "A little strangeness comes well to such initial situations," my stepmother said. "Sometimes people obey rather better those whom they know less well. It is a matter of the paramountcy of the spirit, or the yearnings of the soul," she concluded mysteriously. Then, after a moment's reflective silence, she added, "You may go and listen, if you wish. Go on—I know you are curious."

My heart never beat so madly as it did then, for I knew it to be in its way as much of an order as a request and so I ventured up. The door to Papa's room was closed. I pressed my ear to it and heard a scuffling.

"Now, sir, will you obey me?" came Bertha's voice and then an exclamation of his own that yet was muffled. "A fine time you've had of it in Paris, sir, I has no doubt, but if you have eased your pecker of its longings there will be trouble with the Mistress, that I know. Come, do not struggle—let me get them off. Don't you like a woman handling you? A nice strong woman?"

"My God, what are you at?"

"Just tying your arms to your sides, sir, so you'll come to no mischief. I has to make my preparations, you see, being under orders, as we all are. Take that Miss Sarah now, she won't obey, and has had her bottom well stung for it. Real lovely she looks waggling her hips and showing all."

"I know not the like of this nor what has possessed you, Bertha. Ah! my trousers! I beg you not!"

"All comes off, sir, so as you are fit and ready. Rude, aren't you, with it sticking up like this? Shows you've been a good boy, though, that it should stiffen so readily. Give it a kiss, shall I, for good luck?"

"My God! AH!"

I trembled violently. My moistening palms made marks upon the door.

"A little suck of it does no harm occasionally, sir, though Mistress don't do that often to you, I wager. A fair knob you have and a good girth of it. There . . . isn't it best to be in my hands rather than those of a stranger? Such wicked women there must be in Paris. I'll have you on this chair now, sir, and if you don't keep your legs apart so I can tie your ankles to the legs, I'll pinch your balls and swear I will."

A rustling, a scraping, a fervent gasp from Papa and then a smacking sound. He cried out.

"Your Mama will have spanked you thus, won't she? Come, confess it, or I'll have you sat on pins!"

"S . . . s . . . sometimes!"

I had expected his tone to be outraged. Instead it was sullen.

"Naughty boy, weren't you? Making up for your sins now? Got you settled, ain't we, nice and cosy. I let you keep your shirt on so you won't shiver, but you'll soon have a warm enough time of it. Mistress will want to see you now."

These last words being spoken more loudly, Bertha must have guessed at a listener and could have thought it no other than myself.

"Bertha! I beg you!"

"No, I don't think you will, sir. It's your Mistress as you'll beg. If we were on our own now I'd go down on your pecker as soon as look at it. Often wondered what a beauty it might be, and so it is."

I fled to an adjoining cupboard where often I had hidden during games. Bertha tapped upon the door as she passed and must have laughed to herself. In a few moments I heard my stepmother ascending and crouched down, though it was then utterly foolish to do so for she immediately opened the cupboard door, knowing well enough I would be there.

"Come out, you sillikins," she whispered.

"I want to stay here!" I begged.

"Do you? Very well, then, you may. I will leave the bedroom door a little open. You may peep within. Make not a sound."

Pressing the cupboard door to then, but not completely closing it, she went into the bedroom. Not being able to hear what went on, I was desperate and would have ventured out save that now I heard other footsteps. I opened the door a chink. Gagged and with her wrists bound in front of her came Sarah, naked but for black stockings that were tightly gartered, and shoes. Her head swung this way and that wildly and her eyes stared. Leading her forward from behind with both hands on her elbows was Bertha.

Whether my sister glimpsed me or not I do not know. I believe not, for she was in that state of staring in which one sees nothing clearly. Seeing the door to Papa's bedroom opening, she attempted to back away but received a resounding juicy smack on her naked bum as made her jerk. As they passed the cupboard I crept out just in time to see her being thrust within and a gurgling cry emit itself from beneath her gag. I did not know it then but Papa was also gagged. My stepmother had seen to that.

Ah, what violent struggles ensued as Sarah saw Papa, naked to his shirt upon a chair and prick uprearing plainly to her view! She twisted, she strove, but nothing would avail her as halting step by step she was urged towards him. My stepmother, having positioned herself directly behind him at the back of the plain wooden seat, then seized Sarah's wrists and with quite lightning movements brought my sister's arms in a loop over Papa's neck and with a short length of cord secured her wrist-bonds to a bar at the lower rear of the chair so that Sarah hung haplessly over him with the swollen crest of his charger all but nudging her belly.

"NEEE-EEEEEH!" came her screech thinly through her gag. Her hips jerked back exactly as if she were offering herself to the cane, her legs being forced to straighten on either side of his so that she effected a gap of some three inches between her belly and his cock.

My tummy churned. I thought her then to be put to him, but my stepmother's ideas were other. Unable to kick or she would have fallen sideways and perhaps made more intimate contact with Papa's pestle, Sarah could do naught in resistance now as Bertha forced her legs apart and fastened the sides of her ankles to the legs of the chair.

"Now, Miss, by bending your knees you will be able to sit upon his legs. I leave you to do that at your leisure. You will come to it eventually when your legs tire and must urge your belly then against his cock."

Madly did my sister's head shake then, but all was lost for her—or all perhaps was gained, in longer term. I, skipping quickly backwards lest Papa see me, was then confronted by my stepmother and Bertha who seemed to take little account of my presence and closed the door resoundingly.

"Half an hour should do," my stepmother said, quite as if she were discussing the cooking of something or other. When I said this to her a few minutes later downstairs, she laughed and said, "Well—I am, am I not?"

Bertha absented herself, her duty done.

"What . . . what will happen?" I quavered, for all was so strange that I could not take account of it.

"That you will see for yourself, my pet, if you are minded to. I will have discipline, I will!" she said abruptly and left me then to my own devices which caused me to ever be glancing at the mantelpiece clock. No sound was to be heard from above save once a slight scraping sound as if the chairlegs had moved. I sucked my thumb and waited, being aware that it was a babyish thing to do, but I needed some comforting.

Precisely as the half hour passed, so my stepmother reappeared and extended her hand to me. Her calmness was in counterpoint to my own excitement.

"Come, then," she murmured. I drew back. "You do not want to?" she laughed. "Very well. It is perhaps for the best. I will tell you all that happened." She ascended slowly and many sounds then came to me. The door to the bedroom was re-opened and Sarah pushed along the hallway. I heard the sound of a smack and her muffled squeal. All was over sooner than I thought for then I was in company again with my stepmother who lit a Turkish cigarette and held a look of perfect victory on her face.

"To think that she might have done that voluntarily," she sighed.

"Oh, what?" I could not help but exclaim.

"Have you not guessed? I am sure you have, but want me to describe it to you. Very well. In the end she sank down upon your Papa's legs. Her own, being held wider than his, she settled her bottom nicely upon his thighs and so could not help—after the straining of her legs—from bringing her tummy in contact with his prick. Her head must have sunk forward then on to his shoulder, for so I found them, quivering together yet otherwise still as statues. He had come all up her belly, naturally," she concluded and, throwing her head back, expelled a blue wisp of smoke.

"Wh . . . what did she say?" I asked stupidly.

"She must be pleasured herself, dear. That is requisite. And in particular while the memory of his throbbing, spouting organ is most vividly in her mind. Will you do it, Clara?" So asking she drew out of her bodice a long, pointed feather at which I stared. "You twirl it all around her spot. She will soon come. It is best that I let her. You hesitate, Clara. If you do not, I shall put you upon him in turn."

"She . . . she . . . she will not let me, though," I stammered.

"Hah! Do you imagine I have left her wandering about? She is well secured and legs apart. Her poor cunny must be longing for fulfilment, even though she would deny it. Pleasure her, Clara. Bring her on!"

"Yes!" The sudden exclamation leapt from me. It would be cruel to Sarah otherwise, as I told myself, and so took the feather and hastened to my task. In her room she lay bound upon her bed, naked as she had been and I saw a splash of come upon one stocking top. Thankfully she was gagged still. Her eyes literally spat at me and her straddled legs, which so revealed the hairy pouting of her quim, strained at the ropes, yet I knew I dare not hesitate. Seeing the feather, she made the most agitated movements of her head, then arched her back as I sat beside her and carefully twiddled the feather tip about her spot. How moist she was and the lips of her quim gleaming! Muffled shrieks came from her as the feather swept about her darling place—for indeed I thought of it so and wished devoutly that it had been watered for her.

The bedsprings jolted and sang with every stroke, her thighs quivering madly and her bottom bouncing. The breath hissed hotly through her nostrils. I dearly wished her then not to be gagged, but as so often it was as if our stepmama had read my thoughts, for upon the instant she swept within and sat upon the other side of Sarah, motioning me to stop. When I did, Sarah's eyes closed, opened, and then closed again. Her belly rippled. She had come and I knew it.

"Darling, I am going to remove your gag now," our stepmother told her, brushing strands of hair away from Sarah's moist forehead. "Listen carefully my sweet, for if you scream or utter any untoward sounds, I shall have you put again upon him, though this time in a firmer manner. Mark my words well, for I mean it. Was he not naughty to let himself be bound and gagged for it? Well?"

Opening her eyes, Sarah stared straight up at her, and I saw the wicked skill of our stepmother's words.

"Nod if you agree, Sarah," was said gently opposite me. "He was naughty, was he not—hard his cock at the thought of you."

Sarah nodded. Reaching carefully under her head, our stepmother then slowly loosed the gag, though pausing halfway to put her finger to her lips exactly as though all three of us were at simple play. The cloth being drawn aside, Sarah uttered a shuddering sigh. Her head went limp and she rolled her face away from Stepmama who however took her chin and brought their noses to touch.

"D . . . d . . . don't want the feather!" Sarah moaned.

"Of course you don't. You are not a bad girl, are you? Are you not my treasure? Give me your lips, your tongue now. Be good, be good."

"Glug!" sounded from Sarah but as her lips were submerged so her shoulders relaxed and with infinite tenderness I began to stroke her wet pussy with my fingertips and felt her ardent quivering. Little sobbing cries came from her which echoed into the mouth whose scented lips were splurged upon her own. Receiving a blind gesture from my stepmother who waggled her hand at me, I quickened my motions and with devious changes of hand managed to loose Sarah's ankle bonds, as I thought was requisite. At that she rolled upon her hip and clung to our stepmother so that my hand was removed from her quim but in a second was replaced by the rubbing, stockinged knee of her tormenter who quickly hoisted her skirt for the purpose.

A soft, rounded knee is delicious against the quim, as well I know, and Sarah came again quickly, clawing at our stepmother's shoulders while their mouths remained enmeshed. Then, as if she knew not where she was, she flung herself of a sudden on her back and stared blindly at the ceiling, her legs straightening and the dried sheen of Papa's sperm showing plainly on her belly.

"Naughty . . . he was naughty," she murmured, speaking as though to herself.

"Are they all not so, Sarah? Have I not tried to teach you? Will you not take example from Clarissa? She is Mistress now of her guardian's ways. Cease to deny yourself the pleasures that await you."

"I d . . . d . . . do not know what to do," Sarah whimpered. "Oh, the things you do to me and what you make me feel."

"Better now than later when you are ensnared in some useless marriage and regretting it," said our stepmother in a practical tone. Sarah was half won over and she knew it even as I myself did. Once again Stepmama drew my sister into her arms and stroked her hair. "Will you not take the cock now even as Clara must?" she asked softly, smiling at me over Sarah's head.

Sarah shook her head, her face submerged between two thrusting breasts.

"Must I cane you then? Must I, Sarah?"

"Neee-oh!" A little whimpered cry and Sarah clung to her.

"Do you want it in your bottom or in your cunny, darling? You see—I give you a choice!"

Again a shake of the head from Sarah and a deeper huddling. Then, smiling ever blandly at me over Sarah's curled-up form, my stepmother murmured to me, "Go and see if his prick is up again and then call Bertha."

CHAPTER TEN

TO VENTURE into Papa's bedroom where he sat helpless and stripped to his shirt seemed to me the most daring of all the things I had yet done, yet I knew it must be. Perhaps it had been too late for me to turn back from the first moment when my stepmother had kissed and caressed me—or perhaps I never wanted to.

My palms moistened again as I opened the door. Papa turned his head and saw me immediately. Our eyes locked like thorns that become snagged together. I knew the sense of both seeing and not-seeing. His shirt being tucked up and caught behind his back, I could see all. His legs were slimmer than I had imagined and were curiously smooth, though muscular and strong, his calves having a fine turn to them while his thighs, being somewhat compressed by his seated posture, looked lovingly strong. His penis lolled thickly over his balls, rather, as it seemed to me, like a big sleeping worm. Beneath it, his appendages, being distended by the pressure of the chair, gleamed not a little and had dark curls sprouting all about.

Perhaps I expected him to make some violent gesture of his head and to struggle equally against his bonds. He did not, but sat passive as though a mantle of fate had fallen upon him and from which he could not escape. So long did we gaze at each other that it seemed an eternity. I ventured perhaps a tiny smile, though I do not remember well and may have added this touch in retrospect. Then I stepped back and withdrew. His thing was not "up," as my stepmother had asked and I wondered what to do. The second half of my instructions was clear, however, and I tripped halfway down the stairs where, leaning over the bannisters and gazing down into the well—which I loved to do—I softly called for Bertha.

"Yes, I know, Miss Clara," she answered back, though invisible.

I hesitated then for a moment and went back along to Sarah's room. She had sat up and had our stepmother's arm around her naked back. Her head was hung and her hair all awry, though in later times it was always carefully pinned and arranged for what our stepmother lightly called "entertainments."

If I digress here briefly it is to say that neatness in appearance and tidiness of attire is always requisite for the female, particularly one who has concluded her training. She wears the best perfumes, fluffs up the pad of curls about her quim, keeps her stockings ever taut and has her boots or shoes polished to perfection. Bangles of gold or silver or various colours, drawn well up the arms, provide an excellent embellishment, as do fancy garters with broad rufflings and tiny rosettes or ribbons.

Some Mistresses affect a severe manner of attire which I do not like myself but which suits some. I recall well the sister of a local curate who was in her early thirties and wore her hair ever in a tight bun which suited her, for she could coil it immaculately, which left her swanlike neck in full view and hid nothing of the pale oval of her face, but as to her I shall return later for I was to mark her conversion one of my signal victories.

Sarah was subdued, quiescent, though I wished her not to be. I would have had her smile and embrace me and our lips to meet, for I always loved her tenderly, as now. An approach sounded.

"Turn over, darling, and kneel," our stepmother murmured to her.

Sarah raised her face a little, stirred, seemed indolent and then finally allowed herself to be manoeuvred over so that her bottom rose as sweet and round as an apple, her breasts pendant. Moving one hand beneath her while she was thus poised on all fours, our stepmother brushed her dangling tits gently with her palm. Her nipples, being already erect, quivered to the touch as did her glossy back and bottom which was caressed in turn. Shifting her right hand down under Sarah's bottom, our stepmother thus cupped and held her fore and aft as one might steady a nervous filly. Upon that, the door swung full open and Bertha led in Robert, attired in his chemise and stockings and with a blue ribbon clasping his hair at the back. His drawers having been removed, his prick stuck up like a flagpole.

Sarah then twisted her head—having her bare bottom arranged to his view—gave a squeal and would have started up had it not been for the soothing motions of our stepmother's hands.

"Shush, dear," she murmured, "bring your bottom back to the end of the bed."

Robert being guided forward meanwhile by Bertha's commanding hand, Sarah once again wildly shook her head and needed to be restrained.

"Please, no! Please, no!" she pleaded as though in anguish whereat our stepmother ceased fingering her titties and ringed her tightly about the waist so that Sarah's shoulders were partly hidden from my view and Robert's as she was leaned upon.

"Quickly, then, Bertha," came the order and a slight downward nod of our stepmother's head which had the intention of showing wherein our brother's prick was to be guided.

Sarah bucked at that, but then our stepmother gripped her hips more tightly the while that Bertha, taking hold upon the stem of Robert's rearing prick, nosed its rubicond head full under Sarah's plump quim and urged the knob within the rich, moist aperture of her cunt.

"NA-AH!" Sarah screeched, whereat our brother's cock slipped out again, so eel-like were her motions. It did her, however, little good, for while Bertha then held him and waited, and Robert stood with the most bleared expression on his face, our stepmother afforded Sarah's bum three hearty smacks which left it rosy-pink and her sobs resounding.

"Now, my girl, you will take it up you," our stepmother said sternly, and with greater purpose then Robert's pego was slipped in to gritting cries from Sarah as she received the first three inches, four—then five—and ah! a sudden jolt inspired by Bertha's hands and he was in her to the root, her bottom bulging to his belly's thrust.

"HOLD!" was then commanded by our stepmother who peered over and down under Sarah's bottom the better that she might view the sensuous conjunction of their private parts. Only the root of Robert's prick then showed and Sarah's shoulders hunched themselves and shook. Her bottom moved infinitesimally and then was stilled. Bertha, restraining Robert, placed her hand under his buttocks and so held him tight in to his sister. Indeed, I distinctly saw Bertha's index finger curl and seek between his cheeks whereat he flushed and bit his lip and strained up on his legs.

I had no doubt that Bertha was tickling his bottomhole, and so it proved, for I have since learned that it is a fine and cunning way to stimulate the male to his best endeavours.

Robert was breathing heavily but was silent, for which I admired him, for the sensation of the spongy grip of Sarah's cunny round his tool must have truly been exquisite. Little hissing noises came from her as if of rebellion and yet wonder. So were they held together, locked in love's motionless combat, for a full two minutes before our stepmother nodded and Bertha—giving a little pinch to Robert's buttocks—made him work. In-out he thrust his gleaming cock, and such a sight I had never known. Sarah began to moan and squirm her hips, causing me to wonder whether she was enjoying or escaping, but the ringing of our stepmother's arms about her waist was inexorable and tight as a vice. Puffing not a little now, Robert half closed his eyes and there came upon his face a look of perfect ecstasy, his sister's cuntlips pouting round his tool which ever glistened with her exudations. SMACK! went his stomach to her bottom in its forward thrusts while I, misty-eyed, wished it full up me instead.

"OOOH-WAH-WAH-WAH! MAMA!" sobbed Sarah.

"Faster!" our stepmother ordained. "Faster for ten strokes, Robert, and then slow again."

Poor boy—he did his best to obey. His lips trembled, his face full flushed and eyelashes quivering prettily like a girl's. Some wicked instinct told me that Sarah might well be sucking upon his tool with her cunny while yet pretending to reject it for in his outward strokes—so close I stood to them—the veins around his penis swelled mightily. Silently I counted, though the flashing of his cock was fast indeed, his knees bending and Bertha but holding the back of his head beneath the ribbon she had made him pretty in.

Eight . . . nine . . . ten. "HAAAR-AAAR!" he gasped and it was indeed a cry of amourous longing such as seemed to touch even our stepmother's heart.

"Come, then, Robert—come if you wish. Full in and give her your injection—NOW!"

It was indeed a benediction in all aspects, for otherwise she would have monitored his every move, though saw (unusually) the urgency of his case.

"OOOH-HAAAAR!" came from him then. His entire being quivered, his stiff cock thrust full up Sarah who uttered a low-moaning whine then sank her head and screwed her bottom into him so that they seemed stuck together as do dogs while from the whimpering sounds that escaped his own lips I knew him to be spouting well in her.

"FEEE-OOOOH!" gasped Sarah, though in a muffled tone, her face pressed into the coverlet of the bed and her toes, as I noticed, distinctly curling and uncurling very much as a cat's paws when they experience pleasure. "Mer-mer-mer-mer!" came from her incoherently the while that Robert's sperm gushed and splashed within her maw, there was received and held in bubbling warmth. Then did Robert quiver mightily, his knees giving a little and his head being allowed to hang back, mouth open, while he expelled his final jets and dribbles.

They were done, Sarah, too—despite herself—had come, for I distinctly saw the shiny glistenings of her sprinklings on his cock as it emerged and would have then plunged in again had Bertha not withdrawn him.

"Good boy," Bertha intoned softly and dear Robert looked fit to cry for pleasure, but did not. His face softened, his legs trembled, and he was led out, tool dripping and slimed well with desire.

"Good Robert," our stepmother called appraisingly after him and then the three of us were alone again while Sarah, sinking down upon her belly, quivered, clutched the coverlet, and lay still. Our stepmother stroked her smooth back gently, running her hand down all over her pert bottom, and winked at me as though to say, "She's done at last!" I watched my sister's long and shapely legs tighten together and then relax. "You may sleep now," she was told and her legs doubled up while she coyly hid her face and was bundled beneath the cover. Her face turned a little on the pillow, showing her profile, and she looked perfectly angelic, I thought.

"She was well seen to, but yet will have better," my

stepmother said in a whisper as she led me out and closed the door behind us. "Does it not make you want it more?" she asked mischievously and well seeing the rising palpitations of my breasts whose nipples felt like thorns.

I nodded, my face suffused and my body feeling hot. I was, it seemed, to be ever a witness, but not a participant. No doubt my flushed expression told its tale in that respect and I could not help—standing as we were upon the landing—glancing at Papa's door.

"He will be released now. Bertha will see to him," was told me gently, for she ever read my thoughts. "It was nice for Robert, but he must not expect too many favours," she went on. "You see, my dear, the male must be kept in check and the female must learn to suppress her own desires if necessary in order to maintain discipline. Both he and your Papa will be looked after well so long as they obey me. All willingness to meet my endeavours to train you all will be rewarded. Sometimes sparingly," she mused, "but still they will be. You have many little tricks to learn yet, Clara. Your calmness is admirable, though. I chose well in you."

I was silent, but felt flattered. Had it not been for Robert's pleasure I might have felt that I had betrayed both him and Papa, but I knew I had not. I was easily converted, perhaps, though no less so than other females who see within the guidance of an unerring hand the chance to loose the shackles of convention and become Mistresses of their own fate.

"The circle is sealed. That is always requisite, Clara. It matters not whose cock a girl is put up to, or takes in hand, provided that the male has learned the mastery of the female and knows his place within the immediate realm. It cannot be otherwise. You have not been hard done by, nor has Sarah. In time you will have the males brought to you, at your bidding. Their training will be such that they will be acquiescent to your every wish, will take pride in it, if you only knew, and hasten to do your every wish. It is a reversal of what normally obtains, but therein lies the pleasure and excitement of it. None are cruelly treated—unless they err—but that is rare. Even when whipped or smacked their cocks stand up proudly, as you have seen with Robert, for they know with brimming hearts and eager balls that, come what may, they will be put to good use afterwards."

"Are there none who resist and will not obey?" I asked.

"Oh pouf, as to them you may ignore them. There are females such, too, but we may discount their existence. They do not serve our wishes and are of no account," my stepmother said crisply. "Should any such approach you with lustful intent, treat them coldly and with scorn. Cowards as they are they will go in hope of another. Their eyes are mean and their temperaments equally so. Even though you whip the males' buttocks you will do so with love. I refer to our submissives, of course, Clara."

I nodded. I had such images before my eyes as I would not have dared to think of months before.

"There are none here who will resist now," my stepmother said. I could feel her nipples hard through her gown as she pressed against me and the long railing of the bannister on the landing came to my back.

"I know," I replied thickly.

"You want to, don't you, Clara?"

I could not answer. My mind ran hot with thoughts.

"I shall cane you first a little. You desire that?"

"Yeth," I lisped in my excitement. She would not do it hard. I knew she would not do it hard. I trembled, clung to her. Raising my gown at the back she explored my knickered bottom with her hand and felt its tightness and its heat. "Oh, b . . . b . . . but," I bubbled.

"It does not matter whose it is. You must learn that or you will never conquer. You may wish to cry a little before the pleasure comes, but you must learn not to betray your emotions to the male. When the plunger is tight up you, grip on it and hold. In no wise shall you speak, you understand? Yes, I believe you do and shall keep you on tiptoe for it. The dawn shall not come before you have had the pleasure of it."

CHAPTER ELEVEN

MY STEPMOTHER was true to her word, though had I anticipated the manner of it, I might have tried to retreat from my fate. Robert was not seen for the rest of the day. Was it to be he? Sarah was quiet but a little more communicative now and seemed not unkindly towards me. I felt sure that our stepmother must have dropped at least a hint as to what was to happen in my own respect for there was a touch of complicity in her manner towards me, little as we said.

When Papa appeared downstairs again all was quiet, my stepmother spurring on such conversation as occurred. Indeed, she encouraged him to read items from the newspaper to us that we might discuss them. Appearing naturally hesitant at first, Papa gained more confidence under her careful guidance for which I much admired her. Sarah blushed a lot, but that was expected of her. In all I knew the net to have been completely cast and tightened just a little, though not so much as to impede us in the generalities of life

"As sheep are guided into their pens at night, so they may be allowed to wander freely in the meadow to graze," she said to me afterwards. Confessing, however, that this sounded a trifle cruel, she went on to say that this was but a rough comparison. "Soon enough my own pets return to the fold of their own accord and do not need to be led. They know where it is, Clara, and what is its purpose, and there they find warmth and safety. And love," she added, "for what is at first a discipline imposed from without rapidly becomes a pleasure. There is naught but love in entering a firm strong cock into a receptive cunny or a tight, warm bottomhole, and ecstasy in receiving it."

"What, though, of a girl who would refuse utterly?" I asked. For at the time of speaking—which was two days after my initiation proper—the question had floated much in my mind.

My stepmother's expression took on a serious mien. "As to that, one must judge, Clara. Some young women can be extremely fretful and give every sign of refusing with all their might. It is easy to be misled in this, particularly when a great deal of sobbing and squealing is involved—perhaps even some kicking. When resistance appears overmuch, then the girl is best left to think over the matter, may be spanked perhaps and then coddled. One must not give up at the first attempt, but try a second and a third. Complete strangers are best left alone. One must learn a little of the tenor of a young woman's ways, how she thinks, and so on. Her bodily movements should be observed, and whether she is given to flirting or not. Beware that she is not to be given up to the lusts of but one individual, for you may rue the day that you brought her to what you thought of as 'training.' She may—once out of your grasp—find herself given up solely to her elder—for he is bound to be that—and will never know salvation. True, the male may be the first to indulge with her, but then he must be brought to heel afterwards and she must have the seeing of it."

"As with Robert," I interjected.

"Precisely so. And you were minded to say your Papa also, were you not?"

"I do not know." I twisted my fingers shyly.

"Bear in mind, my sweet, that your dear Papa is under my care and attention, intends no harm to you whatever, and is fundamentally obedient by nature, as many men are, though they do not always know it. Such punishment as he receives for his seeming sins, he enjoys, for it is a humiliation with promise. His is a privileged position, and he knows it. On the other hand, many males regard being humbled as a privilege, and perhaps also a form of titillation, as Robert does. In a few weeks' time, he would be lost without the occasional luxury of wearing silk stockings and soft, frilly chemises. Such brings his proud pego to a condition of stiffness and readiness he might have never otherwise known. What a darling he is—we must treasure him!" she exclaimed impulsively.

"But if a girl DOES finally refuse?" I insisted, for I wondered in my heart of hearts what she would do in such a case.

"My dear, her wishes must be respected," my stepmother said simply. "If she is one whom you like, then continue to nurture her subtly and perhaps you may still bring her to it, but if not. . . . " she shrugged.

"You would not count her, then, a dullard?"

"How kind you are in your heart, Clara! Not if her personality otherwise pleases. One little trick is to ask her advice upon as many matters as possible. In this wise you may see more clearly into her mind and may even, with guile, make her an accomplice, for while some girls will not do such things themselves, there are occasionally others whom they would like to see doing it."

Her frankness made me laugh as ever, but I have wandered—I trust not to the reader's annoyance—from the scene I was about to describe and which I had imagined, perhaps hopefully, would take place in the privacy of my bedroom. It did not. I was not so much as to be made an example of as to present one, as I was told. There was a subtle and clever balance made in affairs, for Sarah was to watch, as I indeed had watched her. This would give her solace in knowing that she had not been "picked out," as our stepmother said. Conversely, however, I would give the best of examples by not refusing, fretting, squealing or crying.

"This will place you on a rung immediately below myself," I was told solemnly, and though for a fleeting while I thought it a bit of a trick, I soon understood that it was true and that my complicity in what had gone before had not proved in vain.

The appointed time was immediately after dinner, for a full tummy makes for satisfaction, as is said, and I had also imbibed enough wine to make me feel very pleasant indeed. From the dining room I had heard movements afoot, no doubt by Bertha whom I am pleased to say was not otherwise present. Nor was my brother, who was sent upstairs to "study." Papa appeared to sense something, but said nothing, for my stepmother overlaid all with bright conversation and to my slight bewilderment, I must confess, he too retired upstairs unhindered, leaving me with my sister and stepmother.

"We will go into the drawing room, then," was said. I, being the first to reach the door thereto, opened it and saw to my heartbeating surprise that a greater space than usual had been cleared in the centre of the floor and that there stood there now a stout wooden trestle—much as used in sawing wood—upon the top of which was strapped a cushion.

"Sarah,dear, your sister is to be caned. Pray lead her to the trestle, bend her well over it, fasten her wrists and ankles with the leather clamps that are affixed fore and aft and raise her dress up to her waist," our stepmother said.

I stood perfectly still. Sarah evidently wanted to run and gazed all about as if haunted.

"Well, Sarah?" came sharply from our stepmother and, seeing that I was unresistant, my sister took my wrist hesitantly and led me to the stout wooden bar that was placed at waist-height across two sturdy pyramidal forms. Making a strange little sound in her throat, she then bent me over it gently so that my tummy came upon the cushion. My arms, hanging limp, were soon constrained by the short leather straps buckled about my wrists. I felt then such helplessness as I had never known, but at the same time a sort of distant curiousity about my posture, even envisaging other girls in the same pose and with their bottoms bared as mine was about to be.

Squatting down, my sister then drew my ankles wide apart so that they might be similarly affixed. Then, with a certain vengefulness that I could not help but sense (and even, I might say, sympathised with), she bared me to the waist, finding that I—no more than she—wore no drawers and so offered my cleft moon and pursed quim to view.

How open I felt! My legs were straddled a full two and a half feet apart and I felt a thrill of submissiveness entire. Whose cock was I to have? From whose balls would I receive the throbbing emissions of desire? Would I cry out despite all my endeavours?

Perhaps I thought an interval would then obtain. It did not. My stepmother, taking up a cane she had secreted under some cushions, whistled it softly through the air.

"Oh, do not hurt her, pray!" came from Sarah in the background, for which fond cry I loved her much.

"Hurt her, Sarah? Indeed not. She is to be inducted, even as you have been, or rather in a manner that you will be later on. Mark what I say for I will have no truck with disobedience from either of you. You know that by now—do you not?"

My sister evidently nodded, for I heard no word from her. Then came a shuffling of feet as our stepmother positioned herself and ran out the cane (as I afterwards always knew her to) lovingly across her palm. I must confess that I felt a panic then. All such words as had been uttered to me had seemed fine and fair and just, but now reality was upon me. I was to receive.

SWEEE-ISSSSH!

Ah, how it bit and burned, that first caressing of the cane on my exposed globe! Caressing yes, for such was her manner that it skimmed my hemispheres, though I would have thought for an instant that it had urged white heat deep into me. I ground my teeth and closed my eyes, feeling the insurgent heat and stinging deep inside my peach. HOOOO-IITTTT! came then the song of the cane once more, and this time its passage was lower, coming up beneath my bulge so that I all but squealed out loudly and felt the tongues of fire lick all about my cleft.

"What a bumptious young bottom she has, has she not?" our stepmother asked quite conversationally.

"It . . . it is lovely, yes," Sarah choked.

"So smooth, so round, so pert, so beautifully offered. Mark that her hips move well but that she has not cried out. What a young Amazon she will be!"

The compliment was well taken, but not the next SWEEEE-IISSSSH! which I swear stung deeper into me and brought tears splashing on the carpet from my eyes. I wanted truly to scream out to ask her to stop, but knew that such would be my true undoing. I squeezed my nether cheeks which reared and jerked. Slivers of fire shot through me and I felt as if I had been sat in nettles, so awful was the sensation.

"My sweet Clara," I heard our stepmother say, and then to Sarah: "Fetch the oil, my love—that little flask upon the table there."

Oh, was it over? I begged for it to be, shut my eyes tight and felt the swimming of my helpless tears.

"Hold the cane a moment, Sarah. It becomes you to do so, for you will learn to wield one soon enough—though not on Clara. Still, my pet, hold your hot bottom firm," was said to me and then a finger came, well oiled, and rubbed all round and into my rosette, bringing a faint squeak from me that evidently was forgiven. Round and round the fingertip swirled on the perimeter of my rose-hole, urging drops of oil within. A little loving smack then on my burning cheeks and I was seeming done—the wicked route prepared. But no.

"Do you understand, Sarah?" I heard asked and then HOOOO-ITTTT!

"THEEEE-OOOOH!" I gritted, though as silently as can be, for it was indeed a harsh one and bit me deeply as if my poor bottom had been assailed by a thousand wasps.

"I d . . . d . . . d . . . yes," responded Sarah.

"WHAT do you understand, Sarah?" . . . SWEEE-ISSSSH!

"NAR-HAR-HAAAAAR!" I cried within myself and screamed as silently for Sarah to reply.

"That . . . that . . . that we must be s . . . s . . . submissive."

"To their pricks, when I wish it. WELL?"

"Yes!"

Oh, what a heartfelt cry, for she saw the cane raised anew, as afterwards she told me, and thus did our step-mother play off my "punishment" against her confession. My bottom cheeks were raging. I could no more fend off the fire than I could rise. By clenching my hemispheres I sought to draw it in and by doing so felt a certain heat in my belly and pressed my derriere out as much as possible to the cooling air.

"What a divine posture! Is she not asking for it now?" my stepmother laughed and then clapped her hands. The doors were out of my vision, but I heard them open and with that a gasp from Sarah, quick suppressed, no doubt by a quick gesture from our stepmother.

A padding of feet came to my ears. I was alert to all, knowing not whether to writhe my bottom more or still it. I heard Sarah's feet shift as though she had retreated.

My eyes screwed up still against the insurgent stinging and I felt myself ready for naught but a large bowl of cool water in which to plunge my derriere.

"You are well ready for her, I see," I heard my stepmother say. "Obey the rules and give her pleasure. The route will be tight. Give it to her an inch at a time. Sarah—take hold of this."

A little quavering sound from my sister then. I knew it not, but as I learned afterwards a long silk ribbon was looped twice around the root of my conqueror's stiff penis, my stepmother and my sister each standing to one side of him and each holding an end of the ribbon taut so that his movements were at least symbolically monitored. Then came male hands at my hot, throbbing cheeks and parted them as one might split a peach. Hung full over the trestle as I was, and tight secured, I had no means of defense even had I sought one.

"Oil his knob a little, Sarah," our stepmother ordained, ensuring that my sister was as much under duress in obeying as I. I heard a groan of satisfaction of the male at her fingers' touch and then the swollen crest came against my rosy aperture.

I wanted of course to scream, despite all my tuition, and yet withal a sense of lewdness seized me. I had watched Sarah accept our brother's in this fashion—albeit but an inch or so—and had felt much fervoured excitement in the sight. Now I in turn was at pillage and even more brazenly in my posture than she had been. "NOOO-HOOO!" I wished to scream, for now the cork urged in and therewith all the breath seemed to rush from my body. How thick it was, how warm, how pulsing! I felt my hole expanding to receive it, much as does moist, warm sand when the tide has receded and the fingers are pressed down within it. AAAAH! another inch, and from him another groan.

I held my silence even though I wished to cry. The sensation was delirious. I had a cock in me! "WHAA-

HAAAR!" I cried in my head and all about me was a swimming heat. I yielded, yielded, urged a little back and so enforced his knob within my tube. Ooooh, the feeling of it and I cared not whose it was, believing wickedly that it might be dear Papa's.

"It is called buggery or sodomy, my pet, but neither word pleases. Both are ugly of sound and offensive to the ears," my stepmother afterwards told me. "Better," she went on, "to say a girl is corked or plugged or put to it, for the meaning then is clearer and a vision of it better taken. When lewdness takes you then you may work back and forth with your hips in concert with the male, though the most imperious ladies receive their corkings often without movement, and in particular if one male slave after another is put to them."

In this moment, however, I knew nothing of theory but only of sensations. My conqueror, snorting not a little through his nostrils, but otherwise kept quiet by the attendance of my stepmother, had soon succeeded in gaining his libertine entry with half of his pulsing shaft upon which I could not help but squeeze since its girth invaded me to the uttermost. I would have retreated in that moment, perhaps, but had nowhere to move. The instinct, as I learned, is to repel the invader, and yet the faint wrigglings of one's hips invites it. His hands clamped me tightly about the sides of my buttocks and I heard his feet shuffle apart as though to gain purchase on the carpet for his task.

How manly a well-proportioned male looks in such a posture I can well admire—his calves straining, knees unflexed and balls waiting to swing once the full plugging motions begin. Infinitely more beautiful, however, is the subdued—or apparently subdued female—for in the correct posture her ardent derriere is fully raised and thrust out for the amourous assault which she soon learns to long for.

Once the halfway mark is reached, the remaining passage becomes easier, as I now learned. He would have plunged in then, I know, had the ribbon wound around the base of his stiff penis not provided warning tugs. I was intended to feel every inch of his lewd entry and did. The breath whistled softly from my own nostrils and my fallen hair cascaded down on either side of my face to sweep upon the carpet. I wanted to sob, to cry out, to implore, but remembered ever the final role to which I was destined. A humming sound of frustration emitted itself from his throat which I dimly interpreted as a plea for him to be fully at me, but my stepmother was inexorable in her treatment of the males. Indeed, as I had heard from Sarah afterwards, her free hand was at the back of his hair to restrain him further if need be, for I was said to be a toothsome piece whose apple bottom every male would plug on sight and with full randiness were he able to.

A gasp escaped me as the last two inches were rammed up. Such small sounds were thankfully forgiven and with a sense of extreme excitement and ecstasy, I felt my heat-sheened bottom mounded to his belly. The inevitable "HOLD!" came from my stepmother then and never was the compression better felt than when his pego pused away in me, tight-clenched as it was between my ardent cheeks.

I had almost forgotten my stinging—or rather the sensations I had so resented and which indeed had pained me, merged now into an otherness of bliss to find myself male-corked at last. My legs stiffened of their own accord and I presented—fully cleft as I was—the prettiest of sights, or so was told afterwards.

"Had you rotated your bottom eagerly, I would have forgiven you, Clara," my stepmother said afterwards, "for I never knew so sweetly docile a pupil, nor one so eager to receive the sperm. What did it feel like?" she asked me but half an hour afterwards, her eyes sparkling.

"Oh, like a big fleshy poker," I sighed. "At first I

wished to reject it, but was then invaded by delicious sensations of complete surrender. My bottomhole felt larger than ever before and yet was so tight about his cock I thought him never able to move it. When he drew out slowly to the knob I wanted to cry out for its entry, but you stayed him thus and teased me horribly!"

"Yes, what a delicious moment that was, to see you so a-tremble and almost in doubt that the cork would return into the neck of the bottle, so to speak! I leaned forward then, stroked the fronts of your thighs while they quivered and felt the sticky moisture of your quim before permitting him to drive the peg in again. I heard your teeth chatter distinctly and a little mewing cry come from you. You will have no doubts about your pleasure there again, will you?"

"No, never! Will it be as nice in my cunt?"

"Of course, though the sensation is different. The two pleasures are twins to one another, though a true Madame, I think, prefers it up her bottom, for she can judge the full entry of the tool better and feel the squirting of the come. How you puffed and worked your hips towards the end, you naughty thing!"

I giggled and said I could not help it and wished I had had a mirror to watch Sarah's eyes.

"Hah! they were like saucers, Clara! How her bosom heaved and such a sullen look of pleasure on her face that no dissembling on her part could disguise!"

"You have not told me who it was and neither will Sarah tell."

"She dare not speak of such without my permission. There need be no secret in the matter. It was Bertha's husband, Tim—a brawny man with a fine cock that Bertha has seen to it is well trained for its tasks. And why he? Because, as I have told you, my pet, it matters not within all reason, who your provider is. Tim is clean and firm in body, which is all that matters and was the mere provider of your pleasure. Did you feel the jetting of his come?"

"Oh, it bubbled and throbbed and pelleted in me until I thought it would never end and even through the gathering thickness of the sperm I felt his shootings on and on. How delicious!"

"He was kept from coming for a full week, in readiness for the task. Bertha saw to that, massaging his pecker daily."

A cloud passed across my mind. "But, Mama, when he sees me again, comes upon me, oh I shall blush and know not where to look!"

"Tush and nonsense, my pet. This is the very lesson you have yet to learn. You will gaze at him directly, calmly and impersonally. So far from being bold with you, his eyes will drop. He knows you to be the conqueror and not the conquered."

"But were he to come upon me alone—perhaps at the far end of the grounds and I defenceless?"

"Defenceless you never now can be. You received his prick imperiously, my sweet, uttering not a cry nor a protest. He will know your merit. His cock will stir, will rise upon sight of you, remembering as he will the luscious tightness of your orb, the way you sucked on him."

"That is exactly what I mean!"

"What can I teach you, Clara, more than I have done? Had he been untried, not trained, truly the picture might be different, but such a male would never be put to you, nor would such a one be allowed to darken our doors. He regards you now as hallowed, as a female supreme. The very fact of your youth will put him more in awe of you. Call him now and bid him lick your shoes."

"Oh, I could not!"

"Could not! Ha! Do you intend to fail me then?"

"I do not know where he is," I mumbled, for by then my initiation had long ended, of course. The trestle had been removed, Sarah had gone up to her room—there to ponder much, no doubt—and I was alone in the drawing room with Stepmama.

"He waits beyond, outside the door—as fully he expected to. I shall go into the morning room now, Clara. Call him."

"Oh!" The little exclamation passed my lips and then I was alone. My palms moistened, even as my bottomhole felt sweetly creamed. I knew not whether to stand or sit. Finally I stood up, hands behind my back, tight-clenched. I would feel much smaller in his presence, I knew, for Tim was a tall, strong man. I parted my lips, but quite comically only a croak came. How silly and nervous I felt! But then at last I summoned my will. I was to be alone at last, even though for a moment, with a male subject. Such was my stepmother's clear intention.

"Smithers!" I called, for such was his surname and instinct told me not to address him in this moment other than by such.

The door opened immediately and he stood there, then hesitated and entered, closing the door quietly as might a footman. I held my head high although in truth I quivered inwardly. Standing to attention, his head bowed, he waited.

"Here!" I all but barked and pointed to the floor immediately in front of me. Not meeting my eyes, he came forward and the silence about us seemed tremendous. "Kneel! Kneel and lick my shoes!" I said, keeping with great effort a quavering from my voice.

He obeyed on the instant, his nose first scraping the ground and back bowed. Raising my skirt no more than was necessary, he uncovered my buckled shoes and impressed his lips upon the toes of them fervently, one after the other. It tickled a little through the leather, but I liked it. I knew my stance, my high station. I had reached, as it seemed to me, the very summit of female ambitions.

His mouth brushed again back and forth with the submissiveness of a trained dog.

"Go!" I said coldly and therewith, without the faintest protest or raising of his eyes to mine, he lumbered up and retreated, not wiping his lips as I fleetingly thought he might, for that would have been a sign of gross rebellion and discourtesy. Indeed, his tongue flicked quickly about his mouth as though the very taste of the dust on my shoes pleased him. Then he was gone, the door closing soundlessly once more, and immediately after my stepmother entered and drew me lovingly into her arms.

"My little conqueror!" she crooned and it was then as if the gates of life had opened wide to me and I waited upon our new adventures.

CHAPTER TWELVE

"HAD YOU BUT another sister I would have taken triple pleasure," she sighed then as together we walked into the hall and made our way upstairs.

"There will be other girls, though," I ventured boldly and not without a strain of hope in my voice.

"Could you cane or birch one?" she asked me curiously and led me into her bedroom, there to dispense liqueurs.

"Yes, I believe I could, though perhaps at first with your guidance."

"There is a trick to it, Clara—a manner of twisting the wrist so that the cane skims the globe and does not bite too deep, for to allow it to do so would be cruel. The paddle is splendid, as is the strap or birch. Your sister is to have a taste of the birch tonight. You see this here?" So speaking she rose and opened one of her two wardrobes. Within stood a fine birch, its twigs still moist, for they should be softened, said she. To use a dry one—save across a knickered bottom—would be cruel. "What a fire it brings to the bottom!" she laughed, handing it to me and allowing me to swish it through the air, which I did with great pleasure, imagining a receptive naked bottom on the end of it.

"Why must Sarah? Did she not assist you?" I asked immodestly.

"You scarce needed to be put to the test, Clara, but your sister does. Robert has mounted her well and creamed her quim, but she will not be truly settled until she has received the same as you. Did I not tell her so downstairs? Yes, even amid your tribulations you heard that. I shall not belay her hard. Just sufficiently to warm her for the entry of the cock. She will sleep the better for it and already has her nightdress on, I am sure, which will save undressing her. Do you wish to watch?"

I shook my head. It would be unfair to Sarah, I felt, to be spectator to her trials again. I squeezed my bottomhole and imaged her receiving it. Would it be Tim, I asked naively. My stepmother smiled and shook her head.

"No, dear. She must be exercised in a way that will impress upon her even more the male role in these affairs. I am not sure that she will, though. She is less forward in her understanding than you and may remain a novice for a few weeks yet. You may have to birch her on the morrow, Clara, if she complains."

"Yes." The word escaped me before I meant to say it, and yet I did.

"The tests may occasionally seem to you severe, Clara, and yet you must be assured that I judge them finely. Go and tell her that I wish to see her in ten minutes time. Go on!"

The last words were sharply spoken, for I had hesitated. The handle of the birch felt warm to my hand and I relinquished it reluctantly, which she saw well.

"Go on, darling, you will burnish her bottom well tomorrow and that will be good for her—good for you both," she said more softly. And with that I hastened to Sarah's room where she was just getting into bed and so received my message crossly.

"Oh, I am just going to sleep," she declared, though not meeting my eyes, which was a great mistake for her, for when a thing is done it is done, and when it must be done then it must. Such is my philosophy, guided as it is by caring and devotion and a knowledge of the needs of others which they may not recognise themselves.

"You had best go or she will be cross," I said, "but wear only your nightdress, as you are doing, for I do not think you will be kept long and Stepmama said you were to go thus."

"Very well," she replied moodily and sat sideways upon her bed picking at her quilt, I wondering much at what went on inside her. The sight of her thinly-clad bottom, which was so beautifully round, stirred me and it was as though I felt the birch clasped in my hand once more. Even so, I did not linger but bidding her a fond goodnight went along to my room and there left my door ajar of a purpose.

I knew that I had to listen and felt all tense within. The minutes passed all too slowly. I watched my clock with care, half fearful that Sarah might delay or be late in her going, for I sensed punctuality to be important. How quiet the house was when her bare feet slurred at last along the corridor! I heard then a little cry from her as she evidently entered our stepmother's room and then a slapping sound followed by another cry.

"You have seen it once already, Sarah. It is but a cock and a fine one. Am I to birch you, girl? Will you not kneel up? Come, present your bottom. What a lovely one you have!"

"Oh, d . . . d . . . don't, please! I cannot in front of him!"

"What has he to say in the matter—or you? Do you treat this as a mere lewdness of desire, you sillikins?" SWEEEE-IISSSH! The birch sounded distinctly, making such a juicy sound across my sister's bottom, and she wailed. "Will you have another and another, Sarah? He dare not move nor stir until you are presented up to him. Am I not in command of you both and fully so?"

"Ho, ho, ho, he m . . . m . . . mustn't" SWEEEE-ISSSSSH! "HAAAAR! Oh, it burns!"

"And you will do more, Miss, if you do not show your bottom better. I will have you here all night until you obey! Had you but learned a lesson from Clara then you would be silent in letting him perform his rightful duty. Come, William, advance a step or two, but no closer. Did I not tell you what a globe she has and the sweet hang of her tits? You are to touch them not upon peril of being birched yourself. She will learn better, perhaps, from taking your prick between her cheeks than any other."

"Blub, blub, blub!—Don't let him . . . please!"

"Once you are corked, girl, we shall have another song from you. Would you disgrace your sex, Sarah? Come, dear, open your legs wider and push your bottom well out. You want the birch again? There . . . that is better."

"Oh-woh! I shall die of this, I shall!"

"Tush and nonsense! No young woman ever died from it. You are to receive your Papa's cock and sperm up your bottom, my pet, as far as it will go, and merrily he will throb in you, I have no doubt. It is you who are to receive the greater pleasuring, not he. Very well, William!"

"No, no, no! AAAAARGH!"

"More in, William, more in. Get two inches well lodged and so remain. There! You see how well she opens up to you?"

"Nooo, nooo, NOOOO! It is too big! Oh! Papa! Do not!"

"Shush, you little fool! He has no say in the matter. I shall have you birched at breakfast, Sarah, if you continue this disobedience. Very well, William, ease it far full up her now and hold."

"J . . . J . . . Julia, I should not! GAAAAR! How tight and warm she is!"

"How DARE you speak, sir! Have I not forbidden it? Clasp the fronts of her thighs, but no more than that. I will not have your fingers straying to her quim. Think of her as I have instructed you—not as your daughter but as a Queen of Love—one whom you henceforth will obey in all respects. Now work her slowly, slave, while I fondle her titties, for such is my prerogative."

"GOOOO-OOOOH-OOOOH!" A sobbing cry from Sarah. "Oh-woh-woh, it is naughty!"

"Deliciously so, my pet, to have your Papa's cock up your bum at last, and well have you merited it. If you would but be quiet and stately in your movements there would be no need for such fussings. Work your hips gently back and forth to his prick. He is right up you now with every stroke."

"I c . . . c . . . can't! I mustn't! OOOOH! Oh-woh-woh, Papa, take it out!"

"Little hypocrite, how your titties have swelled and your nipples hardened! He will do naught but what I tell him, nor you. There . . . your hips now surge a little—that is good. Keep at your workings. Do not be fretful. William, draw out now unto your knob, but hold it just within."

"OOOOH!" A sudden wail from Sarah. I imagined well the impetuousness of her bottom now, despite her cries. There is nothing more taunting than to have the peg full up and then to have it so withdrawn so that it throbs and titillates the rosette's rim. Sarah's little petulant cries sounded as though smothered, her burning face—I am sure—being buried in the coverlet.

"Now, Miss, he will hold it so for as long as I tell him. An hour even, if I wish it, yes, for the adorable warmth and tightness of your derriere will keep him so. Even though his eyes plead for deliverance he will not receive it, nor you. You wish to wriggle upon it, do you not, but are ashamed to, for it is a luscious feeling, Sarah. Would you break the spell, or stay an hour so? You have but to speak, Sarah!"

A long silence, and then: "Wh . . . wh . . . what d'you mean?"

"Is he not as much in training, my pet, as you?"

How well I imagined my flushed sister, corked just sufficiently as she was not to dare to move and in her secret heart all a-quaver lest it be withdrawn.

"You are m . . . m . . . making me do it."

Oh, what a silly answer, I thought, and felt quite enraged with her. At first I had thought our stepmother overdoing things, but now I knew better. Sarah was really the greatest sillikins of all.

"Very well, you shall stay thus—both of you."

"Oh-woh!"

"J . . . J . . . Julia!" from Papa.

"Have I not told you to be QUIET, sir! Do you not know your place here? You are but the provider of her pleasures, did she but know it. A heel on the back of your neck would suit you better than this posture. Keep it in—just in! Now, Sarah! Well, Miss?"

"Wh . . . wh . . . what?"

"It is for you to command, you fool! Would you be here all night and turn a majesty of movement into farce? Bring him to conclusion. Speak!"

"I d . . . d . . . do not know what you want me to say, Mama."

"Mama, indeed! Well, that is a little better, Sarah. Your bottom pulses deliciously with his prick up you, and well you know it. Be bold in your commands, for they shall be no less than that. Ordain him to effect six strokes in you—full within—and to come."

"HAAAAR! Oh! P . . . P . . . P . . . "

"Do not stammer, girl! Out with it! Sheathe his cock yourself, if you will, for I permit that. Six long, firm strokes and then you'll take his sperm."

"P . . . P . . . Papa! Do it!"

"No, Sarah, that will not do, girl. Enunciate clearly your desires, and let us have no pretence that they are other than that. WELL!"

"Oh-ho-ho!" Another silly little sob from Sarah whom

I could not help but think was truly enjoying having that swollen plum nestling so securely in her hole, for it must have been pulsing fiercely, as though all the time seeking re-entry and fulfilment. "S . . . s . . . six strokes, Papa, and then c . . . c . . . come!"

"Jooo-oooh-oooh-lee-AAAAH!"

Never had I heard my stepmama's name so expended as with one long groan Papa commenced his toil. Indeed I felt a trifle sorry for him that naughty Sarah had kept him so long about it—though I was to learn better in such matters later on.

"MA-MA!" from Sarah, for the slap-smacking of her bottom to his belly was fiercer than before. The gasping of their breaths sounded and the bedsprings sang. That she was truly being plugged I rejoiced in and felt as though I were receiving every stroke myself, so juicy were the sounds. "LA-HAAAR!" she sobbed then and to a deep groan from Papa I knew his come was spilled, or jetting up her deeply as it must, for though I describe her cries as sobs they were other than of despair but of a pleasure she could not conceal and I imagined her round silky bottom ground full into him as the delicious pellets of sperm anointed her, for then came a shuddering sigh from both and a moment of trembling silence.

"Withdraw, William! You have done your duty. To your room, sir!"

No sooner did she speak than was obeyed. I heard the shuffling of his feet and he was gone, his bedroom being that adjoining hers and in the direction opposite to my own so that I had no need to hurriedly close my door.

"Well, Sarah?" I then heard and then the distinct sound of a kiss. "Was it nice? You may answer truthfully, for he is gone. Were you not well served? Have no secrets from me now."

"I don't. . . . Yes."

The confession being wrung from her, another kiss sounded.

"You have been well-reamed, Sarah. You are become a woman now, even as Clara. I wish you not to have shyness in such matters but to put yourself up boldly, though rather at your own wish than mine. A male slave may caress you, if you so command, but otherwise will merely be of service to you or—as we say—will service you. The longer you keep them about it, my love, the greater your own pleasure will be. Do you not feel nicer there, despite your howls?"

"Yes . . . but I should not. Oh, to think it was Papa!"

"Why, you silly, at the very mention of your bottom and your titties, his stalk has risen ere this. I have kept him long and in great suspense for this moment. Were you to go naked now to his room, what do you think would happen?"

"Oh, I don't know—I must not think of it."

"Indeed you must, and most precisely. He would obey your every command—not fall upon you, cock stiffening, as you foolishly imagine. Ask him to merely kiss your bottom and he will. Anxious as a dog awaiting an offered biscuit, he would kneel to you."

"He would not do it to me again if you were not here?"

"Oh, how you miss the point, indeed! No, he would not, nor dare to. Put a halter around his neck and lead him to your boudoir and there he will do your bidding. Have his cock stiffen, if you will, and merely toy with it, then send him away."

"I c . . . c . . . cannot imagine doing it!"

"You will. It is pleasant to play with the males, Sarah. They, too, take pleasure in their own frustrations. If you are not Queen now of your realm, you are at very least a true Princess. Lie on your back now, dear, you will soon come again to the touch of my finger. Did you not come when he was up you? Tell the truth!"

"Yes! B . . . b . . . but with Papa, oh!"

"It matters not who, Sarah. You will limit yourself to none, will bind yourself to none. Only be imperious and less hesitant and you will find your way, as Clara has already done, and she by precepts rather than example."

"Had she not done it before then?"

"Not before tonight, no, and has yet to have her cunny creamed, though needs me not to administer to her in that. Learn from her thereby and you will profit much even though she is younger than you."

"I do not want her to make me do things, though."

"She may or she may not. It depends upon your comportment and behaviour. Be neither sullen nor uncommunicative. Speak quietly at all times and follow your nature. I believe you know it a little better by now. If you do not, I shall have you exercised regularly until you are come to the proper way of things."

"I . . . oooh! you are m . . . m . . . making me come again . . . I shall try!"

"Until you learn to control those nearest and dearest to you, Sarah, you will come to nothing. This is the secret of it. Regard your Papa and Robert with distant love and use them to your own desires. Be stern, be cool, and be commanding and we shall soon have things better ordered here."

"Yes, yes, all right . . . haaaar!"

"There, my sweet, you will sleep all the better for it. I confess that the sight of you two has stirred me not a little. Have Clara bring Robert to me."

"Yes."

Sarah's voice was dutiful. In but a moment or two she knocked upon my door, which pleased me, for normally she would have burst in. I answered politely for her to enter and pretended to have dozed.

"Mama wants Robert taken to her," she uttered breathlessly.

"Very well," I replied languidly and got up, stretching myself, attired as I then was in my cotton nightdress. "You will have to help me get him ready," I declared, for a sudden sense of mischief had come upon me.

"I?" She started back, but I stepped forward and clasped her to me. Our bellies came warmly together and I could feel her springy bush against my own.

"Is it not nice to be naughty, Sarah?" I murmured and kissed her neck. She hid her face and trembled.

"I dunno," she mumbled. I felt stern and, seizing her hair, dragged her head back. With my free hand I felt into her bottom and, pressing the cotton close between her bottom cheeks, felt a dampness there, a stickiness. She wriggled wildly and grabbed at me as though protectively.

"He has been right up you and come in you, hasn't he?" I asked.

Her mouth wobbled. "Oh, Clara!"

"Hasn't he? Has he got a big one? Did you press your bottom right into him as he came? Did you, Sarah?" There was a pause and her fingers tightened into my shoulders. "I shall birch you in the morning if you do not tell," I whispered.

"Hooo-hooo! Yes, he has got a big one. Oh, all the things you make me do and say!"

She was still at that song, I thought with annoyance, and may be ever would be so. Some young women are, ever secretly rejoicing in their naughtiness and, once tickled and teased or birched, allowing their drawers to be pulled down, they ever wish to be overcome. Reluctant as she was, I drew her along into Robert's room where he lay waiting in his stockings, shoes, chemise. His prick lay thick but inert over his balls. A sense of wonder was in his eyes at the sight of us both in our nightdresses. Before he could move—if indeed he intended to without instruction—I had clamped my hand firmly over his mouth.

"Bring him up, Sarah," I commanded.

Her hand wavered and then reached out as in turn she bent over the bed, lifted the limp worm of his tool and began massaging it hesitantly until I spoke to her sharply and told her to look me full in the eyes while she did it.

This she obeyed, face flushed and lips rather prettily apart. Having done her duty, Sarah was sent back to bed while I took our brother into Stepmama's room. I knew well enough what she intended. Within minutes Robert lay groaning and hissing his pleasure between our stepmother's thighs which she kept wide apart, lying upon her back. The oiliness and clamping of her cuntlips was delicious to see around his stiff weapon. Raised up as he was told to be on his forearms, Robert was not allowed to kiss her or otherwise touch her. Eyes haggard, he stared down at her swollen tits, for she had discarded all save for her corset and stockings. Her thick brown nipples burgeoned to him, but were forbidden to his lips. He grunted as he worked her, but she lay inert, a dreamy expression upon her face. Now and then her bottom would give a little jerk as his balls smacked into her, but her eyes were pools of mystery, hazing over only when she came which she did a full dozen times, I swear, for his slowly-ramming cock glistened the more with her every libation.

"Not yet, Robert, not yet," she said again and again when his breathing grew coarser, for she knew every sign of the male's impending spills. Thus she kept him at it, finally raising her beautiful legs and drawing them full back as she commanded him to come and he did so, quivering and shuddering, till every drop was spilled, absorbed, sucked in.

"Off with him, Clara—he is spoilt," she uttered when at last it seemed he would sink down on her, though straining every tendon not to do so.

His cock dripped as I drew him out and led him stumbling back to what she thereafter frequently called his "cell."

"You are a good boy now, Robert," I murmured to him and sat him on the bed like a child until I had him undressed and put into his nightdress which was an old one of my own. "Get into bed," I told him and he did so, huddling up and with his back to me.

"I w . . . w . . . want . . . ," he mumbled.

I, halfway to the door, turned and asked sharply, "What?"

"To . . . to . . . to d . . . d . . . do it with you," he said and hid his face.

"You know you may not say such a naughty thing, Robert, you KNOW you may not," I told him and waited for his reply.

"Yes, I know," came his whisper.

"Do as Mama tells you and we shall see," I said and then went out, myself all a-tremble, though he knew it not.

CHAPTER THIRTEEN

THUS WAS THE FIRST new chapter in my life all but rounded off. To the outer world all would have seemed normal, and indeed did so, for no visitors noticed a change in Papa, Robert or anyone else. But to live in an entirely closed world was unhealthy, Stepmama said, and exhorted Sarah and I to spread our wings, to entertain and to seek out subjects. By day Robert wore his normal attire. At evenings I would have much fun in dressing him up, even to putting him into one of Sarah's corsets which fitted him admirably so that he looked quite adorable in knickerless state thus, stockings taut and tightly gartered, and well-polished shoes.

Sarah, having been prised more out of her shell, would tickle his balls and cock with just her little finger, which she learned well to do, until he had a fine stand, his prepuce drawn back and his knob aglowing. Even so we monitored our own desires as our stepmother taught us to and would accept the males but once a week, which of occasion made me fret and want for more.

"You shall have more when you have tamed your own subjects," I was told. "The males must not be spoiled, Clara, or they will take airs upon themselves."

I birched Sarah sometimes and she would then respond by coursing the softened twigs across my own bottom until I came up to a fine heat. Such amusements never took place before the males, however, for it was not seemly for us so to do. Even so, they must have silently remarked the glowing heat of our bottoms when we were tapped or tupped or pistoned, or whatever our word might be for the evening. Sarah gradually grew silent when it was done to her and would lay her cheek sideways on a velvet cushion, her eyes wide with wonder as the shaft urged back and forth and only a gentle quivering of her bottom was to be seen. With the cock firm gliding in her she would come and breathe more quickly when she did so, her eyelashes fluttering prettily and her eyeballs rolling up.

"To feather your sweet pussies when you have the prick up your bottoms would be delicious, but you are accepted now as almost the same rank as I in the household and so must not be seen to be playthings," our stepmother said, to my own disappointment at least for Sarah still obtained some hesitations. Seeing her apparently incurable in this respect, our stepmother paid her the curious compliment of blindfolding her when, instead of upping her bottom and thus keeping her expression mostly hid, she was put on her back to them which—if our stepmama was feeling mischievous—might be in the drawing room upon a tigerskin. To Tim or Papa or Robert it was a sign of uncaring that she was not put out by whoever's prick she received, though that was not really the reason, but it sufficed to allay their thoughts and so kept her "queenly" in their eyes.

Once or twice our stepmother would make Sarah tipple heartily before putting her down, which was always done in the absence of males, for it was to be seen by them that everything she did was voluntary. My sister would then be arranged prettily on the tigerskin with her skirt wreathed up and most neatly fanned out on either side of her hips. Her bush was dark and showed beautifully against her snow-white belly. While she lay there with the blindfold on, our stepmother would unbutton Sarah's corsage so that her firmly jellied tits came into view, the nipples then being teased to fiery points. Sarah would then moan and toss for in the meanwhile I, taking a soft brush, would fluff up her mass of pubic hairs and so tickle her with the bristles at the same time. Becoming passionate, she would seek our mouths, but these were refused.

"All your desires must bubble on the cock," she would be told. Thus all her will was required to hold herself still in readiness and anticipation when the male was led in, by which time Sarah's knees were flexed and her thighs straddled so that the pouting of her cuntlips was well in view and glistening not a little from our endeavours. Then the male would be put down on her, he being ever restrained to thread her well and thoroughly until her bush was well creamed with his come and she would lie languid and satisfied, being allowed her own time in which to get up.

I had taken at this time to writing thoughts down on paper. Not only thoughts, for I attempted also to describe such "exercises" as above, and found myself a muff at it, or so I thought.

"Show me what you have written," my stepmother asked once when I complained to her of my difficulties. She then sat reading earnestly such a scene as I have here described, with much bumping of Sarah's bottom on the floor and the sweet but breathless look on her face. "It is not so bad as you think," my stepmother concluded at the end of three full pages, "for what you are attempting even the greatest of writers have failed in, which is to say how to describe even the conjunction of two pairs of lips or the first meeting of the prick to the cunny's mouth. Such things escape the pen as oil does water. Fret about it not. You have come within good measure of it." Thereat she laughed and added, "I see you have described the crest of your Papa's cock as like a garden bulb nosing into loam—that is most amusing! The desperations of the writer are even greater than those of the painter, believe me, for words do not have colour and are flat. Shall you write more?"

I nodded, for I was a little flattered by her attentions and by her question which plainly directed me to proceed. She then bid me write in chapters and not endlessly—"all at a gabble," as she said—and hence I did and so have built my narrative upon those early efforts.

At this time—so much have I condensed events in this chapter, not wishing to repeat myself—I had reached the age of seventeen and so my titties and my bottom, not to say my pouting slit, were truly worthier of all attentions. My stepmother had not added, however, to our entourage, saying that to do so would encourage laziness in myself and Sarah.

"I could bring men and maidens to you both, but I will not, for then you would be like fledgling birds forever feeding from their mother's mouth and learning not to fly," she told us one day, adding that she meant to hold a garden party, and so closely did she run her sentences together that I knew there to be a meaning in it. No sooner had I thought this than she went on: "The guests will be varied but carefully chosen. There will be no merriments, but you are to observe them closely. The rest I leave to you."

"Shall we have some of them to stay, then?" Sarah asked carelessly.

"Most certainly not. Not, at least, until you have them trained. You must go afield in your endeavours."

"Oh, I could not!" my sister exclaimed, "I would be too shy."

"Would you really, Miss? You were not too shy to up your skirts last night. You must pay a penance, Sarah, for that remark and you will not be blindfolded on your next occasion but will gaze steadily into the eyes of your jockey the while he rides you. I will take no comment on that from you and no rebellions. Close your eyes but once and I will birch you afterwards until you really howl. That is understood?"

"Yes—oh, perfectly," Sarah exclaimed, her face aflame, and rushed upstairs.

"There is no taming of her, Clara, but no matter. She must be driven more to boldness and will be so, for she ever tries to hide behind my skirts."

"Well, she will come to it," I replied vaguely, for my mind was rather on future events than a repetition of present ones and so I looked forward to the garden party muchly. Of my stepmother's skill in compiling the guest list I will say this—that she chose with great cunning so that while there were many dullards among the arrivals there were a handful who offered what might be called possibilities. These, as came to me during a pleasant afternoon among the water ices, the strawberries and cream, comprised a young married couple of superior mien, and the local Vicar, his brother and his sister.

Of the married couple, the young woman was called Jennifer, or to give her her full names, Jennifer de Vere Lacey. She was patrician in features, of just above middling height and of some twenty-four years. Her figure was splendid, adorned as it was in a fashionable grey silk dress set off by a superb hat with feathers, flowers and ribbons. The buttons of her corsage spanned tightly down between her fulsome tits and I had a true mischief to see her eyes if of a sudden she were seized and the buttons were undone. As to her husband, he was foppish in appearance with a slightly drooping moustache and the clear skin of a woman. He shared her slenderness which boded well for his appearance when naked. Seeing me appraise them, my stepmother sidled up to me where I stood in the background beneath an elm tree and murmured, "Married couples can be quite fun, Clara."

Before I could reply, and indeed wondered how she was able to read my thoughts, she had gone to move among the guests, I taking upon myself the role of a watcher. Occasionally I would circulate also to offer pleasantries and see to it that glasses were filled, for in this manner I could better judge the tonality of voices, the shades of expression in their eyes, the way they moved their bodies and their hands, and other things that told me much. In so doing I fastened upon Maude, the Vicar's sister. She was at my guessing of about thirty years, possessing a superb bosom and a small waist, a pleasantly rounded face with full, slumbrous lips and a voice that spoke of timidity.

How strange that I should feel above them all, and yet I did, yet I was as the donkey between two bales of hay and could not choose until my stepmother—sensing my indecision—murmured to me that Maude would be the easier.

"Why do you think so?" I asked.

"She is a spinster. Think what she must privately suffer in the caves of torment, thinking of cocks and balls and believing herself to be cast aside by life. I know her type. She will have beautiful plump thighs and a very well-furred nest that oftimes seeps desire within her drawers. See to it that they come off, Clara."

"How?" I began, but she was off again, and wisely so for I would never have moved on my own without this urging and prodding of hers. Thus it came about that I inveigled my way into the good graces of Maude and was soon enough to be found visiting the Vicarage. There I learned the true relationship of the trio, for Maude and her younger brother, Vivian, had been adopted in infancy by the Vicar's parents. The Vicar, being named Edwin, received me with a kindness which attached itself visually, as I noticed, as much to the lower half of my being as to my upper. Even so I passed a first frustrating afternoon for Vivian, being somewhat shy, though in his twenty-fifth year, seemed to me a perfect subject as I thereafter told my stepmother.

"Bide your time. Cultivate them. Things do not happen in a flash unless one has them well immured in one's own household," she told me. "Have patience. Maude is ripe to be mounted and will become, I do not doubt, a secret worshipper at the altar of Priapus. Get well into her good graces, that is the first thing. Affect piety, if you must. Become affectionate and you will learn how to turn her."

The challenge thus being presented to me, I spurned it not, and indeed intended to win my spurs, for if I retreated from the challenge of this trio then I would be hard put to test myself again. To get into another friendly female's bedroom is never difficult and this I first obtained by saying that I much desired to help her brush her hair. The afternoon was sultry and much suited to my intent. Being flattered that I had become so loving of her and evidently an admirer, this Maude let me do. When I unpinned her hair I found it lustrous and full and, she being seated before her mirror, I lifted it and ran my fingers through it with a sigh while meeting the reflection of her eyes.

"Why do you sigh, Clara?" she asked innocently—if, that is, any woman can put a question innocently.

"I want to cuddle you," said I and in so saying let my hands fall beneath her arms so that my fingers came just under the heavy bulging of her tits. Colouring not a little, she could not bring herself to ask what I was at, save to ask awkwardly and with a little laugh,"Do you? How loving you are! Why do you?"

"Because you feel nice," I responded and with much boldness passed my palms full up under her heavy gourds and felt their fleshiness and weight, at which she blushed.

"Clara, you should not," she said thickly, but a measure of excitement already pulsed in me.

"Are you not told that you feel nice?" I whispered and moved my lips about her neck which I had bared by raising up her hair.

"There is no one to tell me," she uttered and then herself gave a deep sigh as I more openly fondled her breasts and felt her nipples stir.

"They are too discreet and shy, are they not?"

"Oh? Who?" was her response, but her face was suffused. She began to breathe heavily as my fingertips kneaded her proud gourds with more and more insistence. I soothed her forehead then as one might a child's and felt it damp with excitement. An intense thrill ran through me, for I knew I had stirred her and that she was loathe to rise. Her stool being of the swivel type, I turned her about so that she came to half face me. Without hesitation I swooped my lips full upon hers and, swiftly gathering up her skirt, felt first her rounded knees and then her thighs, the skin of which was lustrous, silky, smooth.

"I know not who admires you most, Maude—Edwin or Vivian—for their eyes become haunted at the sight of your swaying hips, the bulging of your breasts, your. . . . "

"St . . . st . . . stop it!" she moaned and made to twist her mouth away, but having tasted her saliva and passed a little of my own into her mouth, we were closer than she knew. "How can you speak this way, Clara, it is sinful. Oh! what are you at? Oh goodness, no!"

I had dropped to my knees and, her skirt being already raised, plunged my face between her thighs while all too late she endeavoured to clamp them together.

"Stop! I will not permit it!" she moaned, yet even so I managed to lever her thighs apart and, scenting the muskiness and feminine odours that lay between, moved my mouth up to her crotch where, beneath her drawers, I felt the mounding of her bush. I pressed to it and sought the lips between, pressing the cotton there to feel her moisture. "HAAAAR! Clara! You cannot!" she choked. "Oh! I have never done this before! Please stop!"

One knows it when a woman means such or does not. The slight perspiration twixt her fleshy thighs excited me. A screech from her and I had found the bow-ties of her drawers.

"Oh-ho, Clara, no!"

"How I love you," I murmured from my furry haven there. Already my tongue had moistened the strip of cloth sufficiently to let me feel her lovelips in their splendour. Her hands beat feebly at my shoulders and yet I felt her weaken. Groping blindly up her hips, I loosed her nether garment so that it sagged about her seat.

I remember ever to this day her strange soft cries of hope and yet despair. Smaller than she, yet I managed to draw her up, wherewith her drawers fell to her ankles, cramped her steps, and with a low cry she fell upon the bed. Then like a small tigress I was upon her. Her gurgled sobs, her moans, went all for naught. Little as she would seeming have me do, I bared her to her waist and found her nest with urgent lips and tongue until she wilted, quivered and lay still.

"Maude dear, you have come," I said proudly while she stared at me with hazy and apparently unseeing eyes. Her bush was sprinkled with her own dew and my saliva, the clump of dark hairs glistening and the rolled lips of her slit most moving to see.

"Wh . . . wh . . . what have you d . . . d . . . done to me?" she cried and buried her face in her hands.

"Something pleasant, something sweet," I laughed and forced her mouth to mine and kissed her deep. "Did you not like it? Oh, do not pretend you did not, for we all do."

Her long tongue engaged mine at that. For some reason my words appeared to stir her, perhaps because she had desired for so long for someone to say those very words to her, though I believe she would have denied it.

"But how young you are!" she murmured, startled at her own boldness, yet continuing to allow me to peck upon her lustrous lips. I knew her then for mine and stroked her bush with seeking fingers that found her oiled innerness and perked her lovespot up until it quivered like a little penis. "I have never been sinful," she exclaimed softly in wonderment.

"You silly, why not? And besides, that is only a word. Oh, do keep your legs open for I want to teach you to."

"Why, you naughty thing!" she giggled but being more at ease now and with a little puffiness in her face which showed that she wanted to come again, she permitted me to caress her and stirred her bottom luxuriously as I did so.

"I shall make you naughty," I replied, and before she could reply slipped my tongue within her mouth anew, rolling it all around her own until she trembled and clutched me and spilled her salty juices to my hand. Being well oiled between her thighs by then, I glided my hand under the heavy bulge of her naked bottom and inquired the tip of my forefinger gently around her puckered rosette, making her jump. Indeed, she tried to evade my finger there but I would not have it and, thrusting one leg over hers, kept her pinned, though ever with a saucy smile upon my face which fully disarmed her.

"N . . . n . . . no, not there!" she mumbled, but her mouth was ever now receptive to my own.

"And why not, pray, if it is nice there. I will make you wriggle, Maude, I will!"

"Oh-woh!" she choked, for I had slipped the tip of my finger in and held it so. "That is m . . . m . . . more wicked, Clara," she gasped.

"Is it?" I smiled, for she was all of a wonder that I knew so much and would do so much at my age, yet this very fact intrigued her and perhaps brought her on more quickly than if I had been a full-grown woman. "I do not think you know yet what is nice and what is not," I chided her, though lovingly. Her mouth was open and she breathed gently through her nostrils while my finger eased within her orifice to the first knuckle.

"Oh, Clara, t . . . t . . . take it out!"

"I will not. You have to learn. Has not Edwin at least fondled your bottom ever?"

"My goodness, no! The things you say! Such improprieties can never be."

A sudden urge came over me at such doltishness and I sprang upon her in such wise that before she knew my intent I was perched with my legs on either side of her shoulders facing her, my skirt up and my knickerless state hovering but inches above her eyes.

"Lick me, Maude!" I demanded. Placing my hands beneath her neck I drew her face up until her lips splurged underneath my quim whose moisture of excitement bubbled to her mouth. For a brief moment she spluttered and would have struggled, but I held her firm, for my posture allowed me so to do, and in a trice had my cunny warm upon her mouth. "Your tongue, Maude!" I insisted. She hesitated for an instant, but the effluvia of my pouting sex already enflamed her nostrils and with a muffled sigh she drove her tongue within so that I squirmed and rubbed my honeypot all about until her lips and chin were oiled.

To demand and to receive is ever exciting. I tightened my stockinged knees to her head. She slurped and choked and slurped again, her tongue ever working like a small snake within me so that when I spilled I salted both her nostrils and her mouth, but kept her under for a longer moment in defiance until I felt her more submissive and finally eased myself up from her very slowly as though defying her to move.

She did not, but wiped her mouth and gazed at me, all words lost and thoughts a-tumble.

"Wait!" I commanded sharply and with that stood up

and smoothed down my skirt. I wanted to see if she would wait. It was needful for her to, though she did not then know that. Going to the bathroom—for I had learned my way about the Vicarage—I brought a flannel, dipped it in her jug beside her bed and laved her face, soothing her with words and brushing back her hair. Almost like a doll she lay while then I sat her up, her drawers all pendant at her ankles still.

"N . . . n . . . no one will know, Clara?"

"Know? What is to know?" I turned about and gazed down from the window. We were alone in the house; my purpose was suited admirably. "You are no less than you were, nor I. Indeed we have gained, Maude. What sin or loss is there in that?"

"I do not know. I believe we have been wicked."

So fretting she drew up her drawers, I hearing the sound of her movement but not turning, for it is as well to dismay one's subjects a little in the beginning, and indeed occasionally to do so thereafter.

"You will not tell, Clara?" Her voice was a silly quaver.

"Tell Edwin or Vivian that I have had your drawers down? Do you not think they have removed them themselves with their eyes before this? Have they not seen in their hot minds the cleavage of your cheeks beneath your skirts, the valley deep between your splendid breasts?"

"Ha! No! You must not say that!"

"Indeed, why not, for it is the truth. Would they otherwise be men? A prick well wrapped in linen, hidden up, is still a prick, my dear."

"Oh, the things you say! I had never thought to hear the like of it!"

I turned. My eyes were sultry and yet not forgiving of her words. "I have pleasured you, Maude, and you have pleasured me. If our cunnies were not meant to be tickled, would they have been made so? How your clitty budded when I fingered you! Will you deny the work of

Nature so and its rich promise of eternal bliss?"

"You have me all about with my mind and I know not what to think."

I giggled and deliberately changed the mood. Impulsively I kissed her once again. "It was nice, though," I declared, "and shall be again, for I mean you not to fall again into your old and dried-up ways among the musty books and household chores."

Even so, my apparent confidence was confounded by what I might do next. True, I could have asked my stepmother, but pride held me from doing so and, upon my return home she tactfully asked me nothing, save in mischief to say (and perhaps to test my mood), "Do you want to be put up this evening?"

She adored seeing me being plugged or corked and ever said that I looked prettier than Sarah with my smaller and even tighter bottom rounded up and back well-dipped and jiggling of my tits as the plunger worked me.

"No," I said moodily and retired early, there to think, though it got me nowhere and I felt myself the architect of my own frustrations. I had arranged to see Maude the next day and she had not dissented—indeed was ready for more, I believe, provided she could be "forced" to. By some instinct, however—and such, as I now believe, as fate fashions for us—I went not to the Vicarage straight away but took my own pony and trap to the church. Why I did so I cannot explain save that it was indeed "kismet," or fate, as my stepmother afterwards opined.

Leaving my pony tethered and grazing by a tree, I walked slowly to the doors and looked all about but could neither see nor hear anyone and so thought my aimless journey wasted. Nevertheless, I ventured within, endeavouring not to let the big door latches clang or squeak, and passed down the nave. As I did so a sound came to me and I halted, rather breathless in my daring.

"Ah! Oh, sir!" I heard and the voice was that of a boy and not a girl. "Hoo-hoo! It is too big!" then came to me and with my innocence long lost the full import of those words struck me like a knell.

I tiptoed forward, hearing as I did a certain grunting and then a voice I knew well to be Edwin's.

"Ha! my sweet boy, is it not nice, not juicy, firm? Do you not like it?"

My cheeks reddened. The youth, whoever he was, choked and moaned. I heard the slap of flesh to flesh. Even my neck felt enflamed for there is nothing that I abhor more than congress between males, and this I instinctively knew was afoot. The sounds of lust were all about. Stiffening my resolve, though I wished not to see what I must see, I passed along and opened a side door. There truly did all wickedness meet my eyes. I would fain not describe it save that the untrousered youth was bent over a desk and Edwin's corker well plunged up his nether parts. In my carelessness, however, the iron ring of the handle slipped my grasp and sounded sharp against the door. Edwin's head jerked up. Full-flushed as his visage was, his eyes encountered mine, his cock stopped working. It sufficed. Quick as a flash I closed the door, was gone, and—running madly—sought my own retreat.

That he would not, dare not, follow I felt certain and so, despite my trepidation (which in truth was anger, well disguised), I gained the trap and quick rode off towards the Vicarage and the waiting Maude.

CHAPTER FOURTEEN

I CONTRIVED my expression well upon encountering Maude, affecting sorrow and amazement, but refusing to say anything, despite her questions, until some wine had slaked my thirst.

"What is to do? What is to do, Clara?" was constantly asked. I had slyly, though with apparent agitation, loosed my bodice while I drank, for it is ever a good thing to draw the eyes to that which might the better evoke visions such as words confirm.

"I will not bandy words, Maude. You are become a woman of the world now. You have spoken to me of sin. I will tell you what is sin. Do you know Edwin's habits?"

"No, no, I do not. What do you speak of?" She wrung her hands and stared at me. Even in the moment I thought how fulsome her bottom would be to the birch, upon which my own surname is so well and truly founded, as it were.

"I passed by the church there to pray, Maude, and saw that—within a vestry or whatever it may be called—such as no eyes should ever see. Shall I tell you plain? There is no other way to it. Edwin had his prick full up a boy's bottom—one of the choirboys I imagine," I said almost languidly.

How she gaped! How she protested yet in vain that it could not be true! Yet such was the tenor of my voice, and so well modulated was it between sorrow and anger, that she could not help but bring herself to accept. Springing up, she paced back and forth, oftimes burying her face in her hands and declaring with many sobs that she knew not what to say, for all the world was topsy-turvy now and no greater sin had she ever heard of. Indeed I am quite certain, despite my titillation of her the day before, that she had no concept of a male weapon being inserted in the fundament and even endeavoured to say so, though in a long and rambling way.

"The Ecclesiastical Court will hear of it, I have no wonder," I murmured as though in uttermost despair.

"What? Oh dear heavens, no! We shall all be ruined and turned out! We have no other place to go," wailed she, and thus unknowingly handed me the key to her future pleasures and her fate.

I waited then until she had ceased sobbing.

"At the least there must be punishment, Maude."

"Yes, but not that way, not that way. Oh, he will be unfrocked!"

"I, too, have thought of that, Maude, and would not have it so. Are you not angry—angry—that such a thing should occur and such a waste displayed?"

"A w . . . w . . . waste?" Her jaw gaped. She descended her bottom into her chair again. I pondered the moment, rose and went to her, accommodating myself upon the rolled arm of her seat. I stroked her hair.

"You know of what I speak, Maude—let us have no dissembling. The male should be put only to the female, in whatever wise. I will say of Edwin in his defence but solely this—that his cock has too often been deeply stirred by your voluptuous presence and so in this wicked way he sought to exercise it, or one might almost say exorcise it," I murmured.

"You . . . you . . . you do not know what you are saying," she mumbled, her face all red and fingers tight together.

"I know well of what I speak, Maude. Vivian will come to the same fate if it is not prevented. Even the rustling of your skirts makes their balls swell, as I have observed. You have never thought to look. Even so, Edwin must be punished and the matter covered up," I said crisply, knowing well that she wished to be diverted from what I had said of herself and so she greedily seized the point.

"How, though—how? The youth will speak!"

"I will attend to the youth, Maude. There is but one way to deal with Edwin now, and that in secret that your future may remain secure. He must be humiliated beneath a woman in such wise as will never make him stray again. You alone can effect this and so save your heritage and your home."

"I . . . I . . . I . . . would not know what to do. Edwin has always been master and. . . . "

"Shush!" I interrupted her, "he will be no more so. You shall be the Mistress of your realm. I can but advise you what to do. Should you fail. . . . "

"Oh-woh, Clara!" sobbed she.

"SHOULD you fail then he will be unfrocked," I continued coldly. "Now I will tell you what to do, so listen carefully and interrupt me not or I shall go from hence, will say nothing to the youth, and all will be undone. Well, Maude?"

Her eyes, brimming with tears, came up to mine, but I marked not her sorrow for I knew how rapidly in such matters all moods change. Before the day was out her drawers would be down and she would be panting to the urging of the prick—though this I carefully did not explain to her. Her wonder at my instructions was such that she appeared dumbfounded, yet with the sword of Damocles above her very head she had no way to turn nor any other recourse to seek. Much further weeping and protests came, but I would have none of it, brought her wine and made her drink her fill, one glass, then two, then three that she might be merrier in the matter, as I said.

A trifle blurred by then she was induced to go upstairs while I waited for Edwin's return. He was not too long about it, for which I was thankful. He paled upon seeing me and would have retreated, for I had kept myself quiet in the drawing room. Upon his entry, throwing down gloves and hat carelessly as he did upon a sofa, I sprang up and barred his way back to the door.

"We have much to speak of," I said coldly.

"My God—Maude!" he choked, believing I had told her.

"She is not your god, though she may yet become your goddess," I replied, which of course cast him into full mystery so that he ever looked towards the door.

The Edwins of this world are many. Outwardly rumbustious in their ways, they seek to dominate the female kind and do so in multifarious ways, for they are the purseholders as a rule. Even so, it is a most curious phenomenon which I have now often observed whereby their eyes will glitter with a certain interest when they feel the tables might be reversed. Indeed, such is a moment they appear to hunger for and greet with all amazement and no concealed interest and arousal until they find themselves well put down by which time their fate is sealed.

Thus it was with Edwin, though as for myself I had him at a fair disadvantage. He had nowhere to look and nowhere to hide. I had seen all, even to the protrusion of his stiff penis between the youth's cheeks. The name of the latter I quickly gained, Edwin stutteringly assuring me that he would reveal nothing for the boy had been well rewarded for his "efforts."

This confession truly caused my lip to curl. I will not, however, burden the reader with the details of the conversation that followed. The form of it is something that may be guessed. Given a choice between facing an Ecclesiastical Court and my own judgement, I had him on the carpet in ten minutes, hands to his sides and lying on his back. Having effected this—to his great amazement at whatever was to occur—I fetched a length of rope with which I had armed myself from an old clothes line and, despite his shamed protests, slipped it beneath his back and wound his arms most tightly to his sides. Even the strongest man cannot rise to his feet thus, and so I had him. Passing quietly from the room, I then called Maude down. Ever flushed with the wine she had taken, she descended both nervously and cautiously, but I tugged at her sleeve impatiently, telling her that Edwin had accepted his punishment and that she must therefore give it.

As we then entered the room where he lay bound, his head jerked around and his eyes bulged. I had told him nothing of his stepsister's role in this and his dismay was evident. A croaking sound came from his throat but died as I strode and straddled him, my feet on either side of his hips.

"Get down on him, Maude!" I instructed sharply, adding for good measure, "You know otherwise the penalty!"

Her face was a picture, her legs visibly shaking as she advanced upon him, as I had previously told her to and stood nervously with her feet in line with mine and on either side of his shoulders. Edwin closed his eyes immediately, though he would have had a fine view up her skirts.

"DOWN, Maude!" I barked and at that she wavered, wilted and then drew up her dress so quickly that I scarce had time to see her knees before she plumped her knickered bottom on his face and enveloped him in the tentlike darkness of her skirt.

"GLUMP!" came from Edwin. Maude's colour rose to her eyebrows. As usual she gaped.

"Firm down. Wriggle your bottom on his mouth and nose until the latter is up between your cheeks, Maude!"

She gulped, she would have whimpered had I not stared her out. Flexing her bent knees deeper, she settled herself more fully and thus gave her stepbrother more intimate acquaintance with her knickered parts. A gargling gasp came from him and then a muffled silence.

"He is not to work his tongue up you, Maude," I murmured, the more to make her blush. His arms strove against their bonds, but that availed him naught. Squatting down myself across his thighs, I then held Maude's eyes squarely while I tried the buttons of his trousers. They were not too tight, although already a firm projection rose beneath them. Maude shook her head wildly and would have moved had I not snapped my fingers. Her hand went to her mouth and she stared as then I loosed all, groped within his coverings and drew out his fine tool. In but seconds, 'neath the warmth and weight of her resplendent bottom as his face was, it rose and quivered in the air, knob rubicond and large.

Maude whimpered, though whether from the sight of it or her sensations on his mouth and nose, I know not. Her eyes became anguished, though I knew not then the true cause of this extra agitation. Her teeth chattered and her arms wavered out to me uncertainly.

"It is nice, Maude. You are in full possession of him," I murmured and toyed once with his monstrous weapon, then let it go. It stuck up straight as a ramrod and a full nine inches long.

"I w . . . w . . . w. . . . " she stuttered, her hips working.

I guessed then for the first time at her agitations. The wine had filled her belly and she needed to pee. The anguish in her look grew more, filling me with vast amusement. Should I let her? Stepmama had said nothing of this and yet the punishment would then be dire. Maude squirmed and looked most desperate, which prompted me to rise. Curiously enough I had no interest in Edwin's prick other than it should service her eventually. Before she could move more, for her feet were already shifting, I moved behind her and bore down with both hands on her shoulders.

"Nooo . . . noooo . . . NOOOO!" she whined.

"Yes, Maude, yes!"

"Haaar-aaaah! I c . . . c . . . can't hold it!"

"You have the perfect receptacle beneath," I chuckled the while that Edwin's legs kicked up in vain. Had I but known it, the first trickling of her deliverance had already seeped through her drawers and wettened his face. I heard a choking sound from him, cupped fast her chin and drew her face back under mine.

"NA-HAAAAR!" gasped Maude, but all was now too late. Upside-down kissing is quite pleasant as I had discovered in games with Stepmama. My mouth fastened hungrily on Maude's, her cries gurgled in my mouth, and then with a low gushing sound she pissed full merrily upon her Edwin's face while he, spluttering and jerking, received the golden flood, strained as it was through the cotton of her drawers.

As she did so, I felt Maude's mood change. Her tongue coiled out and answered mine and her bottom writhed. The release for her was delicious, as it ever is, and she could no longer contain her excitement at the brazenness of what she was doing. Gargling the more, Edwin kicked more fiercely but was held. He was all aflood as indeed the surrounding carpet was where it trickled down his chin and from his hair.

"Suck him!" I hissed, quite beside myself with glee.

"WHA . . . AAAAART!"

"Do it, Maude!" I, in the prime position, thrust her forward until her face was well down over his erection, seized her nose and so causing her mouth to open for air, plunged it upon his yearning cock. She snuffled—oh! I held her, though, and mouth filled as she was no protest came. Truly my stepmother would not have approved of it, I felt sure, yet such moments of inspiration come to all. Besides, Edwin was coming already. I knew that from Maude's choking sounds and then the thick dribbling all about her lips. Seizing her hair, I drew her up again while yet he spouted twice and then once more. Frustration thus was served and I forgave myself. Maude panted, hung her head back and sobbed. I helped to raise her, legs tottering and stockings wet.

"Go upstairs, Maude, bathe and change," I instructed crisply.

She was only too glad to escape, hot-rushing from the room and blundering into the side of the door while Edwin sneezed and shook the droplets from his face.

"You will STAY," I told him firmly. He was too far gone in mad desire to speak. I could not leave Maude on her own—to do so would have been unwise—and followed up. In the bathroom she was already removing her dress and wrenching down her soaked drawers.

"I can't believe . . . !" she moaned.

"Let us have no nonsense about it, Maude. Here, place this bowl beneath you so that the water will run into it. Edwin has learned his first lesson, but not his last."

"The shame of it! I do not know what has come upon us—oh woe!"

"How ridiculous you sound! Do you know it? I would help lave you but I will not spoil my dress. All is not saved yet, Maude. I have yet to apprehend the youth and mend his ways. As for your part, you must keep Edwin well to heel."

"I cannot, dare not, and besides Vivian will be home soon."

"Your 'besides' interests me, Maude, for it reveals that you already have a mind to it."

"Clara, you do not comprehend. Once you are gone Edwin will berate me somewhat terrible!"

"Will he indeed! Dry yourself, my dear. Let me powder your bottom. What a magnificent one you have! No—you do not need your clothes, not yet," said I, grabbing up her things and casting them without, at which she waited, extending both hands in foolish pleading, though—as I noticed—she feared to say more then. "Stay, Maude," I commanded, much as one might speak to a pet and with that I bounded out, locked the door to her faint cry and descended to release Edwin.

Trousers down, I led him up, he being then forced to stumbles for the wrapping of his garment around his boots caused him to.

"Speak not or all shall be revealed of your sins," I told him, by which he could take to mean either what had occurred before his arrival or what was happening now. Maude let out a shriek as we entered and endeavoured to cover herself with a towel, but I snatched it from her.

"He will need it to dry himself," said I blandly while Edwin, unable to keep his eyes from her large firm breasts, bared hips and bottom, was pushed roughly to the basin, there to sluice and wash as best he might, though splashing water all over his vestments as he did. I told him roughly to remove all, whereat both were naked as the day and, surveying one another with furtive and shameful eyes as they did, I distinctly saw his prick twitch. Indeed, to my profound irritation he did his best to conceal a nervous grin as, in endeavouring to hide her nubile charms from him by half turning away, Maude displayed to him the ample rondeurs of her well-cleft bottom. Thereupon to her vast relief and much cupping of her hands over her thick pubic bush, I opened the bathroom door and bid her follow me, snapping at Edwin to stay.

"Did you not see the look in his eyes when he perceived you naked?" I asked.

Maude put her hand to her mouth and stared. "He . . . he is hateful, oh hateful, and you made him put it in my mouth," she blurted.

"There is still time enough to have him reported. Both

of you," I said carefully whereat she made to move past me and run into her bedroom, but I seized her arm.

"No, Maude, you will listen to me. Have you forgotten what is at stake? Have you?" I insisted.

"N . . . n . . . no, I haven't! Oh, what to do?"

"You DO as I instruct, Maude, and take him first in hand. Your stepbrother's virility is undoubted. He must be milked twice a day and given solace once a week."

"M . . . m . . . milked? Given solace?" she stammered.

"By drawing the sperm from his stem, my dear, you will profoundly quieten his desires. By offering your own bottom to his cock you will divert him from less manly occupations and pursuits. As perhaps with another youth who will run immediately to the authorities and inform them of his wickedness."

"Oh no, oh no!"

"What other response could you give? You will be the one who benefits from this, Maude, for have I not warned you that Vivian may go the same way? You, temptress, have disturbed them deeply. Nightly they dream of burying their burning, throbbing shafts in your quim or bottom, and thus do you betray them and drive them through the streets of fearful sin by not appeasing them."

"I had never thought of it—never!"

"If you had not, then fate has ruled. Go, Maude, and bring him to me by his cock. I will show you what to do. Hasten now for I have not much patience left."

"Oh-woh!" The same silly cry and she turned back—I hastening into her bedroom where I sat legs open on the side of the bed. At their entry, and each as redfaced as the other, I smiled at her.

"Bring him closer, Maude. Why, the devil of it, you naughty girl, you have his penis stiff again already! An excellent beginning. Fetch a clean towel and lay it across my lap. Hurry now! And you, sir, stand quite still in front of me."

"If we. . . ." he began feebly the moment that Maude had gone.

"No!" I replied sharply before he could finish. "Be still and be silent! You have no other means of comporting yourself now whether in her presence or mine. Your cock quivers lewdly, though it is scarce half an hour since you last spilled. Ah, Maude, how good you are," I greeted her return. "Spread the towel across my thighs so. Good. Now stand behind him—closer—closer still! It matters not that he can feel your nipples at his back or your bush pressed to his buttocks. All the better, in fact, to bring on his excitement, for you are to deal with him thus each morning and each afternoon. Woe betide him should he disobey. Coil your arms around him now, one hand beneath his balls and the other at his cock."

Maude grimaced, quivered and hid her face behind his back as she obeyed. His loins jerked—for which I had to admonish him—and his features twisted.

"Make him come, Maude," I murmured as at my bidding her fingers began to move up and down his thick tool. "His sperm will fall upon the towel and there be safe."

"Oh, Maude, your hand, your lovely hand!" groaned he. I let him have his say, his little say. It bided him no good, for a certain and sudden ferocity was to be observed in the faster movements of her fingers. Perhaps she wished to get it over or perhaps excitement had risen in her, for such a staff so swollen up and stiff is beautiful to feel in one's warm clasp. A gritting sound came from him and he made to feel behind him with his hands to touch her thighs.

"No! No, Edwin, NO!" I barked at him whereat he wavered, ground his teeth anew, his legs trembling. "Your stepsister has your cock in her hand as she frequently will in order to quell your more libertine desires. For this you will afterwards kiss her feet and thank her. Your lips will then travel upwards to her knees and to her inner thigh, but not beyond. You will know her scent but not her compliance, unless she wishes it. Is that not so, Maude?"

"Yes," came her breathless tone from his back where I suspected her of grinding her pubis to his buttocks. She had passed the bounds of modesty and was fair to be fucked or corked and did, I believe, know it. No female can withstand such temptations for long when the male becomes submissive.

"Stop, Maude!"

My cry was sudden and unexpected to myself. It had come upon me that he was too easily come by his pleasures. It was a practice my stepmama also followed. "See how haggard their eyes become when their sperm is not let loose. They are as ravenous dogs and should so be treated," she told me several times when "withholding grace" from Robert, Tim, Papa or Charlie and sending them upstairs with cocks still stiff.

The look she described and which I had often seen was apparent to me in Edwin's eyes. Maude's hand seemed reluctant to cease its massaging, but she did, while he—uttering a moan—beseeched me silently, all in vain.

"It is too soon," I declared simply.

"Ah, what agony you put me through between you! Have I then deserved so much?" groaned Edwin.

"Has not every male?" I responded sharply and to the surprised awe of Maude who I believe was becoming not unaccustomed to her state of nudity in his presence. I spied then upon a chest exactly what I wanted—a pair of long kid gloves and a kerchief. One of the gloves I seized, commanding Maude to hold Edwin tight which she did by winding her arms rather lovingly about him from the rear.

"My God, what are you at?" he gasped.

"A simple sheath to tame your impetuousity," I said

and with that slipped the sleeve of the glove down over his rampant cock which, to my satisfaction, it covered fully. Then, gripping it tightly about his unbending stem, I wound the kerchief fast about and tied it in a knot. How comical and how absurd he looked thus with the fingers of the glove dangling limp! Despite my suppressed hilarity at the spectacle, I saw a purpose in such binding and covering of the erect organ and quickly determined to use it in future.

"Turn him and stand him in the corner, Maude. He will pay a penance thus," said I.

"I beg you no! Let me dress and have an end to it!" came from Edwin, but I would have none of that. He was a strong enough man and did he not have some semblance of a gentleman in him still could have pushed us both aside and made his retreat then, scorning my threats perhaps to expose him.

All was too late for that, however. He had tasted Maude, had seen her, had been fondled by us both. He was as a youth whose Mama and sister play naughtily with him and then spank him and make him hope for more.

"Half an hour and then you will be seen to, Edwin," I said not ungently as he was urged somewhat like a recalcitrant schoolboy indeed into a corner by the wardrobe and there made to face the wall, head bowed and penis bobbing stiffly in its sheath. "Put a robe on, Maude," I then instructed and she, glad to be able to cover herself at last, obeyed.

"Maude!" came Edwin's frantic cry as we went out, but I would not let her turn back.

"I want to dress," moaned she while I bustled her downstairs.

"You have to see to him, do you not?" I replied crisply, whereat she did her best to hide a nervous grin.

"I did not know he was so bad," she murmured foolishly. "Oh, but do not go, Clara, for I will not know what to do."

"You fool! He has you in his very balls by now. When I have departed, there is no need to tell him so. Keep him standing as he is, remove his sheath and with quick fingers bring him off. Let his sperm bubble over your fingers, Maude, and you will hear his groans of satisfaction well enough. Aye, and devotion!"

"You think so? But what of Vivian? He may come upon us at any moment."

"Then you must treat him equally so. Do you wish ever to remain a simpleton and for me to read you all your lessons?"

"V . . . V . . . Vivian is my brother, though!"

"His prick will throb no less stiffly for that, my dear. Set him to housework—make him do your bidding. Have Edwin ever empty his purse before you. Keep them in control. This is the way of modern Woman with her males."

"Do . . . do . . . do you do so, then?"

"It is not for you, Maude, to question my ways. Perhaps it were best that you saw to Edwin now while I am here. I shall not accompany you. Go—do it!"

"But, Clara, will you not. . . ."

"Go, Maude, upon this instant!"

Robe floating all about her she was gone. Positioning myself at the foot of the staircase I listened. In her fervour or her nervousness, she was quick enough about the matter. Edwin's groans and cries came clear to me. In a moment Maude descended again, her expression a daze, her hand exceedingly sticky.

"What a lot he comes!" she murmured as though to herself.

"Are you not Mistress of your domain?" I laughed and, drawing her to me, tied her robe about. Even so a sense of *douleur* seized me. I could no more control affairs in the next twenty-four hours than I could fly to the moon. For all I knew she might confess her own actions as sins to Edwin and be berated by him. In her then tearful state she would be fit prey for his wicked tool and would no doubt have him well sheathed up her that very night while Vivian palely loitered, as it were, and would never be seen to.

To be "seen to," I might say, was a phrase well beloved of my stepmother and later by myself. It was understood that if a girl had been "seen to," she had been put under. Few others understood the phrase in its inner meaning and so it could be used in company.

"You will attend to all that I have told you, Maude," said I now in departing. She would have clung to me if she could.

"I shall do as you say, yes," she said dolefully, for she wanted me much to stay. The moment must be taken on the instant, however, or all is lost. Even as I made my exit, Vivian was to be seen approaching on his horse across the field.

"Oh, I have only my robe on!" she exclaimed so foolishly that I could have whipped her there and then.

"Do you need to have more in order to receive your younger brother?" I asked coldly and then was gone even while her hand reached out to me and one bare thigh showed out between the folds of her peignoir.

"But Clara!" came her cry whereat I retreated swiftly down the drive where she could not follow and waited patiently the reining-in of Vivian's steed, he gazing down at me uncertainly, then doffing his hat before he dismounted. Maude stared at us both like a wraith from a distance, peering foolishly from behind the Vicarage door.

"Your sister waits upon you, Vivian. See to her every need—obey her in all respects," said I to his great and gaping wonder and then mounted my pony. I had no intention of seeking out the youth in the matter. He would be one of several in any event. Taking up the reins, I regarded Maude steadily, daring her to move ere her brother approached. Upon his reaching the threshhold, he stared back at me and then entered while Maude held the door.

I had much to tell my stepmother, but also much to berate myself with.

CHAPTER FIFTEEN

"YOU CANNOT expect complete success upon every occasion, Clara," was the response I received upon telling my tale. So saying she regarded me with a loving smile. "All that you have told me is to your entire credit. You achieved much in a short time. That Maude will waver, I have no doubt, nor that Edwin will put his prong to her and not in a submissive manner that you and I would wish. Even so, you have done her a service. Vivian will share the spoils, no doubt, once she has become accustomed to taking the cock. She may play them off one against the other, though may not come to our ways."

"That is the pity of it," I said, though feeling now that I had criticised myself overmuch.

"Do not fret, my sweet. One needs constant enclosures. We may play pretty games here within and have the males entirely to our whim, yet we are bound to limit ourselves by so doing. Even so . . . " She paused in order to tease me, I knew.

"Go on," I said eagerly.

"This first period, if I may call it such, has been necessary, Clara, in order that I might train you all fully, but greater pleasures may now be in store for us. Under my guidance your Papa has acquired sufficient wealth not to require him to venture out very often. Our investments are secure, as is our future. There will henceforth be new arrangements here. The males are to be re-accommodated in smaller rooms, their furnishings made simpler—even spartan, I would say. Finding themselves resettled thus, they will know their future more firmly even than now. They are sufficiently docile to obey me, as you know. The larger bedrooms will now be put to other uses. Heaven knows that we have enough. I have, though you little know it, been making the most discreet enquiries as to the forms of entertainment most sought by the gentry. True, I have been taking risks in so doing, but it is surprising how one brings people out when they know that they can rely on one's total confidence. The gentlemen are easiest to lure, of course. Why should they venture to Paris for entertainments they can find here?"

My expression showed plainly that I thought such words a betrayal, and she laughed.

"Come, come, Clara, let us have a little subtlety in the matter. I use my bait as well as does a fisherman. Wives know not that I have spoken to husbands, nor vice versa. It is a matter of guile, subterfuge, and the enchantment of promises."

"Oh, you are a witch!" I laughed and hugged her. There was someone, too, I had not forgotten. Her name spilled from my lips.

"Miss Jennifer de Vere Lacey, yes," responded Stepmama. "I, too, have had her very much in mind. Her history is interesting. She is, unfortunately, an orphan and was brought up by wealthy female relatives who had a penchant for nurturing young ladies. It may well be guessed therefore that she may have been imbued with a preference for the Sapphic pleasures of life, but this I have been unable to enquire into as yet. We shall see."

"How?" I enquired eagerly, for some people leave an imprint on one's mind and the young lady in question had unknowingly done so to me. A young female of outward remoteness is ever a challenge and infinitely more so than males of like ilk who turn within themselves, become bachelors and devote their withered lives to collecting butterflies, old coins and the like.

"In an interesting manner, Clara. I have acquaintance with the parents of her husband who revealed to me but recently that they intend to sojourn shortly in Nice where they have a residence. I ventured to declare that I had intended to France myself and, having so beguiled the mother, find myself invited to join them. Jennifer will be there as will her husband. You, my pet, will accompany me to improve your French."

"Do you mean my French kissing or my French tonguing?" I asked impudently, being scarcely unable to contain myself at the news for I was eager to put the house behind me for the while.

"Those, too! It will be a useful period for Sarah, in any event, for she will have to prove herself here. I have told her that I wish to find *alles in ordnung* on our return and the males no less obedient to all female whims than they are now."

"Oh, when are we to leave?" I asked excitedly.

"By steamer from Dover on Friday. We have but four days to prepare and many frills and furbelows to buy, for I am determined we shall not be outdone in fashion by the French ladies. Were I, of course, an ordinary wife who had to seek her husband's permission—and one that I am sure would not be forthcoming—I might also have to beg him for the financial means to travel and sustain myself. What a joy that I do not have to do so!"

"Yes!" I exclaimed and even in such a simple matter of economics saw even deeper the wisdom of her ways. She had reversed what Society is pleased to call the natural order of things, which when considered is a wholly unnatural one wherein males strut the world as lords and masters and ladies can but peep at them with seeming awe from behind their veils or fans. With this event my stepmother also made me aware that in removing people from their normal environment one could the more easily pluck at the strings of their emotions and desires, for in other surroundings the first trappings of convention are easily discarded.

However, I must hasten my narrative forward lest the reader become tired of my philosophising.

The father of the brood, Horace de Vere Lacey, was a man of slightly raffish aspect who had a penchant for fast fillies of both the four-legged and two-legged kind. Having been a little in his cups when in the presence of my stepmother prior to our departure, he had boasted not a little of his prowess both on the field, in the bed, and even upon the dining room table where he hinted that he had put many a housemaid to his prong. That he should so tell a lady of relatively brief acquaintance may appear astonishing, but my stepmama had such a way with her that by bringing a certain expression into her eyes and remarking, however lightly, on the carriage or form of a young woman—whether a servant or not—she could extol many a confession from an unguarded male whom she could make feel quite a devil in her presence.

With ladies she was quite other at first and would act protectively towards them against the males, which they were quick to discern while liking much her total femininity. Thus even Jennifer softened in her presence and would dart her eyes occasionally at her when my stepmother was not looking.

The sea passage was a little rough, and Lady Millicent de Vere Lacey taking it somewhat badly was so well attended to by both of us that she several times clasped our hands as if to aver a lifelong friendship with us, remarking several times how mature and thoughtful I was for my age.

As for Jennifer's husband, Clive, I marked him well. He had avoided military service and worked in the War

Office, or at least did so from time to time in the lax fashion of many a Civil Servant. I discovered him also to be a year younger than Jennifer, which placed him at twenty-three. He was clearly the apple of his mother's eye and Jennifer would frequently wear a distant look when his Mama saw to the tidying of his cravat or straightened down his jacket.

Such details boded well, however, as will be seen. Jennifer looked no less beautiful, patrician and austere than I remembered her. I quite enchanted her by remembering whole verses of my favourite poetry, a form of literature which she inclined to like also. Once settled in the house at Nice a friendly atmosphere was enjoyed and nothing on my stepmama's part was hastened. The bright, clear and sunny atmosphere of the Alpes Maritimes enlivened us all, not least Mr. de Vere Lacey who was as often to be seen sitting adjacent to Jennifer as he was to his wife. Jennifer in turn seemingly took less interest in her husband when he was in the presence of his Mama, and herein lay the clues to our adventure.

One afternoon, our host declared his intention of visiting a perfumery which was in part owned by an acquaintance of his. I normally would have been delighted to see a place where many delicate scents were concocted, but sensed that my stepmother wished it not, and for the best of reasons. During the past day or two she had taken much to talking with Millicent of her son and in a most admiring manner so that the lady was even more pleased with her and preferred her company, as it seemed, to her husband's.

Thus, to cut a long story short, our host was suffered to depart with Jennifer who promised to bring us back such phials and bottles as could be obtained from a factory which would be pleased to advertise its wares. And thus, too, was the scene set for a first, pleasant diversion. With the departure of the two—and I wondering much how Jennifer would comport herself with her roguish father-in-law (though I did not doubt her coolness in his respect)—we sat for a while in the garden imbibing chilled champagne and then retired within to the cool of the drawing room where Clive seemed quietly pleased to find himself in solely feminine company.

My stepmother indeed was quick to remark upon this to his Mama when for a moment he absented himself from the room.

"How quiet and well-mannered he is," she observed as though with pleasure to his Mama. "You must have brought him up well, my dear, and nurtured him with loving care."

Millicent, so quick to be pleased in this respect, replied modestly that she had done her best and much wished him ever at her side.

"Yes, what a shame it is that such presentable young men are torn from one," my stepmother said. "His mode of dress is a model of propriety. I vow that in all truth he prefers your company to any other. How dutifully he stands when you tidy him and pat him all about as though he were a young boy again. It was ever your pleasure to dress him nicely, I am sure. He is not so brashly masculine as some and indeed, if you will forgive me for saying so, I have often thought that young men of smooth skin and pleasing visage were better dressed as we than in stuffy coats and trousers. Why, I remember my own dear Mama who would frequently attire my brother in my drawers and chemises rather than have him cavorting about in sailor suits or velvet jackets and trousers."

Millicent uttered a little laugh and brought her hand to her mouth. "Oh! Was that really so? I have often wondered at such things. Indeed, there was a time when Clive was but fourteen or so that I myself put him for fun into his sister's things. Oh, but I fear dear Clara will be shocked at this!"

"I? Why no," I declared, "for to the contrary I am much taken also by such things. Oh, Stepmama, may I tell her?"

"Of course, my pet, we are in private company, are we not, and no one to disturb us," came the careful reply. I then, leaning forward, made my eyes to shine into those of our hostess, as though complicitous with all her rising thoughts.

"My dear brother, Robert, is of the like," said I, "for several times I have put him into stockings, drawers, chemise, and much he liked it."

"Did you kiss him, then? Was he sweet enough to be kissed in his soft finery?" my stepmother asked archly, giving Millicent quite a joyful look as though my confession laid a seal upon the matter.

I bit my lip, looked coy, glanced down and made so much play of being shy upon the matter as intrigued Millicent.

"We would not blame you, dear, for I am sure he indeed did look sweet," she murmured to a sound of approbation from my stepmother.

"He was most fervent when I did so, though I scolded him for his boldness. Being dressed as a girl, a strangeness came over his character for I had perfumed him and made him sit most obedient while I saw to his good looks, the flouncing of the chemise and the fit of his drawers. When indeed I scolded him, a meekness came over him and he obeyed my every wish so that I truly had him docile as a little kitten," said I, then gazed at both nervously as though I had said too much.

At that moment, as chance would have it, Clive returned from his perambulations upstairs, entered, looked upon us all and hesitated, divining perhaps that we were in more private conversation than had hitherto been the case. Upon that, my stepmother took the initiative.

"Clive, dear, would you wait a moment in your room?" she asked, and so softly did she put the words that he blushed, mumbled something, and withdrew again. Then, turning to Millicent, she went on, "We may now speak in greater confidence, my dears, for such amusements have a great excitement for ladies of our temperaments. Clive's very obedience is a token of what we have been saying, is it not, Millicent?"

The lady sighed, causing her impressive breasts to rise and fall. "My husband ever interfered," she said complainingly.

"Tut-tut, of course they do—if permitted to. I have known such cases and have also known how the intruding spouse might be quietened in the matter."

"Have you?" Millicent leaned forward quite eagerly. I had no doubt that the turn of conversation was exciting her much. My stepmother stretched herself langourously.

"It is something of which we may speak later, Millicent. For the nonce let us attend to the matter of your dear son and what I divine to be his secret, dearest wish. His wife, though senior to Clara in her years, is yet too young of mind to understand such matters, or perhaps is insensitive to them."

Millicent sniffed and I saw clearly a deep jealousy there. "Yes, I believe so," she replied stiffly, my stepmother then gazing upon her with an air of great sympathy and understanding.

"Will you permit me, Millicent, the greatest of favours? I intend to take myself upstairs for a while. A few words with your son, perhaps. You will excuse me?"

Not waiting for reply, she was gone and so smoothly that the room seemed emptied of her in a second while I observed the conflicting emotions that passed across the face of Clive's Mama. "What . . . what do you think she is at?" she asked me in a low tone of great secrecy so that I was hard put to avoid smiling.

"Perhaps it is as with my brother Robert. He was . . . he was very naughty sometimes when clothed as I wished him, yet—oh, I must tell you the truth!—tears of delight came into his eyes when first I soothed my stockings up his thighs, drew up his knickers and smoothed down his chemise. Was it not the same with you and Clive?" I asked with careful shades of shyness in my voice. "Oh, please, will you not tell me for I felt quite naughty myself and yet so much excited that I put convention to the winds."

A flush rose in Millicent's cheeks. My youth perhaps inhibited her. "There are moments that others would consider unseemly, I suppose," she ventured. "Dear Clive, he so liked the feel of silk all about him. You put . . . you put your brother's knickers on yourself, my dear?"

I evidently was the one to make confessions, for then she could hide behind my words in a manner of speaking and play upon those as would further her own excitement while, as it were, keeping her own hands clean in the matter.

"I undressed him as one might a little boy, though in truth he was seventeen. How immodest you will think me, yet I much enjoyed it, for all his parts were vibrant at my touch and so remained when I drew his knickers up."

"My dear, how truly naughty of you and yet. . . . "

She was given no time to finish the sentence for the door then opened to admit my stepmother. "All is well, Millicent. Will you come up, and you, too, Clara?"

A flush then rose deeper on the face of Clive's Mama. Her hand went to her throat. She rose, toying with her pearls. Hesitance lay full upon her and yet her eyes were truly lustrous with an inner glow. "All is well—as you would wish it, Millicent, and I—come," my stepmother said and extended comfortingly her hand. Nothing then was said as we entered the hallway and ascended the stairs, though rarely was such an air of conspiracy upon three females. The door to the bedroom inhabited by Stepmama stood half open. Without hesitation she entered and drew us in. There in a further corner stood

Clive, his back to us. Shy as a girl, he was attired in one of my stepmother's frilly petticoats and indeed nothing else save, visibly, for stockings. At our entrance his shoulders quivered, his head not turning. The look on his Mama's face was a perfect picture. Her breathing sounded heavily.

"Will you not be seated, both of you?" we were asked and two armchairs indicated by the fireplace. A solemn silence then obtained, Millicent having a better view of her son since my back was partly to him.

"It would be foolish, I felt, to delay a matter of great desire to us all, Millicent. Clive, you may turn and face the room."

A shuffling then occurred and he did so, his feet uncomfortably squeezed into a pair of my stepmother's shoes. His lips were rouged, his eyelids shadowed. A look of perfect wonderment was on his face. Upon being almost face to face with his Mama, he blushed and hung his head.

"So timid, is he not—but that should be the way of it," my stepmother purred. "Raise your petticoat, Clive, and let us see your drawers. Ah! do they not look well on him, despite his protrusion," she smiled, for the outline of his erection was clearly visible beneath the pink silk of the knickers which he displayed by holding out the sides of the petticoat in fanlike fashion, well drawn up. "Of course, he was in two minds about it, Millicent, but your own future coaxings and demands upon him will further the matter. Jennifer will not have brought him up so well, I am sure, despite her probable endeavours. Will you show him your drawers, Millicent, or I? I would have matched the colour of his to yours had I but known it."

Millicent's face was suffused. Her hands clutched at the arms of her chairs, yet nothing in her aspect denied the rising pleasure in her frame. Seeing her apparently bereft of words, my stepmother laughed not ungently and said, "Very well, then, I shall show him mine. Step forward, Clive, a little closer to me."

He swallowed, he gulped, he did so, still holding up the petticoat since he had not been told to lower it, and this aspect of his immediate obedience pleased me much. Millicent in earlier years had perhaps advanced him more than she thought or had cared to confess. A few steps brought him between our chairs and the end of the bed where my stepmother stood. Bending and gathering up the hem of her gown, she then raised it slowly—not to the total disinterest of Millicent's sly eyes. Her rounded knees being revealed in fetching, patterned stockings of a dark shade of blue, there came then in our view her swelling thighs, her broad and pretty garters, pale rims of thighs and then above the puckered legs of her directoires which were baby-blue in hue. Being well mounded to her bottom, they displayed her rear cheeks perfectly.

An awed silence fell upon the bedroom. My stepmama crooked her finger beguilingly at Clive and beckoned. He hesitated for but a second or two then shuffled forward again, his eyes on her eyes, for they so commanded him. A trembling hiss came from his mother's nostrils. She appeared to have some difficulty in breathing and sat bolt upright in her easy chair. Toes to toes he then stood with my stepmother whose bosom rose and fell in her excitement, she wreathing up her gown about her waist.

What a strange sight it was and yet how enervating! I wriggled with pleasure and gazed in awe.

"A certain lewdness, Millicent, excites them," murmured my stepmother without taking her eyes from his. "It is requisite in all training. Lower your drawers, Clive—exhibit yourself!"

Millicent's hand went to her mouth. Her eyes came out on stalks. Clive's hands trembled visibly and sought for the waistband of his drawers, his face now flushed. My stepmother stood unmoving though with the slightest of taunting smiles about her lovely lips as inch by inch was now displayed the rubicond head of his stiff penis, followed by its straining length and then at last his dangling balls. A quivering sigh escaped him and he let the drawers glide down to nestle at his ankles.

"Clive—bring it to me," my stepmother intoned in her lowest voice which yet caused the very air to tremble with expectancy. The demand in her tone was undeniable. He had but a a few inches to move before her breasts moulded to his chest. His knees bent awkwardly as if he sought to position himself, his face just slightly averted from her own. Then, with a little gritting cry from him that sounded as might a voice heard far across some fields, he touched his knob up underneath her crotch so that the rounded plum of it quivered just against the silk of her drawers. His jaws clenched. How dearly he yearned to ram it up to her and feel the lips, the pad of deep curls there, yet knew he was forbidden so to do!

"Good Clive," my stepmother murmured. "Stay still now as you are, however much your knees may tremble." The glow on her face was lovely to see. Clearly she could just feel the quivering of his crest up to her crotch, yet no more than that. A quarter of an inch—no more—extended its fine gap between the privates of the pair. A whimper came from Clive but was ignored, my stepmother's head turning gracefully sideways to Millicent.

"You trained him well, my dear. It needed but a small touch or two from me. See how his jaws clench and his teeth grit. The mature female is offered and yet forbidden. Would you have me milk him for his efforts?"

Perhaps Millicent did not know the term, though guessed it. Her eyes answered for her and my stepmother nodded. "Rise then, at the least dear," she said to Millicent and stepped back to a great quivering from Clive's hard stem. "Remove your drawers and hold them out beneath you," she snapped to him while I assisted Millicent in getting up, though in that moment she scarcely seemed to know where she was. My stepmother, however, extended her hand to her and drew her close, then kissed her cheek. "It is you who must handle him, my dear—see how patiently he waits. Has he not been good? Would you have him dressed again as a male and returned to his fond wife?"

"I will see to him!"

Millicent's voice cracked out suddenly and as though protectively. Clive hung his head again, the drawers now looped in his hands and held in front of him beneath his stemming cock which, being of full girth, was pleasant enough to see.

"Do it then in full sight of us, Millicent, for you will never otherwise behave as he would have you do."

"I know. Ah, the dear boy, look how he stands—so patiently as years before he did," Millicent declared, now having become thoroughly bold and evidently itching to take hold of his tool.

It is a matter of taste or habit as to how the female performs this solicitous act which also is one that underlines the male's submissiveness. Millicent chose to do so by standing immediately behind him and thus bringing his bared buttocks to press into her belly. My stepmother then smiled and nudged me, our senses all aflare, as with one determined hand Millicent worked her left arm down between them and, gliding her hand beneath his bottom, cupped him firmly with her fingertips under his dangling balls. Then, with her right hand, she took purchase on his upright prick which caused him much to moan and quiver while the drawers that he held formed a sort of basin shape beneath him. His breathing came deeply then as did her own as she commenced to frig him, her beringed fingers forming a loose ring of undoubtedly divine pleasure around his fervent cock.

A look of determination now was on her face, as I saw. The fingers of her left hand beneath him tightened, causing him to jerk. His head hung down, as though a naughty boy's. His calves trembled mightily and he made to move his prick within her clasp but at a sharp "No!" from her he desisted. Clearly, Milicent was a little more advanced than we had thought. Her attractive, rounded face was set. Determination in her was uppermost. I wondered indeed how Clive had ever escaped her clutches, for his enjoyment was evidently intense. His eyes rolled and the most fervent cries escaped him, though muffled as they should have been.

"Hold the cloth properly!" she scolded him, referring to the drawers, though I sensed then that in the past a towel or some such must have been used.

"MA-MA!" he groaned.

"Are you coming?" she demanded.

"In a . . . in a . . . in a minute . . . OOH! AAAARGH! OOOH!"

"Come on, come on, you bad boy. You know I do not give you too long about it."

"MA-MA! HAAAAR! OOOH!" He trembled mightily, his prick strained up, the crest gleaming and swelling more than ever. Her motions quickened, her fingers passing full up and down the entire length of his rampant weapon. His mouth opened and his eyes were glazed. Then with a shuddering sigh he released the first jet of his sperm. High it soared and then fell in an arc to splash upon the waiting drawers. Another came, another. His thighs wobbled but she held him still.

"Come, darling, come—oh, you naughty thing," she breathed, her face pink with excitement while we stood still and took our quiet observance. Another pellet of white bubbling sperm followed and then another. Then came the trickles and the final pearls. His shuddering sighs were music to our ears. A thick pool of pearly come lay in the drooping knickers and her task was done.

"There!" she breathed victoriously and her voice all a-tremble while Clive suddenly wrapped the soaked garment round his cock and jerked. His final tribute then spat out and so weak did he seem that he almost fell. "Go to your room, Clive!" was heard then from his Mama and without looking back took his laggard footsteps hence and closed the door. My stepmother clapped, a look of shining pleasure on her face. Before Millicent knew what she was at she was thrust upon her back down on the bed and my stepmama upon her.

"Have you not had it in you?" Millicent was asked.

"No!" The face was a woman's but the voice a little girl's. I could not restrain myself but fell beside them and raised her skirt. Her stockings gleamed. My stepmother half rolled from her, held her down and meshed her lips to hers.

"You will, though."

"I will not! Oh no! AH!"

Her cry came as my lips came to her dell, pushing aside the loose crotch of her drawers as I did so. Her quim was rich and moist, salty and musky to my seeking tongue.

"We shall make you, Millicent!"

"You will not! Oh, never! OH!"

The sound of passionate kissing came from above. I felt blindly up my stepmother's legs while tonguing Millicent. It took her not long to come in her excitement. Thrice she coated my tongue and lips with her delirious spendings and then lay limp, her praises softly uttered by my stepmama.

CHAPTER SIXTEEN

"THEY WILL be back soon, will they not?"

Having retired back to the drawing room and there taking wine and biscuits, Millicent put on an air of agitation that however was purely in respect of her husband and daughter-in-law. Immured still in his room and unregarded, Clive brooded on the mystery of it all. As Millicent had confesed, she had not so handled him since his marriage two years before, though had longed to do so. Jennifer was cold to him, she averred, and had no understanding of such things.

"I think her not a dullard, though, Millicent. We must take care in making our judgements. In presenting yourself to her as you have—and she mindful ever of your husband's wicked ways—she has taken an impression other than the truth of how things stand."

Millicent coloured up and would have denied the matter, but fighting inwardly with herself under my stepmother's mild but enquiring gaze, she finally confessed that such might be true.

"She would not know how to handle him even so," she remarked with evident jealousy in her voice.

"Has she need to do so save as pupil to yourself?"

replied my stepmother craftily. "Oh yes, I know, my dear, there is the little matter of your husband. We are aware of his intrusiveness. I think him ruttish, too, if you will forgive the term."

"He is," declared Millicent flatly, "but . . . but what did you mean by pupil?"

"I mean that there are arrangements to such matters. I suspect him of wishing to mount your daughter-in-law. He has perhaps fondled her already to her dismay—perhaps even her aggravation. Therein lie embers to be kindled, Millicent."

"Oh! You would have him possess her?" She all but sprang up and I saw jealousy once more in her expression.

"You would have him interfere and your precious prize lost again? How shall you keep Clive in training once he has returned to the marital fold?" Thus my stepmother challenged back and Millicent put to silence for a moment.

"I had not thought of it thus," she mumbled.

"Then you must. Let there be no hesitations on the matter. Leave things in my hands, my dear, and all shall be well. You will have not one male servitor, but two. Yes, your husband as well! Do not tell me that he cannot be quelled—put down. I know better. Do I not, Clara?"

"Oh yes, Stepmama," I was glad to intercede. "Papa is most docile now, as is my brother," said I coyly to Millicent whose eyes were as saucers upon hearing that. Her fingers worked together with a nervous excitement. She sought to know more, but my stepmother was adamant that practice preceded idle chatter, as she put it, and that to begin with Jennifer was to be left to our hands.

"She will not mind, I am sure, spending an evening alone with Clara and I," she declared. Thus—though futher talk followed which spun around the subject rather than entering into it—all was settled, at which Millicent took herself upstairs to attend, as she said, to Clive. She was not long about it and in no time at all brought him down, once more in his own attire. She would have been loving with him, had him sit beside her and hold his hand, but this was not my stepmother's way. In minutes he was set to cleaning our shoes, but his activities no longer interested me for the nonce. It was Jennifer I was looking forward to. She made no difficulties, nor asked any questions, about being left alone with us that evening while the more closely related trio went to dinner.

"What a strange boy he is—how he adores his mother," my stepmother remarked to her when they had gone.

"He is not a boy but a man," Jennifer answered, yet her eyes looked troubled.

"A boy at heart, my dear, as we within ourselves are still girls. At school, I do recall, there was as much kissing between girls as between boys and girls. I have ever thought it nice so to be. Have not you?"

A pretty colour came into Jennifer's face. She made seemingly to reply while I tumbled down as though casually beside her on a chaise-lounge.

"I do not know," she said thickly.

"Oh, but I think it's nice," said I quite bubblingly whereat my stepmother laughed and said, "That is because you want to kiss her, you little minx."

Jennifer said "Oh!" in surprise and turned to face me. Her lustrous full lips, short aquiline nose, large eyes and flawless skin all attracted me. "What?" she responded in soft surprise while I flung my arms about her neck in girlish and impetuous fashion so that before she knew it our mouths met and merged in the most intoxicating fashion. I felt her shift uneasily despite that. She would have stirred, perhaps sought to break the embrace had my stepmother not then sat down on the other side of her, pushing her shoulders back against the wall and saying in a merry tone, "How sweet to see you both kissing!"

At that I think Jennifer grew embarrassed at such open display and raised her hands, though weakly, to fend me off. My tongue, entering her mouth, had found her own and was there wantonly indulging itself. A gurgle escaped her and the pressure of her hands weakened, my stepmother settling matters by drawing her sideways and shifting her own body so that the bemused but already partly excited young woman found herself lying prone. Perched on the edge of the long, brocaded seat at her side, my stepmother pressed upon her shoulders with a deliberation that she must have felt for she strove to rise but was impeded.

I, kneeling over her then, gazed down at her flushed face lovingly. "Jennifer, let me tongue you," I murmured, to which she replied a startled, "WHA-AAART?" and cried, "Oh, let me up!"

"She wishes to tongue you," my stepmother said as though explaining something to a child. "Let her."

"Oh! B . . . b . . . b . . . !" Jennifer stammered madly, but already her dress was being raised. Beneath as I had suspected were two of the most elegant legs I had ever seen, swelling up from well-turned calves and dimpled knees to lustrous thighs that gleamed above her stocking tops. Rosetted garters clasped the sheened silk tight. A cry escaped her and she wriggled but was held.

"Clara will tongue you—be still!" she was commanded and with that my stepmother scooped one arm beneath her knees and drew them up so high that they all but touched her tummy. At the same time she held her chin in quite a forceful manner with her other hand—a trick I was to learn, for it holds the "victim" helpless, though I did not wish her so, nor my stepmother.

The posture, with her legs drawn high, exposed her completely and in a trice while she squealed and tried to bump her bottom all about, her drawers were loosed and with some quick fumblings on our part, pulled down. Ah, what a treasure came then to my eyes! Her bush was neither sparse nor thick but perfect in its texture, forming a delightful triangle upon her Venus mount. Between the curls and tendrils of stray hair her cunny peeped, its lips quite small—delicious to the tongue.

"WHOO-WHOOOO!" the first cry, as though of amazed pleasure, rang from her as I protruded my tongue and roamed it all about the succulent dell. Her legs kicked, drummed on my back and then were still. I flickered in my tongue and licked, my nostrils tickled by her downy curls. She moaned, hips twisting, then I sought her spot—the little rosebud of desire. How quickly it perked up! A trilling sound escaped her throat. Her muskiness and feminine odours flooded my face with the warmth of love.

"THEEE-OOOH! No! NAH! Not there!"

My fingertip had sought and touched her rosette which she evidently would defend. I roamed the tip around the puckered rip and dipped it in while twirling then my tongue. Another cry escaped her and her hips churned.

"DOH-DOH-DOH-DON'T!" she moaned, but all was too late. Holding her chin still and taking her slumbrous mouth, my stepmother began kissing her despite her seeming sobs of wilfulness. Her tongue sought to retreat, as I afterwards learned, but the passion of the moment was already overcoming her. Feeling the gentle lowering of her legs, I let them rest upon my shoulders and bore their weight gladly in my ministrations to her pleasure. I had worked the first joint of my finger by now into her bottom hole, making her squirm fretfully, yet her emotions betrayed her for no sooner was she thus plugged and my finger and tongue working in unison than she sprayed my mouth and chin with salty bliss.

To my great pleasure her tight warm bottom then began to work up and down as though urging me on. I circled my tongue around her risen bud and heard her throbbing moans as I did the succulent sounds of their tongues and lips. Again her belly shimmered and again she came. Twice more did her tribute inundate my lapping tongue and then with face besmirched by her sweet outpourings I let her legs glide down and rest upon the seat, there lying splayed.

"How she came!" I murmured—my stepmother straightening then while Jennifer lay inert, only the faint quivers in her pale belly betraying the echoes of her pleasure.

"How wondrously she must take the manly shaft," came the reply, whereat she stroked the young woman's face and moved damp tendrils of hair from her smooth forehead. "What a pity her husband is such a weakling, yet he can be further trained, I suppose."

At this, Jennifer sat up with a sigh and put her back to the wall. "What do you mean?" she murmured, yet almost as though to herself.

"His Mama nurtures him—did you not know?" my stepmother asked inconsequentially.

"N . . . n . . . nurtures? What?" Her half-closed eyes opened. "I do not know what you mean! What do you mean?"

"His cock was well brought up this afternoon while you were out, my pet. Was it not, Clara—and dare his dear Mama deny it now?"

"By you? OH! Pray give me my drawers." Her hand waved weakly and then fell.

"We were not the final instruments of his pleasure, Jennifer, nor would lie to you upon the matter. His Mama milked him of his sperm while he, poor weakling, suffered her frigging, his eyes all wild and lured by dreams of lust. Are not men ever so?"

"I do not believe you! Oh, it could not be so!"

"I believe you know it is so, though have not utterly confessed it to yourself nor made images in your mind of the matter. How often does he thread you in bed? Once weekly? Once a month? Is he shy? Is your hand needed to stir him to erection?"

"He is shy. Oh, why do you ask? What conversation you have got me into! Please may I not put on my drawers?"

"You are too proud to say how well you have been pleasured. That is the truth of it. As to putting on your drawers, you will need them less about your bottom than you have been used to. Opportunities have passed you by, but shall not in future. I ask you once again—how often does he take you?"

"You seem to have the knowing of it already," Jennifer replied sulkily and then burst out, "Oh, why should his Mama do such a wicked thing? Is is true, Clara? Tell me it is not?"

"My foolish, beautiful one, it is. Nor was it horrid to see as you might think. Made to stand—and in such pretty finery as she has put him in before—he held his legs apart. They were not face to face and neither did she raise her dress or show her bosom even to his gaze. Is that not so, Mama?"

"It is, my pet. The young man has his whims and she has hers. Until your marriage, my dear, she spermed him regularly and thus kept him tamed, quiescent, as all males should be. As to your father-in-law, Jennifer, that is another kettle of fish. Have his hands not sought around the proud bulb of your bottom—touched your tits?"

"How do you . . . ? Oh! I am shamed!"

"Do you not like it?" I moved to sit beside her, touched her arm, and wore an air of great naïveté.

"It is h . . . h . . . hateful! Yes, he does. Would feel right in my drawers were I to let him."

"Jennifer, we must speak more plainly. Truthfulness becomes us on both sides, for matters now will change." Thus saying, my stepmother sat before her on the floor. Jennifer's legs being still bared, she pressed her lips to her thigh most tenderly and made her start. Seeing her lips linger and her tongue extending around the rich rim of flesh above her stocking top, I drew Jennifer's lips around to mine and felt to my surprise a softness greater than before.

"You think of his cock, though," I murmured to her lips.

"I doh-on't!" she trembled, making her mouth quiver deliciously to mine, but her voice betrayed her. The tips of our tongues touched, making me quite spoony with her.

"You do not get enough of your husband's, hence you think of others. What is there in that?" came my stepmother's voice while of deliberation she held the young woman's thighs apart, admiring them as much as I, as Jennifer could see. Perhaps indeed that tiny point weakened her.

"I do . . . I do think of his cock, but I do not like him. Oh!" she exclaimed at her own temerity and covered up her face. I drew her hands away and rubbed her nose to mine playfully which I believe softened her the more.

"You do not betray yourself by so speaking, my sweet," purred my stepmother, caressing Jennifer's thighs as she spoke. 'We are your accomplices and not your enemies. Dear Millicent's actions are in trust to us, as yours shall be."

"Mine? Oh, but I could never . . . !"

"Shush, child, for you are almost one at heart and yet withal a proud young woman. You will not be brought to him, but he to you, as Clive was brought to his Mama."

"I do not wish to think of that! How could it be?"

"You will think of it, Jennifer. What help have you now save to do so? There is nothing so lewd in such motions as you believe. The male is brought to the female for her satisfaction. Once given, then he is removed, or put to further service as you wish. Your pleasures have been limited until now, though need not be."

Jennifer twisted her fingers, turned her rings around

and knew not where to look. A silence obtained. We waited for her to speak.

"If, if . . . if I gave in to him once—oh! I know how it would be!"

"Foolish girl, have you not imbibed each word I spoke? His prick is all you seek, and briefly perhaps, for there will be others when you find your way and learn to conquer and not to submit."

Jennifer gazed at her nervously, though there was also a tinge of curiousity in her look. "You will not always be here," she mumbled.

"Nor shall I have need to be, for once quelled and mastered he will remain so. How proud and cold you can look when you wish it! Why, you are halfway there to your own salvation."

"It is true, Jennifer." I soothed her arm. She could not mistake the meaning in my eyes. I tugged at her sleeve. A thought had struck me, and proud I was that it had perhaps escaped my stepmother. "Come—come to the room you have with Clive," said I. She hesitated for a long moment and then uncoiled her legs. Her drawers lay on the floor and she would have picked them up had I not drawn her with me.

"What is to do?" she asked.

"You will see," I replied. Her uncertainty as to our truthfulness was melting rapidly. I uttered, however, a little prayer as we ascended with my stepmama in train for I relied on old habits. Not mine, but those of Millicent. Fate proved me right. Reaching my hand beneath the pillows in the bedroom where Clive had been sent to wait, I drew out triumphantly the underclothes he had worn.

"They are not mine!" declared Jennifer and sought her nightdress quickly as if to assure herself against some trick.

"No, my dear, they are Clive's now—his uniform of

petulance, submission and sin. Show her the drawers, Clara!"

I had forgotten that small touch and opened them. The stains of sperm lay dry for her to see. Her eyes opened and her hand went to her mouth. "Oh then, it is true!" she gasped.

"What else but truth have we purveyed to you?" my stepmother responded. "Yet do not think of revenge in sheathing his father's prick in your cunny. There is no revenge. It shall be on his part an act of equal submission to the power of Woman."

"Oh no! I cannot, I cannot!"

My stepmother sighed and made her sit upon the bed. For a full moment she gazed at her soulfully and then turned to me. Her lips formed words that I well could read: "Fetch the cane!"

CHAPTER SEVENTEEN

MOST WICKEDLY, no doubt, the thought of caning the adorable Jennifer thrilled me to the core. I, who have trained many a young lady since, knew this to be a prime occasion. A cane lay in my stepmother's luggage. She was ever ready for all occasions. Taking it out, I fondled it lovingly and envisaged the proud bottom that was soon to receive it.

Pray do not think, however, that there was viciousness in my thoughts. I have never wielded the cane cruelly nor would ever do so. It urges, it impels, it conquers the proudest. When I re-entered the bedroom my stepmother had already rolled Jennifer over in the guise of "tidying" her underskirt beneath. Thus she was bared and, being in that frame of mind that young women are when they know not which road to take, permitted the fondest of kisses to fall on her sumptuous orb, deep cleft as it was and smooth as ivory.

She made to stir as I entered and would have glimpsed the cane before it seared her had not my stepmother deftly clambered on her back and held her down. A shriek rose: "What are you doing?"

"Oh, Jennifer how lovely you look," I murmured, not

sarcastically but with all sincerity, for such girls do when well put up to it. Her garters had been adjusted, her stockings made taut. The moist fur of her cleft showed well beneath her globe. I raised the cane and knew she sensed a danger.

"No! What are you at?" she cried and tried to heave.

SWEEE-ISSSH! The cane seared across her peach and brought a shrill cry from her of the uttermost dismay, leaving a thin pink line in its fiery wake.

"You will LEARN, Jennifer," my stepmother murmured and with her knees full clamped against the young woman's sides, held her firmly down. HOOOO-ITTTT! Ah, what a song the cane makes in the air! The tip was thin and caught her in its passing, bringing from her throat a horrified screech.

"STO-HO-OPPP IT!" she cried and then "Oh NO!" as again I swished it in. Her hips jerked violently, her bottom screwing all about and showing flares of red upon the creamy skin.

"You will take his prick tonight, my love, you will learn. Whose cock shall she then take, Clara?"

"Her Papa's. I mean, her Papa-in-law's," I corrected myself quickly and awkwardly and covered up my foolishness in giving her another which brought a high-pitched scream from her.

"More slowly, Clara," my stepmother admonished me, and I knew my impetuousness. There is a rhythm to the matter, as I have long since learned. Each stroke must be measured and absorbed.

"Why are you do——doing this? I can't bear it! OH!"

"You will learn to obey your superiors in wisdom just as the males will learn to obey us all. Shall you take his cock tonight?"

"NO! YEEEEE-EEEECH-OW!"

I had accorded her another, sweeping it now up beneath her bulge and bringing her to strain her lovely legs. In utter anguish she shook her hips, my stepmother bouncing gently on her shoulders as she faced me. Upon Jennifer's superb bottom was now a pink criss-cross of stripes.

"You will take his cock tonight, Jennifer." My stepmother's tone was implacable.

"I won't, I won't, I can't I—NEEEE-YNNNNG! Ah, stop it, do! MAMA!"

Thus do they all cry out, but it avails them nothing. I have known Mamas to listen and smile, knowing their pets to be receiving only what they themselves once needed to endure before the fleshy peg rammed in between their cheeks and brought them to a bubbling bliss.

"DOO-WAH! DOO-WAH! DOOO-WAH!" I heard Jennifer sobbing incoherently, her bottom now aflame.

One must be merciless. One judges well. Her cheeks perhaps had not yet been cleaved, but soon must be. Her cunny had not bubbled often enough on a prick. The waste of it was sad. She would make a superb mount as Clarissa had done, though I knew little enough of her developments save what my stepmother had told me and that she ruled the household now.

I raised the cane again, though loathe to stripe her hard. My stepmother motioned me. I let it sink.

"Give her a moment," she murmured, "for I wish her every act to be voluntary. Do you hear me, Jennifer?"

Naught but heartbroken sobs answered her. Then came a noise that stilled me as a statue. The three had returned all too early and we were uncovered! Jennifer did not hear, so completely absorbed was she in the raging heat of her bottom and the long hot tongues of fire that licked all through her.

"Go! Go fetch them!" my stepmother hissed to my astonishment while I had expected panic to ensue. She, quicker than I, saw advantage to the matter. I ran to the door and encountered Millicent, Horace and Clive in the drawing room.

"Quickly!" I cried.

"What is to do?" exclaimed Millicent in alarm, but I

wishing not to attempt explanations then turned about again and proceeded back upstairs with they scurrying in my train and expecting perhaps some fearful accident.

For Jennifer it was indeed an accident, though decidedly an ill wind that was to blow her good. I entering the bedroom anew and all seeing the pair upon the bed—Jennifer with her striped and wriggling bottom and my stepmother sitting astride her—stopped still in great amazement. Hearing their arrival, though unable to see them, Jennifer shrieked and sobbed at the same time.

Millicent and her son filled the doorway. Horace was a step ahead of them into the room and so enjoyed a prime view. My stepmother did not hesitate and neither, thankfully, upon her words did I. Jennifer's cleft orb, so adorably pink and pale and red and cream all at the same time, was lifted sufficiently to offer her pouting quim as well to his astonished eyes.

"Come—quickly—service her, you fool!" was said to him by my stepmama. Her eyes seemed to sparkle with fire, conveying their messages of demand to me. No sound came from Millicent or Clive who were clearly too petrified with surprise to speak.

"NO-WOOOOH!" Jennifer moaned, bucked violently, but was held down by her rider whose upraised skirt revealed her own lush thighs and stocking tops.

"You must! Come!" said I to Mr de Vere Lacey and upon that, and with a daring I scarce thought I possessed in another household, placed my hand upon the front of his trousers, felt there an unrising and nipped my fingers onto his swelling stem.

"Oh!" Millicent moaned, and then to him, "Do not look!" So saying, and being stood beside him, she covered his eyes with one gloved hand, the token of her words being to give permission to her husband to do what we intended. The unexpected clasp of my fingers in his most intimate region in any event stirred him almost as much as the wanton sight of his daughter-in-law. Meekly, as it seemed, he permitted himself to be drawn towards her, I then more boldly fumbling with his buttons.

"Ah, the poor girl, how she needs it!" declared my stepmother whose own enticing presentation of part of her nether charms added to the voluptuousness of the scene. She was forced meanwhile to clamp her knees more tightly to Jennifer's sides and indeed while I was bringing Mr de Vere Lacey's long, thick weapon into view was forced to smack her bottom hard, producing sobs and cries that resounded everywhere and brought small answering noises as if of both sympathy and excitement from her mother-in-law.

Our male—for such I thought of him then with my fingers encircling his stout tool—breathed heavily as well he might, my stepmother modulating her expression beautifully so that it came somewhere between command and invitation.

"Ah, my heavens!" groaned he.

"Do it!" I demanded and drew his cock closer to Jennifer's rosy orb, pressing the springy monstrosity down a little so that its rubicond helmet then encountered the pleading of her lovelips.

"NEE-OOOOH!" squealed she at that first tentative touch of it.

"IN! In her!" my stepmother said, her nostrils flaring. I sought his heavy buttocks with my free hand, felt beneath and pressed his balls with my fingertips. He jerked and sank his knob within his daughter-in-law's offered maw.

"HO-HO-HO!" came simultaneously then from the young woman and her mother-in-law. Indeed their rising tones quavered and warbled together like those of wild doves. Horace's eyes were glazed, his mouth open. The oily lips of Jennifer's quim appeared to sink back on to his stave, absorbing all but half of it, though in reality he was pushing and I was assisting.

"AH-HOOOO! NO-WOH!" gabbled she, "he mustn't, he MUSTN'T! WHOOOO!"

"Ah, my delicious one!" croaked he, his face appearing to shine with glory as inch by inch the peg secured itself and brought her blazing bottom full against his belly where it stirred and wriggled violently.

"Be quiet, sir!" then spat my stepmother at him, no doubt to his profound astonishment, though such fleshly thrills were escalating through him that he might have forgiven anything said to him. The trilling sobs and moans of Jennifer were music to our ears, for as he now began slewing his cock in and out of her so she bucked deliciously and thereby served to further his lewd efforts.

Millicent, meanwhile, retaining one gloved hand to hide the libertine view from her son's eyes, passed the other down around his prick. "Ah, you bad boy!" she murmured quite illogically, feeling the risen stem through the cloth of his trousers and he managing a peep now and then at the astonishing sight upon the bed whence the juicy slap and smack of flesh to flesh now came.

"BLUB-BLUB-BLUB!" Jennifer now sobbed, but the nature of her excited squirming, which restrained itself to lewd contortions of her hips, was evident to one's seeking eyes. In all truth she was enjoying the lusty poke despite herself, and panted in between her cries.

"HOO-HOO-HOOO!—you bad boy!" came Millicent's moan, for she could think of nothing else to utter to hide the indiscretion of the moment. With a tremoring excitement which indicated that she was perhaps not fully aware of her actions in such open circumstances, she loosed Clive's trousers and brought to view his own eager prong which throbbed and quivered in her gloved hand.

"Your skirt, my dear—conceal his view!" my stepmother cried helpfully, whereat taking the hint as an instruction, Millicent pressed upon her son's cock and brought him groaning to his knees. Leaning against the doorjamb now she moved him in his kneeling position towards her, raised her skirt and looped it over his head. His shoulders, too, disappeared. He was truly in a tent of darkness and feminine mystery, his stiff stem, waggling, pleading. Millicent's eyes then opened wide. Her jaw sagged. Her expression to say the least was bleary, her eyes never leaving her husband's sturdy, shunting buttocks. A faint guzzling sound was heard. Clive, it seemed, was at the fount of Venus—though through her drawers.

"HAAAAR!" Millicent moaned, though her febrile cry was somewhat lost in the cacophony of groans now echoed by the pair who were cock to cunt. Occasionally and with mischief I would smack her father-in-law's buttocks as they pressed out momentarily—a salute he did not seem to resent for it appeared to make him work her faster. His teeth gritted, his face suffused, a tendon strained upon his neck.

"I c . . . c . . . cannot but help myself—I must come!" he blurted.

"Come, then, you may—full in her and give the girl the benefit of your dose. Do not withdraw, sir, until I so instruct you!"

I wondered whether Mr de Vere Lacey thought himself in heaven or in a dream. His expression was that of a man who is utterly lost in pleasure. Rotating her hips, Jennifer appeared to urge him on. Meanwhile, Millicent had curiously, though praiseworthily, recovered herself a little. Placing one hand behind her neck in a langourous pose, as though she wished to make up for her untoward wildness, she extended down her other arm and pressed her hand imperiously against the back of Clive's head which showed as a bulge 'neath her skirt and so held him. Her thighs moved inwards. A moan escaped him. She was evidently clipping his ears tightly 'twixt her garters. It could do him naught but good.

Such reflections and observations distracted me momentarily, for Mr de Vere Lacey was coming. His puffing cries announced it, his emerging and dipping cock gleaming brightly where Jennifer had lubricated him with her own spendings.

"THEEE-EEEEH!" I heard her cry, and not unjoyously as his thick jets of sperm spattered her within, the veins around his tool pulsing visibly. The succulent sound of their parts thus merging in such liquid fashion was a perfect pleasure to hear. His buttocks tightened, as did his balls which I held upon my palm by delving under him and guarding his retreat.

"Hold in—hold in!" my stepmother spat at him and with a lightning movement of her hand—full facing him as she was and the crotch of her knickers showing now—grasped his hair, which brought a yelp from him. I simultaneously squeezed his balls and thus produced another. He trembled violently, hung his head back and was still, with Jennifer's hot bottom tightly balled into his belly and—I felt sure—her succulent cunt drawing upon him still until the last pearls of his sperm were spilled.

Perhaps remorse or dire embarrassment then overcame him for he would have withdrawn, but caught between us as he was his options were indeed few.

"Not yet, not yet! Hold him in, Jennifer—oh, the wicked man! Squeeze on him tight," my stepmother exhorted, thus making Jennifer accomplice to her will.

Jennifer stirred not nor uttered then a sound. All sensations being so vibrant in her, she was absorbed by them, her lovelips gripped around the root of him.

"M . . . M . . . Madam . . . !" croaked Horace feebly.

"Dooo-dooo-DOOO!" stuttered Millicent in the background. She was coming, I believe.

"We have him, Jennifer. We will take him out. Lie down, curl up, you need have no fear of him. The raging bull is weakened; he will be spermed again later," my stepmother ordained. I seized then the back of Mr de Vere Lacey's hair and gripped it tight as I did his balls. He uttered a wild "YEEEEK!" but in that moment also my stepmother dismounted from Jennifer's back and took his cock as it withdrew. Slimed with love's spendings as it was, it retained a girth and length that was still admirable, though growing limp.

A pleasurable murmur escaped Jennifer's lips, though I did not then look back to watch her subside. With a kick from my stepmother's toe—as the older of the males was spun round helpless in our grasps—Clive was pushed to one side. Millicent's flushed face met ours.

"Put him to his room—a small one beside my own. You will not handle him, Millicent, until I tell you."

"N . . . no!" stammered his mother in assent. In passing by her at the doorway, her husband could not bring himself to look at her, of course. With the subsidence of his wild passion his strength had weakened sufficiently for us to hold him so. Never was one man more bewildered, I am sure, finding himself led by two females into one of the smaller, unused bedrooms where a thrust from both of us pushed him on the bed from whence he stared up at us wildly.

"Your virility, sir, appears to be in little doubt. It will be put to use again before the dawn has broken. As to your daughter-in-law, you have offended her deeply. Such steps as she may take will have my full consent. Be dutiful and no scandal will befall you. You will know better than to defy me soon, or Jennifer. Some cord, Clara, bind his wrists and ankles!"

"Madam . . . !" began he wildly but like a tigress she was upon him while I—having had a drawer indicated to me—took out the waiting cord and was soon at work on him. That Jennifer had sucked on him divinely I had no doubt, for his cock was of a sudden smaller and flaccid, and grunting sounds of dismay—though mingled with awe and not a little fear—came from beneath my stepmother's majestic bottom that was plumped upon his face. Her knees pinned his biceps—a trifle painfully, I felt sure, but for the moment that was to the good. It weakened further his resistance to the cause. In a trice I had trussed him as she wished. We had him prone. With a sigh of satisfaction, my stepmother rolled from him heavily, much squashing his florid visage further in the process, but stayed not to gloat.

My arm was taken. I was urged without, his faint cries following.

"He will be seen to again," she said, loud enough for him to hear.

CHAPTER EIGHTEEN

UPON THE landing we encountered Millicent.

"I have sinned," she moaned, "and you have admonished me!"

"Happy hypocrite that you are, my dear, why think you that?" responded my stepmother, and went on. "You were too hasty, perhaps, but such moments overcome us all of occasion. Moments of orgiastic pleasure are to be controlled at all times. I admonished you merely that dear Jennifer might feel I had no favourites. Now that both males are well subdued, we may alter our tune a little. Disturb your husband not," she said, inclining her head towards the room where we had taken him.

Millicent curled her lip, though flushed with pleasure at what she had been told. "Oh, him!" she uttered in scorn.

"You may well scorn him, Millicent, but he is now better fit for use, is he not? I feel certain you were not unaware of his lewd fondlings of Jennifer, but perhaps were a trifle in fear of him and so said nought?"

The inflexion in her voice was tactfully placed. Millicent nodded. In such circumstances women may often be induced to agree to things upon which they might have otherwise had doubts. Thus can one urge and guide—prepare the paths.

"Good," my stepmother declared as if she had received her spoken assent. "All has been seen. There need be no furtiveness in future, Millicent, in such matters. Did you not eat well? You returned early. Fortuitously, however," she added with a smile.

"The food was not to Horace's liking," murmured Millicent as if that were in some wise her fault.

"Other things will be. Do you have doubts, hesitations? I think not. He was well up her, serviced her well, and she has been the beneficiary of pleased surprise, I have no doubt."

"You caned her! Did you not force her?" Millicent asked in even more surprise.

"As to that, my dear, young women must be oftimes led. Were you never put to males in your youth when you most doubted that you should be?"

Millicent simpered and gazed at the ground. "Of occasion, yes," she murmured.

"So came you to your ways in sweet revenge. Consanguinity is ever useful to this end. You do not seemingly intend Clive to service you, though?"

"I think not." A deep flush invaded Millicent's features.

"As you wish. It is not of paramount importance provided that submission is forthcoming. Even so, were he to have two Mistresses, one would occasionally bring him to the other in order that his duties might be fulfilled. Think on this well, Millicent, for we are not yet ready to depart until all is well settled and the females seen supreme."

"I will. I will think on it." Millicent turned away, her features flushed. "But if I wish. . . . " she began, only to be interrupted swiftly.

"The wishes of the subordinate females are not always paramount, Millicent," my stepmother told her.

"Are we not equals?" Her voice made to flare but then subsided.

"We shall be when I better know your merit. Come, Clara, we must see to Jennifer. The sweet girl has suffered much in the cause. You, Millicent, may go to Clive. Remove your shoes and sit upon his bed. Dangle your legs idly before him while he kneels and sucks your toes. He will gurgle happily at that, I have no doubt."

"Oh!" Millicent giggled rather girlishly and was gone, quite certainly to do as she was told. The male submissive's sucking of a woman's toes I had not heard of before. It is a pretty little trick, and pleasing to the female. Her free foot may tease along his upright prick meanwhile, should she take the whim to do so. Of occasion the teasing makes him come and then he may be punished for his sin in emitting sperm before he was told to.

Jennifer, as may be imagined, huddled up tightly at the sight of us, but we would have none of that, stretched her legs back down and made her lie upon her back. The thin striations of the cane no longer stung but sent a warm glow through her being.

"Were you not well feted?" my stepmother asked her teasingly, chucking her lightly beneath her chin.

"Oh, please, go away," Jennifer mumbled, but such was only to hide her confusion. Her curiousity was far stronger. She could not resist asking where "he" was.

"Put down, my pet, of course, and in due time will soon become accustomed to it. Millicent henceforth will have no truck with his nonsense, nor we. You did not see us lead him out? Oh, what a shame!" my stepmother laughed, "for Clara grasped his balls and hair and I his prick. How docile men are when their lust is expended! He is upon a bed, well-tied and docile."

"He will not always be!" she quivered and raised her hand as though in pleading and grasped the front of my stepmother's dress.

"You think not? Millicent has seen him at you, his cock ploughing in your furrow. Yes, every second was observed, and Clive put down to kneel before her all the while."

"Clive! Oh, he is weak—how weak he is! I, his wife, who should have been defended!"

"Did you wish to be once the pulsing and tingling of your parts had met and made acquaintance? I think not. Shamed you felt at first, but then excited, he put to pleasuring you and well observed. The glory was not his but yours, my pet. Your bottom formed a divine altar of love whereat he worshipped with Priapus, but once expended then he had done his duty."

"His duty? Is that the way it is! I do not want to see his face—oh, no!"

"When he is put to you? You have no need to yet, but there will come a time when, mounted on your belly, you will gaze up at him impassively, or—better—you will straddle him and sheathe his cock yourself while he lies prone, obedient, arms at his sides. He will learn soon enough the lessons of obedience, for Millicent will not touch him otherwise. He will be in a blind alley, knowing better to crawl than to walk. Upon command he will lick your feet, your thighs, your pouting cunny, as a dog might, yet will not attempt you."

"I never wished to be beholden to any male."

Jennifer pouted as she spoke and spoke as though to herself.

"Nor shall you be if you are bold enough. Come, sit up and let us have some wine."

"You c . . . c . . . caned me!" Her voice trembled. She gazed at me accusingly.

"For your own good, my sweet." I smiled at her beguilingly and helped her sit, though she made to fluster awkwardly. My stepmother departing to fetch refreshments, I bathed her face and brushed her hair, she feeling mollified at this attendance on her.

"Did you not like it? Oh, be truthful?" I asked.

"What?" she responded, though well knew what I meant and tried to tease a grin from off her lips.

I made a real merriness of it and tickled her, whereat my stepmother entered with a tray and smiled to see us so. The act of laughing had given Jennifer greater release of her spirit.

"Is he really as you said?" she asked.

"Have you not eyes to see? Come."

Such conspiracies between women are ever stronger than those between males. Being persuaded along the corridor, though timidly at first, the miscreant was shown to her view, his trousers full rucked down below his knees, cock limp, and haggard eyes that stared back to our own.

"See if he may be brought up, Clara," I was told and being not uneager to show my prowess in front of Jennifer, lolled upon the bed beside him at arm's length and caused his prick to stiffen and to rise, massaging my fingers all about at will until his majesty Priapus stood.

"He does not speak, you see, for he may not," my stepmother observed cuttingly and then for good reward raised her skirts and queened him heavily, causing him to splutter much beneath the weight of her knickered bottom and his tool to quiver all the more while Jennifer, bemused, stared on. His breast heaved as he fought for air. I ringed his cock with my fingers and so held it, then beckoned Jennifer.

"Come—hold it," I murmured, though with a fine strain of command in my voice. Her footsteps slurred. His face being completely hidden under my stepmama's bottom, the fact that he could not see her encouraged her. Her arm extended itself slowly. I took her hand and guided it to the root whereat, perhaps to her dismay, the smothering bottom was lifted from his face and my stepmother quickly stood on the floor beside her, daring her with silence to withdraw her hand.

Mr de Vere Lacey's face was sheened with perspiration and his eyes were hot. His lips moved and yet he seemed afraid to speak. I slid in turn from the bed and so Jennifer stood, only the faintest trembling making itself apparent in her limbs and the glowing crest of his penis emerging from her grasping hand. The longer that she held it, the more her confidence appeared to grow. A look now proud, implacable, came on her features that did not fail to convey its message to him. Indeed, he looked cowed.

"Hold him so, for he knows now well enough who his true Mistress is, Jennifer," my stepmother said and turned and opened a drawer. That she had anticipated every contingency and made all ready was apparent to me when she drew out a large broad dog collar and a chain affixed thereto, the sight of which I was well accustomed to.

"Lift your head," she instructed him solemnly and he did so, meekly allowing her to fasten it about his neck, the chain clinking and hanging limp beside the bed. At that, Jennifer gave a little start but her eyes remained steadfast. That she was putting herself on her own mettle, so to speak, I had no doubt. The thrumming of his big erection in her palm must moreover have been exceedingly pleasant.

"Wh . . . wh . . . what is to happen?" he asked then, and thus are the mighty fallen, for to my considerable pleasure his words appeared to be addressed to Jennifer and thus he paid first homage to her.

"You are to be exercised," Stepmama told him coldly and held then the chain taut while I untied his bonds, casting a warning glance at Jennifer not to relax her firm, tight grip. Her knuckles whitened a little. Evidently she was enjoying squeezing him. With his trousers, socks and boots removed, he neither kicked nor strove to raise his arms, but ever kept his eyes on his daughter-in-law's as though pleading with her silently. That he should have done so was the best of chances for it increased her will,

I am sure, and taught her more than many words could have done.

"Bring him downstairs," was then said curtly to me and with that my stepmother swept out and descended the stairs with firm and meaningful tread. At that, Jennifer's eyes appeared to become a little haunted, but I—moving around the bed and behind her—took up the chain and said to him as briefly, "Come!" then added, "Continue to hold his prick, Jennifer, for he has been wicked and well knows it. He must be quelled."

Thus did the bizarre procession occur, Jennifer leading the way and stepping down most lightly while keeping purchase on his cock. I, following at the rear, held the chain taut and kept his head up. Being led into the drawing room, he saw then my stepmother waiting imperiously there, her arms folded.

"On your knees! On all fours like a dog!" she spat to him. The chain clinked once more as I loosened it. Jennifer hurriedly released her grip. Down he sank and looked like a great hound, I straddling his back, the chain drawn tight again. The posture, being instinctive and not consciously intended, amused my stepmama who murmured, "Very well—let him be ridden."

I had exercised the males at home thus. While she took the chain from my hand and held it—and he groaning in anticipation of the as yet unknown—I raised my skirt to my hips and, being knickerless, brought my cunny to rub along his spine where I had ruffled up his shirt. The chain being then put back to my hand, I gritted, "Move!"

Ah, how he groaned and how Jennifer stared! Heavy as I was upon his back he was forced to grind his knees forward little by little, I reaching behind with my free hand and frequently slapping his bared buttocks while he was forced to circle round the room. Coming back to where we had started and my stepmother clapping her hands lightly, Jennifer was then told to mount him in turn—'For you will do it often at your whim," she was told.

He panted, hung his head and waited humbly, cock still erect as ever we had made it and his balls dangling heavily. My stepmother, giving Jennifer's bottom a little smack, urged her skirt up out of sight of him and put her on him. His back all but creaked! Jennifer's cheeks were rosy red and yet excited. A little kick from my shoe impelled him forward yet again, his progress this time being even slower. In truth, Jennifer's feet sometimes touched the floor and so both lightened his burden and urged him forward. Her eyes were bright, her back upright. Upon her rising from him at last, he arched his aching back in humble supplication.

"Madam! May I . . . ?" he croaked, raising his head wearily, though cautiously not attempting to rise.

"You address ME, sir? Address yourself only to your Mistress!" snapped my stepmother.

"I know not what to say to her," he groaned whereat to our supreme pleasure Jennifer strode in front of him and stood with legs astride.

"You may speak," she said quietly.

"Have I . . . have I your forgiveness?" he asked, his eyes upon her legs.

"Are you obedient?" she asked curtly in a tone that owed much to my stepmother.

"Yes." His voice was a hoarse whisper.

"And will continue so to be?"

"Yes! I swear! Even to my dying day. Were you to ask me to lick your shoes. . . . "

"I may or I may not." Her voice was skittish and yet stern, so finely threaded that he would not know what to make of it. Her nostrils pinching with high emotion, she tossed her head and gazed at my stepmother as though proudly.

"He may be put to you, then, but must withdraw before he comes. I will present him to you, my dear. Clara will bring him to you. Should he fail, he will be whipped."

The words came from my stepmother, softly though bleakly. In a sense perhaps it was a command to Jennifer to obey her also. The young woman's lips trembled a little yet her face remained haughty as though she would oppose us, too. Then, upon a gentle touch of her arm, she was guided to a sofa over the high rolled arm of which she was bent, no doubt to her surprise, but she wilted not. I, veiling this from Mr de Vere Lacey's view by stepping before him, waited until Jennifer's skirt was drawn up high about her hips.

Her bottom showed but the faintest of marks by then. Her furred mouth pouted to my view beneath her lustrous hemispheres. At a whisper from my stepmother, she slurred her feet apart. Her legs straightened. From a rear viewpoint all that was to be seen were her shapely legs—her ruffled garters tight about her thighs—the cleft globe poised above, and a hunching of her shoulders down into the seat.

CHAPTER NINETEEN

THE ACT that was to ensue was one of salutation to the female, as Jennifer was to learn. That there is apparent submission in the female cannot be doubted, and yet she holds the reins. In forbidding the male to loose his sperm, she encloses him in the most intimate and tightest manner, and then rejects him, though he may be held long throbbing in her orifice and thus pays homage to her nether charms.

With caution and due ceremony, I brought Horace to rise by tugging on his chain, acting—as it pleased me sometimes to do—as handmaiden to the event, and then to his undoubted dismay led him to a corner of the room and there to wait. Silent as he was, he licked his lips, breathed heavily, his penis straining mightily up his belly. Seeing my stepmother whisper to Jennifer again, I turned him to the wall. Turning my head, I watched her hand glossing all around Jennifer's high-thrust bottom and dipping occasionally to brush her slit. The young woman's hips stirred, though not uneasily. When fretful of occasion, my sister had been treated thus and her orifice oiled. That warm unguent was no more soothing, as I knew, than my stepmother's voice when she was minded it to be. It lured, it comforted, it coaxed, and spoke of pleasures almost beyond one's ken. That Jennifer did not murmur nor attempt to raise her head was to her uttermost credit, for many are the young women who wilt at the idea of the intrusion of the prick between their cheeks.

One becomes accustomed to it, in my experience, after the first rodding there. It pleasured me as much as it did in my cunny, and on occasion more if I were feeling lewd or, as my stepmama would say, "indulgent," for I felt the sperm shoot in more strongly there and loved to feel the balls of the cowed males slapping under me.

The curtains being drawn together, my stepmother then dowsed all the lamps but one which shone with radiance upon Jennifer's offered orb. Having made her sacrifice to Lesbos in this selfsame room, she was now to make another as I had been frequently brought to do, absorbing the pulsing stems in my tight bottom and mewing inwardly.

Mark well that term, for the female in such posture is not craven and hence should hold back the small, imploring cries she might otherwise utter. Neither should she puff or pant, but take great care to control herself, for in her silence the male is then held in greater awe of her. Once his duty is concluded she has nothing to praise him for but on the contrary may upbraid him should his performance lack virility and power, or the necessary rhythms to please her. Sometimes he may lightly clasp her hips, but sometimes not and must keep his hands clasped behind his back. On rare occasions, when the delicious climax is being obtained, he may be called to bend full over her and fondle her breasts, though this is not unduly encouraged, for the awoken female prefers such caresses to come from her own kind, women's tongues and fingers being far more subtle and knowing than the cruder male's.

Until the female has fully proven herself, even so, she must be kept on her toes by her mentor who, if she pleases, will style herself a Riding Mistress and will see regularly to the conduct of the males in pleasuring those whose toes they are often pleased to suck. My stepmother would thus conduct herself at home once a month at least, we being assembled and lectured to before the males were put to us.

The drawing together of the curtains and the dowsing of all lamps save one reminded me of this while both combatants waited for the word of command. Thus on occasion Bertha's daughter, Mary, was brought among us and treated as an equal among the women. She was of my own age, being a little plump about the bottom and thighs, but quite delightful to see when disrobed, for her titties were large and bold, which she inherited from her mother.

The males, having been stripped and bound to the wall-rack in the "pleasure room," with their cocks well stiffened by Bertha, would be left so for an hour while my stepmother philosophised, undressing as she did while Bertha followed suit. Seeing them nude to their stockings and boots would stir us and we would then disrobe also, making much naughtiness about the matter and having our cunnies tickled and our bottoms stirred. Liqueurs would be passed around and much licking would obtain until our erect nipples, flushed cheeks and moist quims sought further fulfilments, I knowing that I might find myself abed afterwards with Stepmama and Mary while Bertha would frot with Sarah and occasionally bring a cock again to her.

When the males were brought down by Bertha, we three girls were put up ready, side by side and with some two feet or so obtaining between our hips which were slung over the back of a sofa. While a perfect silence first obtained, a prick would be put to each of our bottoms, entered an inch and so held. I, being often in the middle, would secretly clasp the hand of Sarah on one side and that of Mary on the other. Our hands would tighten with each further inch that was impelled into us, my stepmother walking all about and observing all. At three inches of such invasion, the males were called to halt and so stood, throbbing in our "rosebuds" with great eagerness and yet the "Ring Mistress" knew she must control all.

Thus we would proceed and I hard put to utter not a sound as the pervasive insurgence increased, the thighs of the males ever trembling as they were called to halt and then again to proceed. Occasionally my stepmother's whip would crack about one or other of their buttocks and their groans would sound. When at last the stems were full embedded, thus we held and gripped them tight, having to guess—if we did not already know—whose penis we contained.

Were the performance to be a strict one (we having perhaps displeased her in some wise), the cries to proceed and to stop ever sounded, so that by her own deliberation there was no rhythm to the matter and much frustration. Finally, however, the corkings would begin, though each male must thrust in and then withdraw in the same moment so that the exquisite sensations of we three were unified.

"Faster!" she would sometimes cry and then we would be corkscrewed deeply. "Now slow—-now SLOW!" she would say after a few such moments and the pantings of the males would sound louder as they obeyed. No movements of our own hips were permitted on such occasions. We received, we suffered, we enjoyed. Our eyes would screw up, our clasps tighten on each other's hands, little trickles and spurts of pleasure emanating from our slits as we were worked.

Towards their climax—and the time of it being ordained by Stepmama—the males would flash their hips and ream us fast, then coming upon their moment would slow down and frequently were made to draw their cocks out almost to the knob as they ejected. Such was a most delicious feeling, for it lengthened the span of their jets and seemed to make them shoot deeper within us, my stepmama ever spurring them on with exhortations and snappings of her whip. Then would the shuddering climaxes obtain and we would grip the roots of their pricks which at the last would urge right in and pulse their last, being made to stay within until they had shrunk and slipped without.

When pestles to pussies were put there was often less ceremony, though the males were not permitted to lie upon us and luxuriate once they had emptied their balls, for such kisses as we received were sweeter from other, feminine mouths. Mostly the males were made to lie prone while we mounted on their stemming weapons and rode up and down on them at our leisure, exhorting them not to spill until we wished it, that we might thereby enjoy our own orgasmic thrills as most young married women never do, the males simply treating them as cockerels do hens. Thus we deprived ourselves of nothing, but gained much, which was the entire purpose of my stepmama's teachings. Our wardrobes were ever refurbished, for we were treated as goddesses, though it was an essential part of the philosophy—and ever is—that the accumulation of worldly goods by way of the male purse is by no means the purpose of it all. To this end my stepmother would frequently cite the cases of Bertha, Mary and Tim whose station in life was much lowlier than our own. Though it was seen to that Bertha received additions to her wages, and that her husband was paid as all manservants are, the prime purpose was to inculcate into him the most profound and dutiful devotion to his wife and daughter and such other of us females who required his virile services.

When Mary was first put up to him at fifteen, she made much fuss of it, as Sarah had done—a matter which bewilders some who think that the male then sees the younger female as his lustful toy. That this is not so emerges with her gradual understanding of the matter and her ability to turn him to her will. If fretful or wilful, as my sister first was, then she was jousted (such again being my stepmother's word for it) by receiving one after another all three cocks of Papa, Tim and Robert in turn until her cunny or bottom bubbled with sperm and she was much quietened and a perfect little angel looked.

We never spoke to the males of these matters, for their comportment spoke for itself. To be exercised was their great pride, for it put them in the forefront and this in turn made them the more humble to be selected for duties. All were trained also to act as maids and thus would assist us in dressing or undressing on occasions when they were *not* to be exercised and then were forbidden to palpitate our bottoms or even touch them with their fingertips when putting on our drawers. Our naked tits would jiggle in front of their eyes on such occasions, but no immediate comfort was given them. On certain days, or as punishment for being slothful in their duties, their pricks would be made to stand and then bound in leather sheathes that they might make no use of them at all save to urinate.

However, I have diverted the reader from the immediate occasion. Jennifer waited with such patience as my stepmother had somehow instilled into her by her gentle exhortations. At a crooking of a finger, I turned Mr de Vere Lacey about and led him slowly to her.

No words were needed. I believe him to have been too cowed and too bemused to utter any. Brought to "post" behind her so that his knees all but touched the backs of her own, I moved fully to his rear and kept the chain taut. His arms hung limp and uncertain. My stepmother, pressing his palms firmly to the side of his brawny thighs, thus signalled him not to move them. Her actions in such moments were ever businesslike. Cupping his balls with her right hand, she then ringed his fleshy, rigid stave with the fingers of her left and forced its springiness down a little until the bulbous nose made contact with Jennifer's sweet, bulging cheeks. Having so adjusted their parts she then brought him against the young woman's tight rosette, whereat he emitted a short "HAAAAR. . . . " and moved his neck against the restraining collar, but I jerked his head back.

Her fingers being clasped two inches below his knob, my stepmother urged it gently inwards, causing Jennifer to quiver considerably and no doubt to bite a cushion which she had clasped under her as a child might clasp a doll in bed. The springiness of her tight cheeks, having been parted to his cock, surged back and gripped it, causing his breath to flood out from his nostrils. A quivering sigh escaped Jennifer and her legs appeared more taut than before as she prepared to receive him in her orifice.

Mr de Vere Lacey's being held still and I at his back with the restraining chain, he could not move but half an inch inwards at a time, I endeavouring to peer round him and making some little success in doing so. The ever-thrilling sight then came to my eyes of a female bottom—and one as lustrous and round as Jennifer's—receiving the male cork or peg or rammer. Her breathing sounded in little rushes now. Her knees bent inwards against the end of the sofa and then once more straightened as three inches were inserted.

How I knew and envied her sensations and wished to fall beneath her and draw her mouth down upon mine as I had often done with Sarah or Mary, and they with me, when we were being serviced! Even so, I knew that Jennifer would not be at her pleasure yet but would be sustaining all the tremulous wonder and apprehensions that come from having one's bottom plugged and reamed for the first time.

The invasion seems tremendous and only with the greatest effort and much prior coaxing does one learn not to tighten the muscles and reject the long, thick cork. At halfway point an easing comes, for there is the sensation of wonder that one has expanded to receive and a first, faint lubrication begins which eases the passage.

"WHOOO-HOOOO!" shuddered Jennifer's father-in-law now in utmost bliss, the sound comfortably veiling her own small whimpers. The lustrous orb of her bottom wriggled a little, whereat my stepmother ceased the progress of his entry and waited patiently for her to still herself. This Jennifer at last doing with courageous effort, my stepmother then nipped his balls gently and so sent him ramming home and firm in her so that his balls, freed quickly from my stepmother's grasp, hung just beneath her quim.

Jennifer moaned, her hands clawing feebly. For a brief moment it seemed she would endeavour to straighten up, but the quivering along her spine was perhaps illusory and he—having my stepmother's fingers clawed into his strong buttocks—was equally held still.

"Dear God, how tight and warm she is!" he croaked, only to be snapped into silence by the lashing of my stepmother's tongue.

"Be QUIET, sir! You are but her servant and her servitor and will be put to her henceforth solely at her own command. Her body is the altar at which you will thus be brought to worship. Arrogance will bring you only punishment, and lewdness will invite her whip as surely as it will your wife's. I put you now upon your merit to pleasure your goddess. Fail in this and you will be denied all future pleasures. Clara—drop the chain!"

I had not expected this, but did so and thus was enabled to view his efforts better. His expression was constrained—so tight with pleasure that he knew not whether to laugh or cry. "HAAAAR!" he groaned and drew his peg half out, so showing better the luscious conjunction of their parts, his prick emerging like a thick root from between the chubby inrolling of Jennifer's bottom cheeks.

Seeming mesmerised by her exuding warmth and elastic pressure, he stayed thus for a moment as though in fear he might eject his sperm too soon.

A humming sound came softly from Jennifer's throat and to our perfect delight she so moved her hips that his cock was once more fully embedded.

"H . . . h . . . hold it in!" she stammered.

"Obey!" cracked my stepmother's voice, causing his legs to tremble mightily and his fingers to work as though he wished to clasp her hips.

There was then a silence as they remained thus, he breathing far more heavily than she. I knew her to be accommodating herself and overcoming all her scruples now. A quick vision of her as I had first seen her at the garden party passed through my mind—tall, elegant and cool with but a distantly enquiring look in her eyes. Uncovered now and put to the prick, she looked no less elegant and was gaining pride in her poise and possession of the once lordly male, bolstered as she was by our presence.

"Perform!" her voice came to him then, "but do not come until I tell you—AH!"

Her little unexpected cry was caused by his immediate observance of her command. His penis began to ease back and forth, drawn ever inwards by the succulence of her enclosure, the tight ring gripping him commandingly. Her hips began to rock gently back and forth in answer to his thrusts, though should not have done, but upon this first entry of theirs into this realm, my stepmother interfered not.

His breath came faster now, whistling down his nostrils which flared as might a bull's. His fingers gripped themselves into his palms, wrists twitching nervously as he strove—with certain merit, I do confess—to prevent his hands from cupping her lower cheeks or hips as he would have wished.

"Not . . . not . . . not so fast! I forbid it!" came from

Jennifer, bringing a look of dire disappointment to his face, though then his pace immediately slackened and the thick root strove more slowly back and forth. My stepmother, being closer to Jennifer's side and ever observant, nodded to me and I knew the dear girl was coming. Small twitterings from between her pursed lips sang of her pleasure. Fully saddled as she was, such lusts arose in her as one constrains oneself not to utter in the presence of a male submissive. Perhaps a full minute passed then while he worked her, in-out, in-out, ever sturdy and long the strokes.

"Now faster! You may come," she breathed.

A gasp of joy escaped him. His loins flashed, her bottom worked, rotating a little lewdly now and then as again and again she attained the peak of her pleasure, the sprinklings of which were to be found afterwards on the cushion she had at first clutched.

The tendons stood out on his neck as surely as did the veins upon his ramming tool. A long shuddering sigh came from him and, breathing furiously through his nostrils, he ejected his pleasure waves of liquid bliss within her much thrilled bottom until the last seeping pearls had been absorbed. Then did he sag, his long cork popping out, smeared and glistening with the emissions of his desire.

I made to utter something then out of habit, but my stepmother touched my hand in warning and instead I took up the chain anew and drew him back. Two paces then separated them. His eyes, hungry on her form, drank in each wondrous curve of his daughter-in-law's most elegant and nubile form. Raising herself a little, she reached back and eased down her gown before slowly turning, her face not a little flushed but her eyes composed.

"Return upstairs," she told him bleakly and in so doing lifted her chin as though in challenge.

His eyes fell. He sought for words he could not speak and then said simply, "Yes."

I released the chain. His retirement was slow, uncertain and redolent of a deep selfconsciousness, but he did not turn. The door received him and he passed through. Jennifer immediately threw herself into my stepmother's arms and laughed, "OH!" as though in wonder at herself. She was clasped silently and warmly, then released.

"Let us see to the others," my stepmother said. Conspirators now settled in their ways, we ascended and sought Millicent. There upon a bed she lay dressed and with Clive beside her naked, his limp cock cradled in her hand. They slept and looked like two babes in so doing.

Had her drawers not been lying on the floor, the scene would have been one of even greater innocence.

CHAPTER TWENTY

"WHAT SHALL we find, I wonder, upon our return?" my stepmother mused while a more restful crossing bore us back towards the cliffs of Dover.

"I cannot conjecture, but I have no doubt that you will put things in order should they have gone awry," I replied. I had seen her witchcraft at work all anew and was much strengthened by it. The little denouement of which I have just spoken added the final resolve to Jennifer and caused her much amusement rather than jealousy. Her progress thereafter was rapid and Millicent duly took second place to her, not by rote of anything said but by silent understanding, for she who had shown the greater boldness drew the greater strength. Even so, the Wills of the two males were quickly redrawn to show the two females as equal beneficiaries, and so all was well, the four remaining in Nice for a further two weeks and Jennifer to report to my stepmother on their return.

As to our household, I had expected Bertha to be left in charge, but having given much silent thought to the matter, my stepmother had finally decided upon Sarah that she might be put on her mettle. I wondered aloud at this frequently when alone with Stepmama, but she ever said simply and wisely, "Let us see," and sought not to draw upon any conjectures of my own nor proffered any of hers.

"Do not birch or cane her if she is in trouble," I pleaded as at last our coach rumbled along the wellknown lanes towards the house.

"There will be no need for that. At least, I trust there will be no need for that. As to any birchings, Clara, they will be performed henceforth by you."

I said nothing but felt myself further elevated, yet could not but be apprehensive for Sarah's sake when at last we arrived. Bertha stood upon the broad, stone steps and I hastened alongside my stepmother to hear her first words.

"All is well, m'am," said she to my vast relief and then, looking up, I saw Sarah waving to me from a latticed window. Immediately I ran within, leaving the two talking together, and raced upstairs. There my beloved Sarah laughed and kissed with me and drew me into her room.

"All is well—Bertha said so!" I gasped unguardedly, such being my relief.

"Of course!" she sparkled and then we kissed again and sighed and hugged one another, I then at last removing my cloak and bonnet and casting myself on her bed to hug my knees, for she was demanding news of me as I of her.

"No—you tell first!'—'No, you!"

So we argued back and forth and our stepmother not then intruding since she had learned all she wished to know from Bertha.

"Well, Clara, you will not believe this, but I had such fortune," Sarah conceded at last. "Do you recall the Weatherbys?" she asked. I frowned, thought for a moment, then said yes. We had come upon them a few times, though not in recent years. I recalled dimly the Mama and Papa of the family and a brood of children among whom were a son, Phillip, and a daughter, Rose, who were but thirteen or so when I last saw them and were twins. This last point burst upon me and I was pleased to remember it.

"That is so and quite by chance they came to stay," Sarah said, "for we met them in the market town and I impulsively invited them. Their dear Mama is pleased to have two less to look out for during a week or so. Rose is quite pretty now and Phillip handsome."

Sarah looked at me and giggled.

"Go on!" said I excitedly.

My sister put her finger to her mouth as sometimes she will do when looking coy, or making great pretence to do so.

"She . . . she will not do it with him, nor with Robert," she exclaimed dolefully, though at the same time biting back a smile.

I could scarce hold myself in for glee. "Have you not spanked or birched or feathered her?" I asked.

"Oh, I tried, but she makes such a squealing of it and Bertha would not help me—said as I must make my way. I have put Rose to her room and made her stay there."

"And her brother? Come, I am sure you have had more success with him. Oh, you naughty thing, tell me!"

"I did not. Honestly, I did not. Bertha, you see, she said that I was to have Rose ready first, for they are both supposed innocents," (at this she sniffed), "and better it is, Bertha said, for Rose to be prepared before she takes their cocks. I would not put her with Papa or Tim at first for that might make her more rebellious."

"Yes, you were right," I began to say and then Stepmama opened the door and looked in upon us.

"What is to do?" she asked. Sarah thereupon rushed to her, was hugged and kissed. Turning in our stepmother's fond embrace, my sister gazed at me not a little victoriously, her eyes sparkling.

"We were discussing what to do, Mama," said I, full well knowing she would have received from Bertha as much intelligence as I from Sarah.

"Very well, my pets, then I will leave that matter in your hands. To all such arrangements as you think fit," she added, turning at the door with a sweet smile and then departing.

Sarah clapped her hands and said, "Oh! She is not then displeased with me!"

"Why should she be, you silly? You have shown your aptitude sufficiently in guiding Rose and Phillip here. How long have they been so?"

"Two days—no, three."

"Why, that is perfect. You had no need to rush matters. Have you fondled her, kissed her enough?"

"Oh yes, she does not mind that too much—has shared my bed. What an adorable cunny she has! I have licked it a little, poured words of praise into her ears and got her flushed, her nipples all erect. But still she will not so much as look at Phillip's cock, nor Robert's—has seen only her Papa's for once when in his cups he showed it all stiff before her, but she ran away, thought it an awesome sight—so big, she said!"

"Will you have me see to her?"

"Oh, *will* you, Clara? She is in the bedroom next to yours and mine. I thought it better so. I held her nose and made her tipple wine, but still she would not warm herself up to the thought of it."

"I will warm her up enough—have no fear of that. You will bring Robert to her first, but not before I call you. Have you milked him well of late? I trust you have, and not only he?"

"Oh yes, for Bertha left it to me. He wears his knickers, petticoats and stockings better now and stands most docile while I frot his prick."

"Good girl—and the others too, I trust. Have you the key to Rose's room? Good, I will take it. Have Robert prepared, though not in girl's attire. She will accustom herself to that later."

"It will be nice for her, will it not—after you have birched her?" Sarah asked anxiously.

"It will be nice for you, too, if you are ever wilful again," said I mischievously, but then kissed her on the lips for comfort and, telling her to leave her door open, to fetch Robert, and to be ready, I took a birch which she had thoughtfully placed in readiness in water, shook it out well, and betook myself to young Mademoiselle Rose, as I thought of her.

"Who is that?" her voice came nervously as I turned the key. Upon my entering, she sat down quickly again in a chair, remembering me perhaps better than I might have remembered her. Her eyes started out as she saw the birch and she sprang up and backed against a window.

"I shall tell Mama if you do anything!" she exclaimed and clutched at the front of her pink dress.

"Oh, shall you, indeed! But your Mama might be made just as busy as you are about to be, Miss. Come here!"

I advanced into the room, quite safe in my knowledge that leaving the door ajar would bring no interruptions. I surveyed her. She was a trifle below my own height, round of face with pretty, pouting lips that soon might be set in penance to suck upon a few manly stalks, though the practice was not encouraged by my stepmama and seen only as an extreme when girls were utterly wilful and in the first stages of their training.

"I w . . . w . . . will not!" Her lips trembled. How sorry I felt for her that her bottom was to be stung, and yet I felt implacable.

"You will lower your drawers, Miss, and bend over!"

"Oh my heavens, what a thing to say! You shall not make me, you shall not! Even Papa has never birched me!"

"Then he is the poorer for it, for you would have been breached ere now. Do you not fancy his cock?" I asked with amusement and watched her cover her face.

"Stop it! You are a dirty thing!"

"We shall change your ways, Rose, and your ways of thinking. Come, do as I say or I shall call Sarah and she will hold you. Will you be so humiliated? Shall you have my brother and yours watch? I will not sting you badly. Do you think I will?"

"Why . . . w . . . w . . . why do you want to birch me?"

When a girl asks thus she is already at the first stage of her submission to the more lordly female. This I have long learned. It is a confession in all essence that it is to occur.

"You *know* why. You have been wilful with Sarah, have had your cunny tickled but will not give in. I will call her." I made as though to move back to the door whereat Rose advanced upon me imploringly.

"I d . . . d . . . don't want her to hold me!" she sobbed.

"Nor your brother to see you—nor mine. Come, you silly, you will understand matters better in but the shortest time. Have you drawers on? Take them off. Raise your skirt hip high and bend over the bed, your palms flat and your legs apart."

"Oh-woh! I do not want to!"

I was closer to her now and she all flushed and both of us closer to the bed. Of a sudden I took her chin in a firm grip and made her stare into my eyes. Her breasts, already full rounded and well formed, rose and fell in her agitation.

"You know you will obey me, Rose, but kiss me first."

My words taking her utterly by surprise and I still holding her chin, I swept my other arm around her slender waist and so held her tight into me with the birch laid at an angle against her bottom. A gasp escaped her but she let my lips all but enclose her own. Her mouth was delicious, as the mouths of young girls are, and her cunny would be also such, I knew. Trembling like a bird then as she was, in part bewilderment and part surprise, I held her.

"Darling, you must," I whispered, for I felt in these circumstances rather to coax her than to continue threatening. 'Your Papa wishes it, and your Mama," I lied glibly, but then changing my mood and my action I spun her around, propelled her quickly to the bed and bent her over. "STAY!" I commanded, for it is a word that novices and initiates must learn and obey immediately.

"M . . . M . . . mama and Papa?" she squeaked, made a feeble attempt to rise and was pressed down again.

"Yes," I declared firmly, though could scarce control my laughter at the situation. Giving her no time to recover I upped her skirt and quickly drew her knickers down.

Ah, what a little beauty! Her legs were trim and nicely curved, her stockings white, and garters pink and saucier than I would have suspected her of wearing. Her bottom, small and chubby, gleamed an invitation she had never thought to offer yet. Holding her neck with one hand laid flat upon it and applying such authoritative pressure as I sensed she required, I ran the tip of my forefinger of my other hand deep up along her groove and brought an "OOOH!" from her. I quested, found the puckered orifice between her springy cheeks and then her tightlipped quim. She bucked and started, but I soothed her then, moving my finger slowly up and down.

The mood then came upon me to smack her first and I did so, ringing her waist tightly with my arm.

"OUCH!" she burst as first my palm assailed her bumptious cheeks and left a pink flare there. Then SMACK! again and then she yelped.

"Now, Miss, you will have more of that if you do not take your medicine," said I and gave her another for good measure, causing her to sob and writhe her hips.

"OOOH-WOOH-WOOOH!" she sobbed, "I don't want to!"

"We will have none of that here, Rose. Be still now and keep your bottom up, your legs apart. Will you obey me or be spanked harder?"

"I w . . . w . . . will, I will! Oh, I will try!"

"What a good girl you are really! Your Papa and your Mama ever say so and would have put you to your trials before this, I swear . . . " SWEEE-ISSSSH!

"YEEEE-EEEEK!"

The cry must have sounded down the corridor, for it was as high-pitched as I have ever heard as the twigs coursed across her bottom leaving sparks of fire in their wake. Her bottom, however, lifted perfectly—for I had brought the twigs right under her and her sweet little quim was displayed to perfection, a touch of salmon pink showing between the rolled lips.

"Rose! Be still!" So I barked at her while her legs twisted girlishly all about and she strove, as all do, to shake off the insurgent heat that assailed her.

"WOH-WOH-WOH! I can't! NEEEE-OWCH! Oh, I can't bear it! Stop it, please!"

"You sillikins, do you think your Papa will listen to you when he takes your drawers down? Your Mama come rushing to your rescue? I think not. Your bottom will be burnished here the better for his later efforts—IF they are permitted."

With what cunning I inserted that phrase and with what surprise she uttered a startled "WHA-AAAART?" but I—accompanying my words with a lighter brushing of the birch across her tingling orb—caused her to screech again, though defensively rather than from any effect of it which could scarce have been called fearsome.

"Do you want your Papa to birch you and then to show you his naughty thing again?"

"No-woh-woh, I don't! AH-HOOOO! No! Don't! NEEE-YNNNG!"

"Come, Rose, come on—push it up more. Oh, you bad, bad girl I will birch you harder if you don't!" SWEEE-ISSSSH! . . . SWEEE-ISSSH!

"AH-HAR-HAAAAR!" she sobbed, her bottom now a lovely rosy red with creamy patches showing in between. Then, dropping the birch while yet she expected another, I seized her neck and, cupping her hot bottom upon my other hand, found her lovespot with my finger. Her cunny, as I expected, was fully moist and her bud erect. "NOOO-WHOOO!" she blurted in surprise, but I had her well, her hip bumping against my knee which I had planted on the bed. "D . . . d . . . d . . . !" came her incoherent stuttering, but then her spot swelled more, its tiny, sensitive point burning to my finger. Her bottom churned and worked, caught as she was in a rage of sensations. With my little finger extended I could feel the greater creaminess of her slit. Her moans sounded, issuing through her sobs.

"Darling, Rose," I breathed, "how nice!" and then, raising my voice, called "Sarah!"

Rose was too far gone then to protest. I had her swimming in the bliss of it and felt her spurting even as my sister led in Robert, naked to his shirt, his prong upstanding.

"HOOO-HOOO-HOOOO!" sounded from Rose whose face was muffled in the quilt. Fresh and beautiful as my brother's prick looked, Sarah brought him quickly to her. Rose, sprinkling then again, felt his knob to her pouting nest and made to jerk. 'AAAARGH!" came her long cry of surprise but already under Sarah's guidance he was embedded. Two inches entered Rose's juicy quim and then a third. "NO-WOH! Who is it! He CAH-AH-AN'T!"

It was the first such resistance Robert had ever met and a look of surprise flooded his handsome features.

"Go on, Robert!" Sarah spat at him and slapped his buttocks. His eyes screwed up. Rose's was the tightest cunny he had yet entered, though not perhaps as tight as my bottom had first been to him. He seized her hips. The movement, otherwise forbidden, was overlooked in the flurrying, writhing passion of the moment.

"Dooo-doo-doo-DOOOOH!" sobbed Rose and then with

the most urgent strivings of his young manly cock he was in her to his balls which hung beneath her nest like two large pendants.

The bed shook and squeaked. A faint squelch was heard as his penis half withdrew and them rammed in again. Rose tried in vain to scrabble forward, but was held.

"Slowly, Robert—she must have full pleasure of it!"

So my voice sounded and he stared into my eyes, his vision bleared, I am sure, by the sucking tightness of her nest. For a long moment then while he strained and worked her, our eyes remained locked and a perfect understanding seemed to pass between us. Panting heavily as he was he seemed to be inhabiting a world of his own, causing Rose's bottom now to smack loudly against his belly while she beat for a moment feebly on the quilt, then buried her face in her arms and uttered the sweetest little moans which in turn were answered by his. Answering my command, his well-oiled pestle moved more slowly. His look became quite agonised. Stepmama would have kept him at it, but a certain tenderness had seized me. It came upon me for a moment that I would take him to my bed that night and bring his mouth and tongue to mine the while we fucked, yet that I knew would spoil him.

"Come, Robert—sperm her," I murmured.

"HAR! HOOO! He mustn't! DON'T!"

Too late. His jaw sagged. The pellets of sperm leapt from his prick, full-embedded as he then was and as his bleared eyes showed. Ramming, the cream ran back along his cock, so fruitfully did he spout, his face softening all the while until he had expended to the last in her and uttered a hugh sigh, his hands falling as though guiltily from her hips while Rose fell forward, squirming from off his cock, and sobbed loudly.

I was not misled by her. Such tantrums often show. The minx would have come a dozen times since I first fingered her. Taking Robert's arm, Sarah led him out, reluctant as he seemed to leave. I would guard the expression in my eyes when next I looked at him, I told myself.

"Oh-woh-woh, you have made me do it!" Rose whimpered and curled herself up, having slyly observed his departure by peeping under her arm.

"And shall do so again," I said, but then cuddled her into me and kissed her all about the face and neck. "Would your Mama not be proud of you? Oh, she would," I chuckled warmly. A little murmur reached my ears and I turned her upon her back and gazed down into her shy eyes.

"I have b . . . b . . . been naughty," said she as though in great surprise.

"Naughty is as naughty does, my sweet, but we have nothing of naughtiness here—only obedience. Bad Robert, he held you, did he not, and should not have done."

"He did, yes." Her voice was sulky but, I noticed, not displeased.

"You will have to punish bad Robert, will you not, and Phillip too, and all the wicked men."

"Yes. Oh! but what do you mean?" She sat up suddenly and sagged against me, waiting as I knew for me to speak. I lectured her quietly then, quelled her protests and made her listen. How much she absorbed I know not, but it did not matter for the moment.

"Come," I said when I had concluded, "tidy yourself, as I must myself. Oh, goodness what a mess I am! Brush my hair and then I will do yours. Shall we do that?"

She nodded, knew not whether to grin or not to grin, but seemed mollified. Once presentable again, I made to lead her down.

"Oh, but where is Robert?" she asked and would have dragged back.

"Why, he has been a bad boy and is kept to his room, darling, and will be spanked by Mama if he comes out. What a red bottom he will have, won't he?"

She giggled and put her hand to her mouth as if she should have not, but could not veil the mischief in her eyes. Even so her feet still dragged, though I maintained patience with her and got her at last to the top of the stairs.

"Wh . . . wh . . . where is Phillip?" she asked in awe.

"He is *going* to be a bad boy with you later—we know that, don't we?—so he is kept to his room also and will be put back afterwards."

"Oh-woh!" Rose gasped but allowed herself then to be led down where tea had just been brought in and my stepmother and Sarah received her as graciously as they might an older guest, flattering her with their attentions and subtle praises—though hinting at nothing that had occurred—until she blushed with pleasure, gazing at me for confirmation that all was such and I nodding.

"Progress her quickly if you can."

The words were whispered to my ear by Stepmama while Rose was diverted by Sarah showing her some new embroidery.

I nodded fervently. I was to be given free rein and was proud thereof, but a further explanation was then afforded me as my stepmother addressed herself to Rose.

"I have word that your Mama and Papa are to visit on Saturday. Will that not be nice?"

Rose's face was a picture. A crumb of cake fell from her lips. A sound was emitted from her throat that might have meant either "No" or "Yes." I am sure that in her mind she fell between the two.

"Rose has been such a good girl, Mama," said I.

"That I am sure of and will continue to be so long as she is in your hands. Where, then, is Phillip?" my stepmother asked in great innocence, causing Rose to all but curl up in her chair.

"Why, we know he is going to be naughty, Mama, so have put him to his room," Sarah said.

"Tut tut! How well you did! They are ever so—Robert

and your Papa and Charlie and Tim. I shall whip them all myself if they do not mend their ways, and so will Rose, I am sure. Will you, my sweet?"

So saying, my stepmama got up and chucked Rose playfully beneath the chin, though taking care to bring her eyes full up to hers and so held her with all the magnetism of her gaze.

"Oh! Oh yes!" Rose stammered.

"I will give her a birch of her own, Mama, for she will need it. Especially after tonight," I added slyly.

"What treasures you all are! I feel quite protected by you! Why, I do believe that if they are to be all naughty then they shall be so in front of us and then we will know the better to punish them. What say you, Rose?"

"Yes." The word seemed impelled from her lips by some force beyond herself.

"Good," my stepmama said crisply and released her chin, then smiled and bent to kiss her forehead, much to Rose's surprise. Then straightening up, she said to me, "Come, dear, we have much to do. Sarah will meanwhile instruct Rose further." Following her quickly into the hall and making sure to close the door, I asked her what was immediately to do.

"Prepare Phillip, my pet, and put him to her within the hour. Have Bertha assist you, for an older woman will overawe him more."

"Yes, Mama. Will Rose's parents truly come on Saturday?"

Her eyes expressed surprise. "Of course, my love. I have so arranged it. Messengers are very quick, you know. I feel certain they may be persuaded to stay awhile. What busyness there will be and so much to do."

With a merry laugh she preceded me upstairs and was gone to her room, to attend to Papa perhaps, though I knew not whether he was about the house or not, so smoothly was all worked by Bertha.

Taking the key she had handed me, I entered Philip's

room. He sat quietly upon his bed reading, but started up when I entered. His face held an expression of awe and I guessed that either my stepmama or Bertha had already spoken to him. Of the same height as his sister, I was thus a little superior to him. His jacket, tie and all save his shirt, trousers and socks had already been removed. The path had already been smoothed for me.

"How old are you, Phillip?" I asked gently, though already knowing.

"Seventeen and shall be eighteen in September." He stammered the second of the numerals and so made it sound like 'aye-aye-aye-teen."

"You are a good age. Your sister is pretty and your Mama—are they not?"

He blinked and nodded, giving a fearsome little start as I approached him and moved my hands down to his trouser buttons.

"Have you not been told to stand still when required, and to do as you are told?" I asked with a sharper tone in my voice.

"Y . . . y . . . yes." He blinked again, having long eyelashes not unlike my own, and stared before him as I drew his trousers down and raised his shirt. A distinct tremor ran through his legs as I held his cock all limp upon my palm. My thumb moved over the top of it and he jerked.

"Be still, Phillip. Unbutton and remove your shirt while I hold it."

Flushed and with lips wobbling awkwardly, he obeyed. The warmth of my palm and coaxing thumb made his prick stiffen slowly in my hand. The looping of his trousers round his ankles held him well. Males are ever vulnerable so. He would blubber when I spanked him, but I would caress him first.

Rose would be well attended to and soon enough. Saturday was but three days away. The world was indeed our oyster.

WORDSWORTH DISTRIBUTION

Great Britain and Ireland
Wordsworth Editions Limited
Cumberland House, Crib Street
Ware, Hertfordshire SG12 9ET
Telephone 01920 465 167
Fax 01920 462 267

USA, Canada and Mexico
Universal Sales & Marketing Inc
230 Fifth Avenue, Suite 1212
New York, NY 10001, USA
Telephone 212-481-3500
Fax 212-481-3534

Italy
Magis Books SRL
Via Raffaello 31C
Zona ind Mancasale
42100 Reggio Emilia, Italy
Telephone 0522-920999
Fax 0522-920666

Germany, Austria and Switzerland
Swan Buch-Marketing GmbH
Goldscheuerstrabe 16
D-7640 Kehl am Rhein, Germany

Portugal
International Publishing
Services Limited
Rua da Cruz da Carreira, 4B
1100 Lisboa
Telephone 01-570051
Fax 01-352-2066

Spain
Ribera Libros S L
Poligono Martiartu, Calle 1, no 6
48480 Arrigorriaga, Vizcaya
Tel. 34-4-671-3607 (Almacen)
Tel. 34-4-441-8787 (Libreria)
Fax 34-4-671-3608 (Almacen)
Fax 34-4-4418029 (Libreria)

Wordsworth Classic Erotica

ANONYMOUS
The Autobiography of a Flea

Blue Velvet

Eveline

Frank and I

First Training

A Night in a Moorish Harem

The Pearl

Randiana

The Romance of Lust

Sadopaideia

Suburban Souls

Teleny

The Whippingham Papers

GUILLAUME APOLLINAIRE
The Amorous Exploits of a Young Rakehell

GIOVANNI BOCCACCIO
Selections from The Decameron

JOHN CLELAND
Memoirs of a Woman of Pleasure – Fanny Hill

SHEIKH NEFZAOUI
The Perfumed Garden
TRANSLATED BY
SIR RICHARD BURTON

PAULINE REAGE
The Story of O

EDWARD SELLON
The New Epicurean

SMITHERS AND BURTON
Priapaia

VARIOUS
The Olympia Reader – Volume One

The Olympia Reader – Volume Two

VATSYAYANA
The Kama Sutra
TRANSLATED BY
SIR RICHARD BURTON & F. F. ARBUTHNOT

'WALTER'
My Secret Life – Volume One
My Secret Life – Volume Two

LI YU
The Carnal Prayer Mat